Ark of the Stars

by Frank Borsch

Translated by Dwight R. Decker

FANPRO

WWW.FANPROGAMES.COM

Published by FanPro LLC

1608 N. Milwaukee · Suite 1005 · Chicago, IL 60647

ISBN-10: 1-932564-88-8
ISBN-13: 9781932564884
First Printing: November 2006
10 9 8 7 6 5 4 3 2 1
Printed in Canada.

Find us online:

http://www.perry-rhodan.us
(Perry Rhodan web page)

http://www.fanprogames.com
(FanPro web pages)

http://www.fanprodirect.com
(online ordering)

About Perry Rhodan

Perry Rhodan the series was born in Germany in 1961. Originally planned as a thirty-issue periodical, its unexpected success prompted the publisher to extend that plan to fifty issues. Now, forty-five years and 2,350 magazine novels (plus a plethora of related products) later, Perry Rhodan stands as the longest-running ongoing science-fiction storyline in existence.

Perry Rhodan the character was born on June 8, 1936 in Manchester, Connecticut, the son of Jakob Edgar Rhodan (a German émigré post-WWI) and Mary Rhodan (nee Tibo). He graduated from the US Air Force Academy and began a career as a pilot. On June 19, 1971, Major Perry Rhodan commanded the atomic-powered spaceship Stardust on the first manned moon-landing, accompanied by three other astronauts.

On the far side of the moon, the men discovered the scientific research vessel of an extraterrestrial race; the humanoid Arkonides had been forced to make an emergency landing. Perry Rhodan established contact with the Arkonides, as a result receiving some of their superior technology. Unwilling to place this unimaginably powerful technology in the hands of a single political power, upon his return to Earth Rhodan landed in the Gobi Desert, rather than the United States.

The world currently was facing the very real possibility of WWIII. With the influence of the Arkonide technology, Perry Rhodan managed to prevent the war, and even bring the various political blocs to a new level of cooperation. He established what he named the New Power, a neutral entity that owed allegiance to all of humanity, rather than a nation or ideology. Further, he declared his new citizenship to the planet Terra, calling himself a Terran. He gained many allies to his cause, among them a group of parapsychologically gifted people known as mutants. The Mutant Corps possessed telepathy, teleportation, telekinesis and other abilities.

Rhodan united humanity—and opened the gateway to the stars ...

Ark of the Stars is a journey into the future of humanity—and into its distant past.

1

The stars called to him.

Venron had never seen them. Not with his own eyes. Only in ancient visual recordings. Secretly and furtively, always in fear that the Tenoy would catch him and the other Star Seekers.

The Seekers had surrendered in utter amazement to the glory of the stars. Had attempted to count them and finally given up. There were too many; one could never succeed in grasping the sheer number of them. And to what purpose? Even in the depictions shown by the slowly but inexorably decaying memory units, the stars were the most beautiful things they had ever seen.

Venron had to see them.

With his own eyes.

He had to be certain that he was not yearning for a delusion.

Venron took off the thick plastic apron and gloves that had protected him for the past few hours from the thorns of the protein plants. The protein these plants provided was the richest available. But why the protein plants so reluctantly parted with their fruits remained a mystery to Venron. Perhaps the tenkren who developed them weren't in complete control of their own handiwork. Or perhaps the difficulty of harvesting had some intention he didn't understand.

A voice wrenched him out of his thoughts.

"Doing anything after your shift?" asked Melenda.

Venron looked up in surprise. He hadn't noticed Melenda come into the supply shed. She was his age, a voluptuous, outgoing woman with long hair and a swing in her hips that he had dreamed about for many nights after she had been assigned to his Metach'ton. But the stars had won out in the end. Now he seldom dreamed of Melenda.

"Yes. I ... I wanted to read some more," he lied. "You know, study."

Melenda looked puzzled. "I don't understand why you want to hide from the rest of the world." She stepped close to him, reached out her hand as though she wanted to take his, but then let her arm drop. "You should occasionally come out of that hole you've dug for yourself. I'm getting together with the others at the bow—Delder's plants have new blossoms. He says a shot of the juice will give you a kick like you've never felt before. And Delder knows his stuff! I bet he'll be a tenkren one of these days. You know the others don't especially like you, but I can put in a good word for you."

"Thanks," Venron said, "but I can't. Maybe some other time?"

"Some other time? You don't even believe that yourself!" Melenda dropped her apron carelessly on the bench and stormed out of the shed. The door banged behind her, making the whole structure shake.

Venron stared at the door for a few moments, then folded his apron carefully and shoved it and the gloves in the pigeonholes provided for them. Then he picked up Melenda's carelessly discarded apron and repeated the procedure.

He did it even though it wasn't logical. No one would come into the supply shed before the next shift, which didn't start until the next morning. But Venron couldn't bring himself to go against his training. "Waste is our downfall," he had been taught since childhood. "Our resources are limited and few!" *Some traitor you are!* he thought. *You even clean up after those you plan to betray!*

Venron left the shed. It was already getting dark. A bicycle leaned against a post nearby. He typed an inquiry on the handlebar screen display; the status indicator showed the bicycle was not in use. Good. It would make things go faster. Venron rode off, cruising with the familiarity of long years through the maze of paths that wound through the fields and gardens of the Outer Deck. He enjoyed the breeze that poured over his skin and streamed through his hair as he rode. On the bicycle, it was easy to forget the high gravity trying to pull him to the ground. The higher gravity of the Outer Deck made their limbs tire quickly during work. By noon, most of the metach thought only of catching their breath and of the Middle Deck, where they would be allowed to return after their shift.

At long intervals, Venron met other metach. Only a few were out and about at this hour; most were sitting with the rest of their Metach'ton and lingering over their evening meal. Why waste time on the Outer Deck where there was only sweat and hard work? He waved in greeting to the people he passed. His pulse sped up each time, returning to normal only when he went around a curve and didn't hear a shout of, "Hey, stop! What are you up to?"

People seemed to assume he was just what he appeared to be: a somewhat distracted metach occupying the time after his shift by taking a spin. His activity was uncommon, but also not remarkable, viewed mostly as a harmless whim.

No one seemed to realize he was a traitor.

In the distance, Venron spotted a young woman on a bicycle, her upper body bent well forward in order to offer less resistance as she rode.

Immediately yanking the handlebars to the left, he shot down between rows of bushes. Sliding off the seat, he crouched down so that he could see the path without being seen, and didn't move until the woman had passed.

It was Denetree. She had tied her hair into a knot as she usually did when she made her rounds. Her legs rose and fell in a swift rhythm. She rode in a high gear not only to develop her muscles but to be able to increase her speed at a moment's notice.

Venron waited for almost half an hour before he dared come out of the bushes. He couldn't have faced his sister. She would have guessed his plan, read it from his face, from his body language. And would have insisted on going with him ...

But that was impossible. Venron had no idea what awaited him. He would look for Denetree later and apologize to her for not saying good-bye.

3

I've done what I could for her, he tried to console himself. He would leave, but would leave a trace of himself behind. He had planned for that.

Venron continued on his way, finally stopping at a remote shelter. The simple plastic construction, a roof supported by four slender poles about the height of a man, would be torn away by even a mild storm—but there were no storms. The shelter sufficed to protect against the artificial rain.

Venron leaned the bicycle against one of the poles, switched it to FREE so the next person to find it could use it, and knelt on the ground. A thin layer of moldering grass and plant stems covered the floor of the shelter. Venron brushed it to one side to uncover the bare metal surface. Near the middle of the cleared space he found what he was looking for: a scratched display screen. Even though it was now fully dark, the screen glowed enough to be readable.

He spread the thumbs and index fingers of both hands, then pressed them simultaneously against all four corners of the display. A keyboard appeared on the screen and Venron entered a random series of numbers.

He didn't need a code: The input was only necessary so that the mechanism wasn't activated by accident. This mechanism opened the hatch to the pressurized air chambers below the surface that would ensure their survival in an emergency. As far as Venron knew, such an emergency had never occurred—and he strongly doubted that the chambers would be of much use if an emergency came to pass. One could survive for a day or a week in them—but then what?

Venron heard a clicking. A square section of the floor lifted creakingly to stand on one edge over a man-sized hole. The Net had released the hatch. Good. The Net had also been informed that there had been a request to open a hatch. Not so good. Everything now depended on how the Net interpreted the action. Playing children opened the hatches on a regular basis. The Net expected it. Testing the limits of their world and what was allowed was part of children's normal development. To a point.

If it was Venron's bad luck that children had been using this entrance a little too often recently, the Net would confine him in the chamber below until the Tenoy came. It would be very difficult to explain what he was doing in the underground chambers: He was an adult who ought to know better than to stick his nose into things that didn't concern him.

Venron climbed down a narrow metal ladder into the dark. Each time he rested his weight on a new rung, the ladder squeaked and sagged. Above him, the hatch closed automatically. Faint light came on, making the outlines of objects visible. Venron looked at the ceiling. Only every third light was illuminated.

Our resources are limited.

Venron had not been down in the pressurized chambers since his childhood. He was surprised by how small and cramped it felt. He was in a long, narrow corridor with a low ceiling, lined on both sides with benches. Baggy pressure suits hung in wall niches, looking like sacks with helmets attached. They would fit anyone of any size or build, and even untrained persons could slip them on in seconds. But they condemned their wearers to immobility. It would be impossible to move through the narrow corridor wearing the pressure suits, especially if the corridor was jammed full of people.

Venron didn't want to imagine it. He already felt oppressed by the confined space.

He started walking, counting the pressure suits as he went. When he reached sixty-three, an opening yawned in the apparently endless row. There was a narrow passageway in the wall where another pressure suit should have hung. Venron squeezed himself inside. After a few meters, the passageway opened onto another corridor lined with pressure suits. Venron turned left and counted the suits again. At ninety-six, he found a new gap and squeezed his way into it.

The throat-constricting feeling that he was caught in a trap gradually subsided. The conditions he had found so far matched the description he had read, which encouraged him to hope that all of it would be accurate. As yet he had not heard the heavy footsteps of the Tenoy racing through the corridors to seize him, nor any warnings from the Net.

Again Venron counted. He stopped at thirty-three. This time, there was no gap. He was looking at a pressure suit that was exactly the same as the hundreds he had already passed. He grasped the suit by the neck ring, lifted it up, and set it down on the opposite side. The suit was surprisingly light. Once, as a child, he had put on a suit just to be daring, and without understanding what he was playing at. The other children had teased him for weeks afterwards because the suit had been such a tight fit. "You're so fat!" they had called over and over again. "Fat! Fat! Fat!" Only Denetree hadn't laughed at him. She simply took him into her arms without a word and held him until he had calmed down.

Venron still remembered how hard it had been to lift the helmet over his head at that age. But he had grown up slim and strong.

Moving the suit revealed bare metal. Venron leaned close, narrowed his eyes and felt the wall. It seemed massive. *Doesn't matter,* he assured himself.

He ran his fingers over the surface, searching for any unevenness. Not an easy task: Dust had settled on the wall over the centuries and hardened, so much so that it had withstood the efforts of the maintenance and cleaning crews that still serviced these chambers at regular intervals. Twice he thought he had found what he was looking for, twice he was disappointed. Then he found the hidden switch, and to his right a concealed display screen slid out of the wall.

An input field lit up in front of Venron.

He mentally repeated the password that he had stumbled across a few weeks earlier when he was looking for new star pictures to show the Seekers. He had succeeded in temporarily isolating a memory unit from the Net without being noticed, a success that could only last a few minutes. A dummy virtual unit wouldn't fool the Net any longer than that. To his disappointment, he hadn't found any new star pictures, only boring construction plans. Without giving it much thought, he copied some of them to his portable memory unit, reversed his manipulation of the system and slipped away.

When he examined his plundered data later, he found—hidden in a dry mass of construction plans and circuit diagrams—a door to the stars.

Would he be able to open it?

He entered the password, and a section of the wall slid back. The hatch was not completely open when Venron dove into the darkness beyond.

From this point forward, he had very little time.

The opening of this hatch, a door most likely unknown to even the highest levels of the naahk's leadership circle, would alert the Net to his location. Venron had to be quick.

Spotlights blazed on and bathed the corridor beyond the hatch with glaring light. Venron felt as though the eyes of a thousand faces were staring at him. Blinded for a moment, he stumbled, then he caught himself and ran. He squeezed his eyes tightly shut, relying entirely on the map that was burned into his mind, the layout that he had memorized so exactingly in the past few weeks.

The plans had overtaken even his unconscious mind, and his nightly dreams of the stars were interrupted by nightmares of winding corridors. He woke up screaming, only to look into the apprehensive and angry faces of the metach with whom he shared sleeping quarters. "Venron," they had whispered. "What's gotten into you? What are you yelling about? Go back to sleep! We have to work tomorrow!"

He never told them what woke him, not even when they threatened to beat him if he didn't keep quiet. Not even when they carried out their threat.

Venron kept his eyes shut. His pulse raced faster, and his lungs drew in air that smelled different, so cold and metallic.

He heard a crackling sound and waited for the peremptory voice of the Net, which from a myriad of loudspeakers would order him to turn around.

It didn't come.

The light grew weaker. He felt a slight breeze. Had he reached his goal? He slowed down to a trot, ready at any second to leap to one side or take off running again. He opened his eyes once more, just a crack. The light was less harsh now, and came from far, far overhead.

In front of him loomed a shape so large that it blocked some of the light as he approached.

Venron stretched out both arms and walked on. When his fingers touched cool metal, he stopped, laid his head back, and fully opened his eyes.

He was in a huge room, nearly half a kilometer high. His hands rested on the massive hull of a craft secured to a ramp that inclined sharply upwards and ended at a hatch outlined on the wall of the chamber.

The shuttle! The schematics had been correct!

Venron cried out with joy, the fear and doubt that had threatened to overwhelm him vanishing in an instant. His exultation echoed back from the walls—and beyond those walls, the stars awaited him!

Venron ran around the hull. The shuttle's lower rear hatch was open, as though the ship was waiting for him. Venron hurried up the ramp and ran through the cargo bay, intent on reaching the cockpit. The plans he had downloaded were not complete. Venron had been able to learn little more from them than that the shuttle existed and was kept constantly ready for use.

And that it was armed.

He reached the cockpit. It was small, with room for only one person, and hung like a transparent blister from the bow of the shuttle. A second, separate cockpit, probably for the co-pilot, bulged from the bow close by. Venron slid into the pilot's seat. Over the gap into which his legs disappeared hung an expansive display screen showing status indicators. Venron touched one and immediately received a more detailed view of that information.

The shuttle did not demand authentication to respond to commands!

Venron had counted on that. Anything else would have been illogical. Among other purposes, the shuttle was intended for use in emergencies. A restrictive access procedure might mean that a shuttle would fail to launch because no authorized pilot was aboard. Further, even an average metach could operate the shuttle by virtue of an interactive help system.

But Venron would have been able to manage even without such a system. He knew his way around computers.

His fingers manipulated the touch screen. First, he verified that the on-board computer was not connected to the Net, then he closed the stern hatch and requested the system status. All indications were green. The shuttle was ready for takeoff.

He initiated engine start-up. The craft shuddered, then, after a few moments, the shuddering transitioned into a gentle vibration.

A control lever extended itself and pressed into his hand. Venron grasped it. A countdown appeared on the display, showing the seconds until the engines were ready for ignition. The time was shorter than he had dared hope. Just a few moments more, and he ...

The image on the pilot's display suddenly changed. Venron now was looking from the shuttle's stern out on the rear part of the hangar. Large doors were sliding open, and through the openings swarmed men and women in the black uniforms of the Tenoy, their weapons aimed and ready.

"Stop right there!" a loud voice resounded through the hangar. It was not the voice of the Net, so it had to belong to one of the Tenoy. It penetrated even the nearly soundproof cockpit.

"Think of the disaster you bring on us!" the voice continued. "And on yourself! Only death waits for you outside! Come back! You can still turn around!"

It was too late for second thoughts or regrets. The Naahk would show a traitor no mercy.

Venron switched the image on the display from the stern camera back to the countdown. Still a few more seconds. He gripped the control lever more tightly, then touched a button. The Tenoy, who had nearly surrounded the shuttle, hit the floor as though cut down by a scythe. The men and women crawled away, desperately searching for cover the hangar did not provide. Venron couldn't see any of their faces; they were hidden by their helmet visors. He was happy about that. He wouldn't have liked to see anyone he knew.

The triple cannon installed under the bow completed its sweep without Venron discharging it. He didn't have any intention of being a murderer. He only wanted to reach the stars.

The cannon was now aimed directly at the closed hatch. Venron pressed the discharge control.

A fireball exploded in front of him, immediately followed by a hailstorm of particles and debris that drummed on the cockpit canopy. A cloud of black smoke billowed through the hangar. Venron pressed the control a second time. There was a second fireball, followed by another shower of debris, but this time no smoke cloud rose. Instead, the smoke was sucked outside as though by a pump.

Venron, who had dreamed of the stars without suspecting what they actually were, who didn't realize that there was a vacuum between them, watched in astonishment for several moments as the atmosphere in the hangar streamed outward. Then he activated the engines.

The shuttle shot out of the hangar. The pressure of acceleration pushed Venron deep into his seat. It went black in front of his eyes—a merciful blackness, since it prevented him from seeing how the Tenoy were pulled by the escaping air into the vacuum where they suffocated. Venron tasted blood and felt something soft and solid rubbing against his teeth: the tip of his tongue, which he had bitten off when he clenched his jaws.

But Venron didn't feel any pain. As he grew used to the acceleration and his blood circulation returned to normal, his eyesight came back.

He saw the stars.

They were brighter than in the films. More glittering. And more colorful. In one direction, they shone red, in another white like in the photographs, and violet in a third. They were close enough to touch. They belonged to him. He had only to reach out his hand to them and ...

A jolt slammed the shuttle. The pilot seat jerked up and Venron would have been thrown against the canopy if he hadn't been automatically strapped in at takeoff. He heard the tearing of overstrained steel, then the display in front of him went dark, along with the light that had illuminated the joystick.

The stars began to spin. Faster and still faster.

Venron screamed, but the stars didn't hear him.

2

"Crawler Six to Mama. Initiating landing procedure. You'll hear from us as soon as we're down."

"Roger. Good luck and good hunting!"

Alemaheyu Kossa, hypercommunications officer of the prospecting ship *Palenque*, switched the crawler's channel to the background. The syntrons of both ships would exchange a constant stream of data without his intervention: position, systems status, instrument readings—an umbilical cord of communication, intangible and yet real.

Alemaheyu's task was to ensure that the stream did not break. Without the data stream, the *Palenque*'s crawlers were helpless, in a sense, blind and deaf. When they ventured out into the endless void of space, there was only one point of contact connecting them with the world: Mama Kossa.

The prospector ship's twelve crawlers were more than auxiliary craft; they were compact laboratories to which an impulse engine, a rudimentary faster-than-light drive, and a pressurized cabin, large enough for a crew of three, had been attached.

Experience had taught the men and women of the *Palenque* that that crew had better consist of people who could stand to be together in cramped quarters for several weeks at a stretch without going for each other's throats. It was a common truth that, after the first week together, a crawler crew felt either burning hatred or unbreakable comradeship. Teams that had worked together for years so preferred the company of their crewmates that they often shared three-person cabins on the *Palenque*, quarters that were only slightly more spacious than the steel cages on the crawlers.

"Crawler Four to Mama," called a shrill, chirping voice. It belonged to the Blue named Yülhan-Nyulzen-Y'sch-Takan-Nyül. Either him or his brother, Trülhan. Alemaheyu could never tell them apart. The brothers were Blues, or "Dishheads," as they were still insultingly referred to on many Terran worlds, the only non-humans in the *Palenque* crew aside from Gresko the Gurrad. "We are entering the planet's shadow in 20 seconds. Exit from shadow projected in 13 minutes and 34 seconds. Don't worry when you don't hear from us, Mama!"

"You, I don't need to worry about. You're big enough to play by yourselves for a quarter of an hour. Have fun, but don't pull any crap!"

In the beginning, Alemaheyu had resisted the nickname. Prospectors were a rough breed, and while the crews had long consisted of a mix of males and females—and occasionally beings whose gender could not be determined with any accuracy—the reference to presumed femininity was a favorite strategy for insulting your coworkers. So when the crawler teams began calling him "Mama Kossa" ...

It was not until his watchfulness prevented, at the last moment, the total loss of a crawler that Alemaheyu understood the nickname was intended as a sincere indication of respect. For the men and women out there in their steel shells, he *was* the *Palenque*, the mother ship, proof that the prospectors, out among the cold and pitiless stars, had not been forgotten.

"Everything all right with you, Alemaheyu?" called Sharita Coho, commander of the *Palenque*.

"Of course. What else?"

"Good."

As always, the commander wore her uniform, an outfit that seemed to reflect an adolescent's idea of a spaceship captain's uniform rather than a practical, utilitarian design. And as always, she wore a beamer at her belt. Alemaheyu couldn't remember ever seeing her wear any other outfit, even away from the ship. Today, despite the uncomfortable warmth of the control center, she had fastened the front of her jacket all the way to the top. She must be sweating buckets—no, boiling alive—but apparently the extra psychological security she gained from the formality of the uniform was worth the unpleasantness.

Today, her sweatiness had a specific name: Perry Rhodan.

A low cheeping tone brought Alemaheyu back to tending his console. Since the unforgettable near-wreck of the crawler, Alemaheyu had formed the habit of checking the data stream at regular intervals. Usually, hourly checks were often enough, but here in the Ochent Nebula, with its five-dimensional anomalies, hyperstorms and unusually active stars, he was checking more frequently.

He called up the data for each of the crawlers in quick succession. Seven of them were on the surface of various planets and moons, gathering rock samples and readings, while the other five were either on the way to a highly promising celestial body or already returning to the *Palenque,* their missions completed. Crawler Four was still in the communications shadow of a Jupiter-like planet five light-years from the prospecting ship.

Concentrating, Alemaheyu reviewed the data streams. Everything looked normal, no anomalies, though Crawler Nine's data did show a tiny deviation—so tiny that he almost missed it.

He zoomed in on the irregularity and directed the syntron to analyze the data status. It found that the crawler's g-force absorber currently would function at 99.93 percent capacity, which was insignificant as long as the vehicle operated on the airless surface of the moon it was surveying. This variance could possibly be deadly when the crawler lifted off and accelerated.

Alemaheyu considered. A hardware failure? Improbable. G-force absorbers were the product of a proven, safety-critical technology in common use for thousands of years. And the crawlers' technology had been selected with especial care: in order to save precious space, the mini-labs carried no redundant components. Every system had to function at 100 percent.

A software error? Alemaheyu went through the crawler's log data. After a few minutes of searching, he found an entry that struck him as unusual. He followed that lead, and finally found the problem. Part of a software update package installed a week earlier had somehow been skipped. This exact issue was a point of contention between him and the syntron specialists. Alemaheyu felt that since the crawlers operated flawlessly, they shouldn't be changing things. But nobody on board listened to him. To the control-center crew on the *Palenque*, he was just the comm officer, not Mama.

Alemaheyu sent the update to Crawler Nine, then tested the absorber with a simulation routine. All the values showed 100 percent.

A disturbance at the entrance to the control center distracted Alemaheyu. The men and women whispered to each other, then he heard a series of "Good mornings."

Their passenger must have arrived on the bridge. The most effusive greeting even the commander herself could hope for from the control center crew was a nod and a murmur.

"Good morning, Perry," Sharita Como said a moment later, confirming Alemaheyu's conclusion. "Did you sleep well?"

"Yes, thank you. Is there any news?

"No. No ores. And no Akonians."

Alemaheyu wondered for the nth time if he should buy Rhodan's story. The Ochent Nebula was a no-man's-land, officially unclaimed by any of the galaxy's great powers. The region bounded the spheres of influence of various Blue races and the Akonians, but up to now had proven too uninviting to inspire any desire to possess it. The number of life-bearing worlds was small, the frequency of hyperstorms high, and the strategic value precisely zero. Anyone who occupied the Ochent Nebula would take on diplomatic complications and outrageous maintenance expenses for new bases on which expensively trained soldiers would die of boredom.

But the sector was hardly deserted. In recent years it had attracted an increasing number of prospectors: Terrans, Blues, mixed crews without a common origin but united by the expectation of a big find and, most recently, Akonians. So far, the prospectors had invested considerable work and capital with nothing to show for it, but the probability of that suddenly changing grew with each day that passed.

A vein of five-dimensionally radiant quartz ... the high-tech relics of an extinct race ... an ore deposit of high purity—any such find could trigger a race of the galactic powers and change the unde-clared cold war that gripped the galaxy to an active conflict.

Rhodan had come on board the *Palenque* to seek contact with the Akonians in order to preempt such a crisis. He wanted to draw the Forum Raglund, of which the Akonians were among the most important members, to Terra's side.

Alemaheyu had laughed loudly when he heard that. Just how naive was the Immortal, anyway? The Ochent Nebula was one of the few remaining galactic frontiers. Did he expect that the Akonians—and even the Blues, who historically could not get along with themselves—would withdraw based on his suggestion, taking a pass on the opportunity to make the find of their lives? God only knew that Alemaheyu had no love for the Dishheads and the arro-gant Akonians, but to dream that they would simply pull out on the basis of a request and an analysis of the galactic political situation? Even they weren't that crazy ... .

"They'll show up yet," Rhodan said, facing the commander.

"Yes, sooner or later," she replied. It was clear that Sharita was not exactly excited about the prospect of having the Immortal on board for weeks on end.

Alemaheyu observed Perry Rhodan from the corner of his eye. He was a man of average height with dark blond hair. The simple uniform he wore revealed nothing of his rank. If Alemaheyu had encountered Rhodan on the street, he wouldn't have recognized the man who had led the human race to the stars nearly three thousand years ago. Rhodan seemed like an average man.

Really.

The *Palenque's* comm officer didn't have any words for it, but something changed on the ship's bridge every time Rhodan appeared. Of course, small, external things changed. The control-center crew attempted, with varying degrees of success, to suppress the curses; the conversational tone wasn't quite as rude; there was less talk in general. But all that was easy to explain. People were like that: they sought tight communities, and when they found them, they closed themselves to outsiders.

But it was more than that. Alemaheyu caught himself sitting bolt upright at his console instead of lounging in his usual posture.

And his work ethic kicked up a notch, too. Not that he would have otherwise been tempted to take his eye off the crawlers—a mama does everything for her children, doesn't she?—but he even conscientiously took care of the bothersome minor duties that human lives didn't depend on.

And it was all because of Perry Rhodan.

It was the same for Alemaheyu as it was for the commander of the *Palenque*. He wasn't able to ignore the knowledge that in his long life, Rhodan had encountered an unimaginable number of people, and had mastered dangers and tests of his skill and courage that Alemaheyu could only guess at. Much as it annoyed the *Palenque's* comm officer, he simply wasn't able to behave naturally in Rhodan's presence—even though the Immortal hadn't so much as hinted with a single word or gesture that he expected special treatment. On the contrary: Rhodan slept in a standard cabin, ate the standard food, and performed standard duties. Yesterday, in fact, he had turned up in a hangar and helped a technician with the maintenance on one of the crawlers.

Rhodan was the friendliest and most sociable passenger the *Palenque* had carried in a long time, and yet it was only with an effort that Alemaheyu could keep from stuttering with excitement when he spoke with the Immortal. It was enough to drive him up the wall.

After greeting Rhodan, Alemaheyu and the rest of the control-center crew went back to their duties. There was not much to do. The crawlers did the actual work. The *Palenque* stood ready in case something unexpected happened. Akonians appearing, or something like that, which certainly wouldn't happen as long as they had Rhodan on board. That was life: if you wanted to avoid something, it was always on your heels. But if you were looking for it, it was nowhere to be found.

"Mild hyperstorm," the hyperdetection officer called out. "Sectors 72Z to 84R."

Not unexpected. Hyperstorms were the rule rather than the exception in this area. Alemaheyu called up the hyperdetection data. No reason to worry. The storm wasn't strong enough to endanger the crawlers. Besides, only one of them was in the affected area.

Alemaheyu made contact. "Crawler Eleven!"

"What is it, Mama?"

"There's a hyperstorm brewing along your course. Rather weak, nothing that should bother your crate."

"Okay. Then why are you calling us?"

"Because Mama always worries." The two men, Alemaheyu Kossa on the *Palenque* and Mikch Theyner on the crawler, laughed. The joke had long since worn out, but they couldn't resist making it. It had been Mikch who had given Alemaheyu the nickname in the first place. "But seriously," the comm officer went on, "it's possible the data stream will be interrupted for a few minutes. I just wanted to let you know so you don't worry about it."

"Too late. Our pants are already sticky and stinky. Catch you later!"

"Be seeing you!"

Alemaheyu had barely finished speaking when the data stream broke off. The crawler had been caught in the storm. The craft would now be thoroughly shaken. It would do Mikch and his people good. Remind them of how comfortable they had it on the *Palenque*, remind them of their place. Very little could go wrong. Without guidance from the *Palenque*, the crawler was effectively blind from a navigational standpoint, but it was operating in a slow, sublight flight. It would be hours before it came near a moon or a planet.

Sharita Coho and Rhodan had retreated to the rear section of the control center and were conversing in whispers. Alemaheyu tried to eavesdrop, but they were too far away. He only caught the word "Akonians" a few times.

A soft chirping reminded the comm officer that it was again time for a routine check. He immersed himself in the work, exchanging a few words with the crews of the various crawlers. Four reported in. The craft had left the planetary shadow and was in the process of landing on a highly promising high plateau after an optical scan of the surface.

Alemaheyu wished the crew good luck in finding pay dirt. When he returned to his status review, he felt a stab of unease. What was going on with Crawler Eleven? The data stream was still out.

"Hyperdetection!" Alemaheyu called. "What about the hyperstorm? Is it still going on?"

"Yes," came the reply. "It'll reach its peak in about an hour."

"Roger," Alemaheyu said. Then he had a thought. "Position?"

"Shifted to Sector ... "

"Shifted? What about the area where it originated?"

"Nearly normal readings now."

Alemaheyu called up the communications module on the holo-screen and attempted to make contact with Crawler Eleven. No result, either from the crew or the crawler's syntron. The comm officer gave the hypercom maximum transmitting power, focusing the beam on the sectors in which the hyperstorm had raged. No response. It was as though the crawler had ceased to exist.

A lump developed in Alemaheyu's throat. He suddenly wished he had a joint to smoke to calm his nerves. But all that would've gotten him was a burst of Sharita's wrath. The comm officer leaped up and hurried over to Rhodan and the commander.

"Sharita," he said, as she looked up at him angrily, "I'm sorry to disturb you, but I think we have an emergency."

3

A vague sense of unease drove Denetree that evening.

She was used to taking off on her bicycle after the shift. Most metach on field duty were too tired afterwards to do more than drag themselves back to the half-gravity of the Middle Deck, eat with their Metach'ton, plug into the Net for an on-line game, or just sit and wait for the next day.

Not Denetree.

Yes, the work was hard, but after a Ship-year—more than half her obligation as a field hand was behind her—she had gotten used to it. In the beginning, only her thighs had developed, and she had otherwise looked like a beanpole. But now she had put on some flesh. Her arms, her entire body had become muscular. In the first months, the effort of cycling had almost completely burned her out. The gravity of the Outer Deck crushed newcomers mercilessly toward the ground, after a few minutes making every movement a torture. There was very little help from machinery in the fields, allegedly to save the always limited supply of energy on board. Denetree felt certain that was true, but exhausting the young metach in performing their service for the Ship seemed to her an equally likely intention. It kept them from getting dumb ideas.

In theory, at least. In practice, Denetree became an example of the opposite. In the unanimous opinion of everyone who knew her, Denetree's endless rounds through the Ship on a bicycle after the end of her shift fell clearly into the category of dumb ideas. Except that it was harmless. Denetree didn't bother anyone, and as long as her rides always took her back to her Metach'ton, and her work performance the next day didn't suffer, no one tried to stop her. Not her neighbors, not the Naahk or the Net.

Immediately after the end of her shift, Denetree climbed on the bicycle she considered "hers." Of course, it wasn't really her own. None of the metach owned their own bicycle, no matter how highly they were placed. The bicycles belonged to all equally—which didn't necessarily mean that every metach could use every bicycle.

Denetree had made a number of changes to the bicycle she used: "optimizations," as she called them. Her bicycle's rims had a smaller diameter than the standard model and the tires were wider with a studded tread—designed for better traction rather than minimal rolling resistance, as was typical. Denetree pumped the tires full enough that only the center of the tire rested on the ground, creating a narrow, smooth strip that made it easier to ride on uneven terrain, but was apparently inferior in direct comparison to the standard ultrathin tires.

The other members of her metach had laughed at her when she rode her bicycle to her shift the first time. "Look, that crazy Denetree has built a plow!" they mocked. "Come on, dig us a furrow!" Only after she had beaten the loudest mocker in a race, handily leaving him in the dust, did they stop their open teasing.

It had been Denetree's luck to end up with one of the heaviest men in the metach as her opponent. He weighed more than a hundred kilos, and she weighed less than half that. Even though his weight should have given him an edge, Denetree beat him, and on the relatively unfavorable surface of the road.

But her bicycle wasn't designed for speed. It had a low center of gravity and a computer-supported gear-shifter, into which she had secretly installed new firmware she had written herself. Those three assets made it possible for her to leave the assigned paths and ride between the fields, and even travel through the Ship's wilderness tracts where only a few metach ever wandered, since they lay away from the settlements and fields.

And the firmware had a second, equally important function: it made the bicycle effectively Denetree's. If anyone else climbed onto the seat, the firmwear switched to neutral. The spectacle that followed had many variations, but only one conclusion: the unhappy would-be rider got off the bicycle cursing, sent a DAMAGED report to the Net over the guidance computer, and left the bicycle in the ditch without another thought. Thanks to Denetree's firmware, none of those reports ever reached the Net. The Net only ever saw a standard green indication from the guidance computer: "Bicycle intact. No maintenance required."

Pedaling furiously in high gear, Denetree left behind the field where she had spent today's shift. Her arms and neck ached. Harvesting jakulent was hard labor. The long-stemmed plants were cultivated by the Ship for the sturdy fibers in their stalks. But choosing which of the stalks were ripe for harvest, cutting them and separating them into their individual fibers was a nasty grind—such hard work that a person was rarely assigned to the work for more than two weeks.

Denetree ignored the pain. She would forget it completely in half an hour, when the exertions of pedaling would bring her pulse to a constant 140 beats per minute, and the blood that pulsed through her veins took the pain with it.

Today, her thoughts were somewhere else.

She was worried about her brother. Venron had become more taciturn in recent weeks than ever before. Not that he had ever said very much, but he had opened up to her, at least, especially when the feeling of being locked in, of there being no way out, threatened to overwhelm him. Then he had laid his head in her lap and looked up at the sky. It hung overhead, close enough to touch—close enough to make one weep—and was always the same. By day, bright, though never blinding; by night, an oppressive, impenetrable black.

Denetree and Venron had endured considerable mockery and nasty remarks over time. Not because of their shared yearning for the stars, which they kept to themselves, but because the brother and sister shared a close relationship. The Ship did not support families. Children were raised in groups according to their ages; siblings rarely knew each other, and only a few cared to. What would have been the point?

By chance, Denetree and Venron had been assigned to adjacent Metach'tons. And ever since they had run into each other that first time, they had been inseparable. A connection existed between them that even they could not explain.

The strongest bond between them was their common desire to escape to the stars, to find a new life away from the prison of the ship. Venron had often wept as he dreamed of that possibility, but Denetree waited in vain for relieving tears to come to her. The hard grip of his hands around her body relaxed to a gentle touch and his breath evened out as he lost himself in the fantasy of escape.

Denetree had never managed to flee into her dreams to find peace. She only had her bicycle, the pumping of her heart, the protesting throb in her thighs, and the endless rounds through the ship that took her nowhere.

Denetree reached the fields where Venron's Metach'ton was currently assigned. The hut that served the two dozen men and women as a shelter, changing and storage room was deserted. They must have finished their shift already. Denetree thought for a moment, then went on in the direction of the bow. All day long, the members of her Metach'ton had enthused over the party that would be taking place there tonight; perhaps the news had reached Venron's Metach'ton also.

After a few minutes, she saw a group of people moving slowly through the fields. She pedaled faster and quickly caught up. It was Venron's Metach'ton. A swarm of bicycles surrounded an electric-powered harvest platform. It was strictly forbidden to use the platforms for anything other than work—energy was too valuable to waste it on leisure activities—but the young men and women didn't care about the rules. Half the members of the Metach'ton had made themselves comfortable on the dirty platform, while the rest rode on bicycles, trying to hang on to the platform with one hand so they could be pulled along. The metach were exhausted from the day's labors, but the urge to feel something other than exhaustion pushed them on.

"Watch out!" one of the men on bicycles called when he saw Denetree approach. "Here comes that pale little speed demon again!"

The group made no effort to stop. Denetree came alongside, shifted to a lower gear, and shot with perfect aim through a gap in the bicycle riders to the platform.

"Melenda!"

The young woman cuddled in the lap of another metach. When she saw Denetree coming, she deliberately turned her head and, her eyes closed, gave the man a long, deep kiss.

"Melenda, please!"

The woman disengaged from the embrace and stared at Denetree in annoyance. "What do you want with me? Can't you see I'm busy?"

"I'm looking for Venron. Do you happen to know where he is?"

"Venron ... " Melenda rolled her eyes. Her pupils were dilated. Had she already been smoking? The jakulent stalks could be used for more than one purpose, especially ones of which the Ship didn't approve. "Oh, now I know who you mean! That lazy slacker who thinks he's too good for us! He was on his shift."

"And?"

"As usual, he did only half his quota. We had to slog away for him so he could he wander around the field and daydream."

One of the men on the bicycles came closer, making a game out of trying to force Denetree away. Without looking, Denetree took her right foot out of the pedal's magnetic stirrup and gave the man a kick.

"And after the shift?"

"Who cares about that?"

The man got back at Denetree for the kick by waving the other bicycle riders into a phalanx that pushed on Denetree from all sides. They would teach the troublemaker a lesson.

"Please, Melenda! Help me! I ... "

The men were on her. Denetree took a blow to her side. Her back wheel and the front wheel of one of the other bicycles rubbed against each other with a shrill squealing. Denetree yanked the handlebars around, then braked. Someone hit her again. The circle around her closed. Malicious faces laughed at her, like children torturing a field rodent. Denetree looked wildly around and saw a tiny opening to the right. She rose from her seat in order to step on the pedals with all her strength. There wasn't time to engage the battery.

She broke away from the crowd but she could not avoid falling. Suddenly, the unfenced irrigation channel was right in front of her, and in the next moment the ground came up to meet her with a metallic scraping. Enthusiastic catcalls accompanied her fall.

Denetree laid in the grass until the crowd moved off. The hoots and cheers gradually died away. Then Denetree heard the shrill voice of a woman say, "Just ask the Net where your brother is!" and the whinnying laughter of the rest of the Metach'ton in response.

"Just ask the Net!"

Nothing could be easier.

She stood up carefully, checking her body for injuries. On her hip was a blood-engorged spot where she had run into the handlebar. Otherwise she was unhurt. She pulled the bicycle upright; its back wheel had landed in the irrigation channel. She had been fortunate: the vulnerable rims had not been bent.

She trembled in rage and humiliation. The metach had no right to treat her like that! They ... Denetree thought of Venron. What must he endure at the hands of his Metach'ton, day in and day out? It was said that nothing escaped the Net; it was there for everyone. Why didn't the Net transfer him to a different group? If this is how they treated him, she didn't think Venron could hold out much longer.

She got back on the bicycle, thinking. Where could he be? Venron had a knack for isolating himself. Time after time, he disappeared for hours, even entire nights. He told no one where he hid, not even Denetree. But she knew he went places no one else had been, because each time Venron brought her a present: new pictures of the starry sky, recordings made by previous generations, even small manufactured objects, like nothing she had seen before.

Denetree returned to Venron's Metach'ton shed and began a systematic search. In increasingly larger circles, she scouted the area.

Could Venron have gone on one of his raiding forays?

Not likely, Denetree decided. Venron's explorations into the off-limits areas of the Ship were the high points of his existence, hours that made everything else bearable. Days of detailed planning preceded each foray, his excitement mounting until it seemed he would burst. When he was planning one of these expeditions, he smiled more often and gave her presents: small figures he made from stolen wood or metal, preludes to the great gift of new knowledge that he would soon bring her.

Venron had returned from his last foray more withdrawn than ever. He had wept a great deal and could only fall asleep if he was clinging to Denetree.

Three days ago, he had given her another gift, a small box wrapped with a fiber band. She could easily hold it in one hand. When she started to open it, he stopped her. "No," he had said. "Not yet."

"Then when?" she had asked.

"Not today. And not tomorrow, either," had been his answer. "You will know when it's time. Until then, hide it in a safe place." No matter how hard Denetree had tried to pry further information out of him, he refused to discuss it.

Denetree completed her first circle of the shed. She had not met anyone. Anyone who didn't absolutely have to remain on the Outer Deck retreated in the evening to the Middle Deck, where they were better protected from radiation and could relax.

She assumed Venron was planning something. But what? More than once Denetree had suspected that he was saying good-bye to the Ship, quietly seeking out his favorite places and spending time with his few friends.

Denetree rode in increasingly wider circles, and to the same extent that the dull pain of exhaustion increased in her thighs, her unease grew, finally crossing the invisible boundary into fear. The paths lay deserted in the last light of day. It was impossible to miss a metach on foot or riding—unless he or she was intentionally hiding. But Venron wouldn't do that: What reason could he possibly have to hide from his own sister?

Night fell. The Net turned off the light.

Venron considered whether Venron might try to hurt himself, then tried to dismiss that thought. Even though no one spoke of the unhappy ones, she knew that many metach took their own lives. The Net, which otherwise reported every last detail of life on the Ship, no matter how unimportant, said nothing about the suicides. But those who took their own lives: they were different, weak or old; they had lost their faith in the Metach'rath, the Ladder of Life; they were not people like her, not like Venron.

Denetree was panting. She rose from the seat, shifted to a higher gear and tried to drive the fear from her thoughts by pedaling harder.

"Just ask the Net!"

The mocking call echoed within her. Yes, the Net would know where Venron was. Nothing—or almost nothing, since it didn't know about the Star Seekers—escaped the attention of the Net. She could report Venron as missing. After that, nothing would ever happen to him again. The Net would take him into its caring protection, turn him over to the Magtar, the psychologists who had settled on the Inner Deck and never left it—and who could never leave it now, because their muscles had atrophied. Despite this handicap, they claimed to know better than everyone else about life on the Ship. They would test Venron until they found something. They would find out about his explorations, treat him with injections and pump him full of their drugs until he could only murmur his name and "Be loyal to the Ship!" Then they would let him go, a reformed member of the greater community.

But he would live.

Unless he was too strong. Then, the Magtar would turn him over to the Pekoy.

Ahead, Denetree saw one of the rudimentary shelters that had been built at regular intervals in this part of the Ship.

He would live ...

The Pekoy would ask questions. Why did he explore? Who else explored with him? Treason was a contagious disease. It would ripen in one individual, then spread to others, growing like an ulcer. To prevent it from endangering the entire community, treason had to be burned out. Completely. If she asked the Net to find Venron, the Star Seekers also would be discovered. They would all fall down the Ladder of Life, and if they were lucky, they would be allowed to begin again at the lowest rung. Maybe.

He would live ...

The Ladder of Life held no meaning for a dead man.

Every shelter contained a terminal for use in emergencies that was fully connected to the Net.

Denetree rode past the shelter, then turned around and stopped at it. There was a bicycle leaning against one of the posts, but no one was in sight. The floor of the shelter and the small touchscreen of the emergency terminal had been hastily wiped clear, most likely by children who had been caught playing with it. They must have run away in order to escape a beating, and left the bicycle behind in their panic.

Denetree bent over the touch screen.

Live, she thought. *Venron must live!*

She touched the display to activate it, thinking hard to come up with the words she would use to report her brother as missing. Afraid of losing her nerve in the last second, she imagined him dead: his stiff, unmoving body, unseeing eyes.

I'm sorry! She apologized in her thoughts to the other Star Seekers, who surely would be exposed. *I'm sorry. But Venron must live.*

The display lit up. But instead of the input menu, she saw Venron.

"Brother!" she exclaimed in surprise. "I was so worried about you! Where ... "

The blare of the display's loudspeaker cut her off. "Look into the face of the traitor, metach! Today, this man, Venron, attempted to destroy the enterprise to which we have all sworn our lives! He has put us all in deadly danger! See his heinous deed!"

Venron's face disappeared. In its place appeared a long shot of a huge room. In the center stood a large, lumpy machine that Denetree did not recognize. At one end bulged two translucent domes like the eyes of an insect, but from the place where the animal would have had a mouth projected a long, three-part device. For a few moments, nothing happened. Denetree thought she saw movement behind one of the domes, but the surface was reflective and showed only what appeared to be the silhouette of a man.

Then large doors opened behind the machine. The Tenoy ran inside. The guardians wore body armor and aimed long weapons at the machine. A voice echoed through the room: "Come back! You can still turn around!"

The device on the front of the machine began to rotate toward the wall of the room, and the Tenoy dove for cover. The device stopped turning.

The image froze. "Observe closely what this murderer did!" crackled the loudspeaker.

The projection spat fire. Once, then a second time.

"Venron, no!" Denetree whispered at the recording.

A gigantic jet of fire shot out from the lower part of the machine and catapulted it through the roiling wall of flames and smoke it had created.

The wall was broken by a jagged opening, and through it Denetree saw the stars. For the space of a heartbeat she forgot her fear. The stars! Venron was not taking his own life, he had found a way to the stars!

A loud hissing noise from the loud speaker dragged her attention back to the display. It looked like invisible hands were dragging at the Tenoy with terrible force. The men and women tried to hang on, but the naked metal floor offered nothing to grasp. One after another they flew through the opening to the stars where, with eyes bulging out of their sockets and desperately flailing arms and legs, they died.

"Venron! What have you done?" Tears flowed from Denetree's eyes, for the first time she could remember. "That ... that's ... what will they do to you?"

The loudspeaker gave her the answer. "The traitor has already met his well-deserved fate. And those who helped him will share it!"

4

The crewmembers of the *Palenque* might resemble a randomly assorted mob hurriedly thrown together in some remote space-port in the galactic backwoods, but Rhodan had to give them this: they were fast.

The *Palenque* came out of hyperspace at Crawler Eleven's last known position less than five minutes after the comm officer announced loss of contact.

"Hyperdetection!" Sharita Coho barked. In her severely tailored uniform, the commander seemed ludicrously out of place among the prospectors. The men and women of the *Palenque* took pride in their individualized personal appearance. Rhodan still found it hard to believe that the commander and the comm officer, for example, belonged to the same ship. Alemaheyu Kossa reminded Rhodan of Jimi Hendrix, an Old Terran rock musician who had died shortly before man's first flight to the moon, except that Alemaheyu had darker skin and usually didn't bother with a headband to keep his mane of frizzy hair under control.

"In progress," replied Omer Driscol, the hyperenergy detection officer. The stocky black man had his face so close to the holos projected above his console that his nose almost interrupted the images. "Last outliers of the hyperstorm ... "

"Those go without saying," the commander interrupted him. "Any results?"

"Nothing so far. Evaluation running." Driscol seemed unaffected by Sharita's curt tone.

Is he just used to it? Rhodan wondered. *Or is he suppressing his anger out of concern for his comrades on the lost crawler?*

Sharita turned her head. "Alemaheyu? Contact?"

The comm officer shook his mane. "No."

"No good. Keep trying."

The skinny Terran bent over his virtual keyboard and typed a series of commands while murmuring to himself. Rhodan thought he heard, "Come on! Come to Mama!" but decided he had to be mistaken. Not even these prospectors could be that eccentric.

"Decrease velocity to half light-speed. The crawler was moving at just ten percent light. We can cover its entire flight path in half an hour."

Tense silence reigned in the control center for several minutes, then Alemaheyu spoke up again. "Sharita."

"Have you made contact?"

"Not with Crawler Eleven, but the other crawlers have reported in. They want to help."

"There's nothing to help with. We're their eyes and ears—and we're at the scene."

"Yes, but they still want to help."

"That's ridiculous! Tell them that they ... "

Sharita broke off when Pearl Laneaux, first officer of the *Palenque*, stepped up next to her and rested a hand on her arm. Pearl towered over Sharita by more than a head.

"What is it?" Sharita snapped.

"Don't do it." Pearl gazed at Sharita with doe-eyes. The two women seemed polar opposites. With her military bearing and spotless uniform, Sharita might have passed as an overeager cadet on a battlecruiser in the League of Free Terrans fleet—but the LFT didn't offer many opportunities to seventy-four-year-olds. Pearl, by contrast, seemed like gentleness personified, a delicate beauty completely at odds with the stereotype of the rough-and-ready prospector.

Their contrasting personalities could have put the two women at loggerheads all day long. And sometimes, like now, they were. But in Rhodan's view, every quarrel between the two top-ranking officers seemed to clear the air like a good storm. When the thunder and lightning faded away, the intelligence of both women had contributed to a decision.

"What?" Sharita demanded, her eyes flashing with anger.

"Don't brush off the crawler crews. Of course they can't help with the search—they know that as well as you do. The gesture is what matters to them."

"Feh! Gestures!"

"Sharita, you know how close the crawler crews are to each other. Don't make it harder for them by denying them the chance to even try to help."

Rhodan saw Sharita's neck muscles strain against the tight-fitting collar of her uniform. For a moment, there was a distinct possibility of violence. Instead, Sharita pushed Pearl aside and called: "You heard her, Alemaheyu! Let the crawlers come. But tell them that the lost time will of course be deducted from their shares. We aren't out here for the fun of it."

The search got under way as one crawler after another materialized near the *Palenque*. The flying laboratories shot back and forth like a flock of birds, performing their task with an agility that surprised Rhodan.

It was no use. The *Palenque* and the smaller craft accompanying it covered the entire sector without finding a trace of the crawler.

"I'm sorry," the hyperdetection officer finally said, rubbing his hands with a helpless look. "The sector has been swept clean. There's some cosmic dust here and there, but otherwise nothing."

"But that's impossible!" Sharita retorted vehemently. "The crawler can't have gone far!"

"Why not?" Rhodan interjected. "It could have accelerated, or even activated its faster-than-light drive. The FTL dematerialization energy signature could have been lost in the hyperstorm."

"I gave no order permitting them to do so. But ... " A grim smile appeared on Sharita's face. "But that doesn't mean much. Who here listens to my orders?"

No one in the control center dared laugh.

"Widen the hyperdetection sweep!" Sharita ordered. "Make it a radius of one light-year. I want a close look at every speck of dust!"

31

The control center crew went to work. Every man and woman bent over the console instruments in their niches. Every ship in the LFT fleet possessed sound and optical isolation fields in the control center that allowed each station to perform its work without interruption or distraction. On most ships, these fields ran almost constantly, with holos ensuring that the control center crew remained aware of the current situation at all stations. On the *Palenque*, a contrary culture had evolved. The prospectors enjoyed the close contact with each other, and Rhodan suspected that someday they would tear out the screening field systems entirely, considering them useless junk.

Now, the prospectors worked in silence, focused on their own tasks yet perfectly aware of their fellow officers. Rhodan heard the occasional muffled curse and heavy breathing, but the report they were hoping for didn't come.

Rhodan caught himself tapping his fingers nervously on the arm of his chair. He wasn't used to sitting inactive in moments of crisis. But the seat he had been given allowed only passive viewing of the data; he could not access the ship's syntron and its subsystems.

Sharita cleared her throat and paced. The fingers of her right hand tapped heavily on the grip of her uniform's holstered beamer. Rhodan felt each tap like a heavy drumbeat.

"Hyperdetection!" Omer Driscoll exclaimed. It was a cry of joy. "Object at distance of just one light-hour. Mass ... "

"Yes?"

"Mass triple that of a crawler," the hyperdetection officer replied tonelessly. "No idea what it is, but it isn't our people."

"Is the syntron getting a visual of it?"

"Just now coming in. The outliers of the hyperstorm are still interfering with detection. And whatever it is, it's moving damned fast. But we've got something."

"Put it up!"

In the middle of the control center, a holo taller than a man appeared, like a window into the blackness of space. The object shown in the holo was nothing more than a dark shadow racing through space, blocking the stars in sections as it flowed past.

The blunt, stocky shape reminded Rhodan of a thumb. It lacked any hint of the flattened appearance to which the crawlers owed their name.

At their first sight of the object, the control crew broke out in angry curses. Rhodan felt relieved at their reaction: he had wondered if the crew of the *Palenque* would ever release its tension.

But at what cost ... ?

"Let's take a closer look at that thing," Sharita ordered.

Rhodan felt a vibration under his feet as the *Palenque*'s engines accelerated to maximum and sent the ship after the object.

In the control center holo, the rotating shadow grew ever larger, its outlines becoming increasingly sharper. Rhodan thought he saw metal reflecting the dim light of the stars. Long, regular lines, and at one end ... a black abyss, framed by sharp-edged tongues of metal that twisted in all directions. One prominent spike looked like it was being pulled back and forth by the rotation of the object, almost as though it was waving. *What an absurd thought.*

"Hey, that thing is waving at us!" Alemaheyu exclaimed. Apparently, he had no concerns about expressing even the craziest interpretations out loud.

"Can the chatter! That thing out there is just a piece of dead metal, nothing else."

Dead metal ... Rhodan thought there was a grain of truth in what Sharita said.

The *Palenque* made a short hyper-light jump. When it reentered normal space, the object was immediately in front of it—at a distance of a quarter-million kilometers.

It was unmistakably a technological artifact. It reminded Rhodan of the rockets used by the human race during his time with the U.S. Space Force nearly three thousand years ago, before man discovered the Arkonides.

Except that this rocket had been torn in half. They were looking at a remnant, and the burn marks on the metal tangle at one end indicated that the split had been the result of an explosion. Had an accident occurred on board? Or had someone shot at the ship? And—Rhodan realized it was the critical question at the moment—what had happened to the other half?

He turned to the hyperdetection officer. "Any other objects like this one in the vicinity?"

Driscol hesitated, then shook his head.

Sharita gave Driscol an angry look. To Rhodan she said, "You are forgetting your status. You are on the *Palenque* ... "

" ... as a guest. I know. Nor am I claiming any authority to command. I just asked a question. And I only took it upon myself to do that because there isn't much time."

"You don't say!"

"I do. And there are other things you act like you're not aware of. That thing out there"—Rhodan pointed to the control center holo, in which the wreckage now took up almost all of the image—"is moving at just under light-speed, and we've matched our velocity to its."

"So?"

"That means we're in relativistic territory. At the moment I can only make a rough estimate in my head since I don't have access to the ship's syntron, but I'd guess that for each minute we spend at this speed, something like a hundred minutes are going by on Terra and the other League of Free Terrans worlds. We've got to drop out of this speed as fast as we can or we'll have wasted any chance we have of rescuing the crawler's crew."

Sharita nodded, as if agreeing only reluctantly. "That's true. Very well. First we'll haul that thing on board—who knows, it might be valuable. And then we'll find our people!"

Rhodan didn't reply. He believed he knew what had happened to Crawler Eleven. If he was right, it would not make the crew of the *Palenque* happy.

The *Palenque* returned to the original search area, combing it for a second time in a series of hyper-jumps, supported by a swarm of crawlers that were just as industrious as they were blind. When this search also proved fruitless, Sharita expanded the search radius.

While this was going on, no one worried about the wreck that had been recovered and which now rested in one of the *Palenque's* hangars. Not in the hanger used by Crawler Eleven—the symbolism would have been too much for the crew—but in the hangar designed to accommodate the ship's space-jet, empty because the owners of the *Palenque* had been unable to bring themselves to invest in the auxiliary craft. It was not a lack of curiosity that kept the prospectors from examining their discovery: the bottom line was that the wreck was something dead, and their concern was focused on the living.

But with each hour that passed, it became increasingly clear that the crew of Crawler Eleven now lived only in the minds of their fellow prospectors. There wasn't the slightest trace of the vehicle to be found in the Ochent Nebula.

Rhodan watched, a helpless onlooker, as the prospectors' hopes died bit by bit. At first, sheer tension allowed them to avoid the truth. The members of the control center crew tapped into the hyperdetector's data and went through it with their own eyes in the desperate hope of discovering anomalies that the ship's syntron had overlooked. Alemaheyu Kossa wrote search programs on the fly that analyzed the incoming and stored data from fresh perspectives. But their efforts yielded no results; all they found were small, scattered clouds of cosmic dust. Exhaustion replaced tension, and desperation grew. It simply *couldn't* be! Their crewmates *had* to be alive! They fought the ever more pressing need for sleep, determined to not leave their comrades in the lurch. But the hyperdetector remained silent, and as the search radius steadily grew, the probability of finding Crawler Eleven steadily shrank.

Finally, Rhodan felt compelled to speak up. "Commander, I believe there is no point in continuing this search."

"Oh?" The glare from the bruised-looking eyes clearly added: *And what makes you think you know so much about it?*

"The crawler's crew is dead."

"And how can you know this? The crawler had enough air and supplies to last for weeks."

"I'm aware of that. But it doesn't matter. The crawler has been destroyed."

"That can't be." Sharita rose abruptly from her seat and stood up straight, brushing an imaginary piece of lint from her uniform jacket. "We have combed the entire area. The last vestiges of the hyper-storm have died out. The hyperdetectors are operating at full capacity. If there was even one piece of debris bigger than a speck of dust out there, we would have found it."

"Exactly."

"What do you mean by that?"

"That in all likelihood, not even a speck of dust from Crawler Eleven remains."

Sharita's right hand closed around the grip of her beamer. "Now I understand what you're trying to say! Those damned Akonians! I'll make them pay! Who else could be behind this? If not them, then it was the Dishheads! I'll … "

Rhodan shook his head. "No. This was not their doing."

"And who else, pray tell? Don't tell me it's the Arkonides, and they're the reason you're here hanging on our … tail."

"No. My mission is what I have told you. I'm here to make contact with the Akonians through unofficial channels and improve Terra's relationship with them. Granted, the Akonians are all over the Ochent Nebula, but it wasn't the Akonians who destroyed the crawler. It was that thing there." The Immortal pointed to a small holo at the edge of the control center showing the hangar containing the recovered wreck. "Or I should say, its missing half."

Pearl Laneaux, who up to now had been occupied with the hyperdetector data at one of the consoles, spoke up. "There's something to that. The thing was moving at nearly light-speed when we retrieved it. An object's mass increases toward infinity the closer it comes to the speed of light. Even a collision with a toy ball moving at that speed would be fatal. Only the tiniest particles would be left of both bodies."

"That could be," the commander allowed. "But why is half of that thing still left? Assuming your suspicion is correct, then shouldn't there be just a single cloud of particles remaining?"

"That's true," Rhodan conceded. "But the thing may not have come apart in the collision with the crawler. What if this rocket had split in two long before? The debris would likely follow only slightly deviated trajectories. One half collided with the crawler, and our search revealed the other half, which despite its high velocity was still in the vicinity of the collision point."

Sharita closed her eyes, took a deep breath, and turned to the hyperdetection officer. "Omer, go through the stored hyperdetector data. Search for particle clouds. Maybe there's one with a mass that roughly matches that of the crawler plus a piece of debris like the one in the hangar ... even though I hope not."

The result came a few minutes later. There actually was a particle cloud in the specified sector, and its direction, velocity and mass were within the parameters of what would be expected after a collision between the crawler and a piece of debris.

Sharita quietly thanked the hyperdetection officer. "At least now we are certain." She turned to Rhodan and stared at him for a moment. "You suspected this all along, didn't you? Why didn't you say something?"

Rhodan met her gaze. "Because it wouldn't have made any difference. None of you would have wanted to believe me. You would have gone on looking anyway until you fell over from exhaustion. And I understand completely. In your place, I would have done exactly the same thing if the lives of my friends were at stake."

Pearl Laneaux opened her mouth, but Sharita waved her off with a militarily abrupt gesture. "I know, I know. He has a point." She straightened the belt from which her beamer dangled. "It's now confirmed. The three crawler crew are dead. Pearl, inform their families. See to it that they get the risk bonus they're entitled to. And now I want to take a look at the thing that is responsible for the loss of my people."

The commander of the *Palenque* stalked out of the control center. Rhodan joined her, and Sharita accepted his company without a word.

5

"Are you sad?"

Lemal Netwar carefully turned his head in the direction from which the voice came. His caution was rewarded; he felt only a fleeting twinge of pain.

He looked at the blank wall. The Net chose not to manifest itself today. It had been manifesting less and less often. Perhaps the projector had broken down and the Net had not found a substitute. It would be one more in a long list of devices on the *Nethack Achton* that had failed.

"Why do you ask?"

Netwar was a large and powerful man; he remained so despite the sickness that ate away at his joints. With his broad shoulders (though lately he found himself slumping), he could have been mistaken for a metach who had been assigned to heavy labor his entire life. But the appearance was deceptive. Nothing could be further from the truth.

"I know you, Lemal." The voice came from a different direction. Netwar made no effort to turn toward it. He was not in the mood to play games with the Net. Here in his private rooms, it heard every word he said, whether he liked it or not. And he had to take it easy on himself, try not to provoke pain by unnecessary movements.

"The wrinkles on your forehead tell me everything I need to know," the voice continued. It resonated with a human warmth that would have convinced a casual listener a real person was talking. If the same listener had been asked if the voice was that of a man or a woman, they could not have answered with any confidence. "It runs straight up from the bridge of your nose and branches out on your forehead to both sides. You always have it when you're worried."

"Always?"

"In 97.355 percent of all cases." The voice sighed. "Why do you compel me to unnecessary precision? To remind me that I am only a machine?"

Netwar did not reply. He often wished he had never begun tinkering with the Net. By doing so, he had upset the natural order of things. He was the Naakh, the ruler of the *Nethack Achton*. The Net was designed to monitor everything that happened on the Ship, gathering information he used to exercise his rulership for the good of all metach. It was what the Builders had intended.

And what had driven him to make changes? He had a lot of reasons. Even good ones. Standing still meant going backwards, was one. To make progress, they had to use the limited resources available to them on the Ship to maximum effect. Netwar hadn't realized what he was getting himself into, was another. The only honest excuse was: he was lonely. The other metach did not regard him as an ordinary mortal. Most worshipped him, many hated him, and without exception they both respected and feared him. If he had tried to discuss his cares and problems, the burden of his responsibility with other metach, he would have met blank incomprehension, even outright rejection.

Netwar had a strikingly sharp mind, but he didn't need to be a genius to recognize his problem. Once, a long time ago, in one of his darkest hours, he had tossed this intelligence to the winds. Naturally, he had reclassified the woman in whom he had confided to lifelong labor in the fields on the Outer Deck, as far away from him as was possible aboard the Ship. This decision was not only for his own good, but for that of the entire Ship.

Soon after this incident, he had started to fiddle with the Net. The Net's hardware was fixed; the Ship had not been given resources to make expansions or large-scale changes to the system, but the hardware was not the important element for what Netwar wanted to do. It was only the skeleton. What he wanted to shape was the software—the flesh—and that he had changed according to his whims.

He was the Naahk. He made all life-and-death decisions on board the *Nethack Achton*. But being all-powerful did not make him all-knowledgeable. It had taken Lemal Netwar a long time to learn the basic concepts of programming, and still longer to achieve the first tiny successes. The Builders had, of course, laid the foundation. They had equipped the Net, the decentralized union of all the *Nethack Achton's* computers, with simple speech recognition and voice control. Netwar wanted to elevate the Net interface to the point that interaction with the Net would be indistinguishable from interaction with a person.

His first attempts had been laughably primitive. The Net had been designed to react to a series of only two-hundred-fourteen precisely defined commands. Naturally spoken language lay outside its capabilities. In order to be understood by the Net, Netwar was forced to use a syntax that was rigidly simple. In the first phase of elevation, he had succeeded only in giving the Net a pseudo-intelligence, essentially the ability to play a question-and-answer game that quickly grew tiresome. The Net had replied to every statement with a question. No matter what he said, he received only questions—never answers.

"You *are* sad," the voice declared.

Now, Netwar regretted what he had done. He had hoped for someone to talk to, someone on whom he could unload his worries—not someone who confronted him with them.

The Naahk said nothing. He tried to concentrate on the data on his master display.

"It's the children, isn't it?"

Netwar immediately lost his patience. He looked up; an absurd gesture, since to look at the screen was to look directly into the Net's face. And it caused him pain, as well. He groaned softly.

"Don't call them that. They aren't children—not any more."

"Oh. So you no longer consider those on board to be your children?"

"We are a community. We must work together to survive. Everyone must serve the community in his assigned place. We ... "

"Spare me the lecture, great Naahk," the Net interrupted. "I wrote that one myself, remember?" Netwar heard an exhalation like a deep sigh come from all around him. Then the voice continued with exaggerated calmness. "I didn't want to talk to you about that. We need to talk about the children."

"Their leader was twenty-two, and the rest were about the same age."

"Please, Lemal. What does physical age say about a person? You, of all people, know better than that."

Netwar ran a hand through his short black hair. He wanted to run away—from himself, from the responsibility he had voluntarily accepted. But the Ship was too small; there was no escape.

"Have it your way," he said ungraciously. "Call them what you like."

"I knew we could talk reasonably with each other," the Net said. "These children did bad things. They explored forbidden territory, asked questions that should not be asked."

"Not children. One child, named Venron. He was alone. You verified that yourself. He accessed the data alone and he broke into the hangar alone. He alone—"

"—condemned forty-three Tenoy to an agonizing death. Forty-three of your best guardians. A crime without parallel in the history of the Ship! Yes, he carried it out alone. But the seed can't have grown in him alone. And it's that seed that concerns us. Venron is dead, forgotten, the past. We have to concern ourselves with the future."

"We?"

"You, of course. With my insignificant help."

"And what would that be?"

"I'm at your side," the Net replied in a maternal tone. "I'm at your side in your hour of need, when critical decisions must be made."

"The decision was made for us. The traitor is dead."

"He is, yes. But the others still live."

"The others?" It was a rhetorical question. The Naahk knew as well as the Net that there must be others like Venron: his confidants, co-conspirators. But Netwar had hoped to ignore that knowledge, to deny it so that he would not be forced to act upon it.

"His co-conspirators. Haven't you looked at his file?"

"Of course. He was an eccentric, a loner. People like him occur occasionally, regardless of our skill in prenatal genetics. Even education has its limits." *When did you become an inquisitor, Net? I altered you to support me, to help me—to ease the weight of my office, not to exercise it.*

"Loners are never alone. The term is a symbol, an imprecision of speech. Loners have families, a friend or two, and they belong to a Metach'ton."

"Should I have everyone who ever spoke with Venron arrested?"

"Of course not. Just a few will suffice."

"On what evidence shall we arrest them?"

Several seconds passed before the Net replied. "Your children are clever. And my presence is not as extensive as it once was, though we attempt to give the opposite impression."

"So there is none," the Naahk said trying to keep his relief from his voice.

"There is no evidence, but it isn't necessary. We know Venron's associates. We'll send the Tenoy to them, intimidate them, and ask penetrating questions. Anyone collaborating with Venron will give himself away under the pressure, and perhaps a few others. And those others will betray additional members until we have the whole conspiracy. The traitors will betray each other. Could there be a more fitting outcome?"

"And if we catch the innocent in our net?"

"Then we will have performed worthwhile educational work. If anyone harbors doubts about his place on the Ship, we will have driven out those doubts."

Netwar looked down at his large hands. He believed in the mission, in the great goal of the Ship and everyone on it. He had sworn to do everything necessary to fulfill their task. But he had taken that oath unable to imagine how heavily it would weigh on him. He had always imagined himself as a kindly ruler, a loving father who protected those in his care. He never would have believed that one day he would order the death of the very people he was pledged to protect, in order to save the larger community.

Desperate thoughts pounded at his brain. He wished that something would happen to take the decision out of his hands. Or that some of the conspirators would show remorse and allow him to be merciful. Or that the Net would give up on this course of action. Or—and this was the height of improbability—that the Protector would return.

Has it finally come to this—hoping for miracles? he admonished himself. *It's time for you to be renewed again!*

"Well?" asked the Net.

The Naahk straightened his spine. "You're right, as usual. Do what you think is necessary."

"I'll give the orders. We'll start with his sister—it's very unlikely that she knew nothing of his subversive activities."

"Fine."

Netwar tried to suppress the thought of what the Net's orders would lead to and concentrated on the master display screen in front of him. He called up the Ship's status data and compared the actual numbers with their corresponding theoretical values, then reviewed area status reports. After a while, his tension faded as he relaxed into the familiar routine of leadership. Proposed changes to the irrigation schedule, personnel decisions, mediating disputes between neighbors—the banal but reassuring elements of daily life— reminded him of his real work: taking care of the community.

"Lemal?"

"Yes?"

"What are you doing there?"

"You can see for yourself. I'm working."

"Yes, but at what?"

"You can see that, too."

"I can. You are doing the wrong work."

"And what would be the right work?" the Naahk asked, though he knew the answer.

"You must speak to the metach. Forty-three Tenoy are dead. Their friends and coworkers deserve an explanation for their deaths—and the hope of justice."

" I will personally call their friends and coworkers to reassure them that proper measures are being taken."

"That is an excellent idea. You should do it right away, as soon as you've given your speech."

"My speech?"

"The metach have a right to know who endangered their community, don't you think?"

When the Naahk didn't reply, the Net continued. "I have taken the liberty of preparing some accompanying visuals." The pale face of a young man appeared on the command display. His jaw was clenched and pushed out toward the imager. He apparently didn't like to have his likeness reproduced. Despite his aggressive posture, his eyes held the look of a dreamer, and an alert intelligence. The Naahk knew this look: it had to be Venron, the traitor.

Always the best, Netwar thought. *It's always the best of us who find life on board too constricting, who yearn for outside, whose curiosity won't allow them to rest. And I crush them ...*

Words appeared below the traitor's chin. "Metach, I am speaking to you today—"

"Get rid of the text."

"Don't worry—it's only visible to you."

Netwar jerked upright. Pain stabbed his joints. "You will not put words into my mouth! Get rid of it at once!"

"As you wish."

The Naahk angrily tugged his jacket straight. Was this what the Net had intended? To provoke him into a rage? He could admit to himself, at least, that the anger would help him fulfill his obligation.

Lemal Netwar spoke to his metach, informing them of the ghastly treason that Venron had committed, explaining the incalculable danger to which his actions exposed them, and describing the merciless punishment awaiting all those in league with the traitor.

The Net illustrated his words with images of dying Tenoy, but as he spoke, Netwar saw only his own face reflected in the display screen.

He studied his reflection, looking for the dreams he had always been able to see in his own eyes, regardless of his current life-cycle phase.

The dreams were no longer there.

6

The wreck seemed to be alive.

The metal of the ruined shuttle, whose temperature had stood near absolute zero for no one knew how long, groaned and creaked as it expanded in the warmth of the *Palenque*.

Under normal circumstances, Sharita Coho would have waited until the temperature of the wreck adjusted to the temperature of the hangar: the thing was dead, and she was in no hurry. At that point, she would have arrived with appropriate staff and the necessary equipment for making a thorough examination of their prize.

Normally. But nothing had been normal since Perry Rhodan had come onboard the *Palenque*. Sharita had known this would happen. She had protested vigorously against taking on the famous passenger, but the owners had stubbornly refused to listen: Rhodan would be on the *Palenque*; they left it to her discretion whether to join him there.

As if she could abandon the rewards of her decades of effort just like that! If Rhodan had turned up only a year or two later, she might have stuck to her guns. But ... maybe it wouldn't be as bad as she imagined, she had told herself.

She felt Rhodan's gaze on her everywhere: in the control center, here in the hangar, even in her own cabin. Rhodan's gaze measured her, tested her—and she couldn't rid herself of the feeling that he found her lacking. Not leadership material.

Sharita shook off these thoughts and focused on the wreck. It was covered with a layer of ice crystals like a thin coating of snow:

the moisture in the air of the hangar had condensed on the cold metal. She laid a hand on the hull and felt the cold slam into her through her uniform glove.

"Be careful," said Rhodan, who had remained several steps behind her. "Whatever they used to build this doesn't seem to tolerate temperature differences very well."

"So I see."

From the corner of her eye Sharita saw movement. She threw herself backwards. A metal strut hissed past her head.

Rhodan was at her side almost instantly. "Are you all right?"

"Yes, I'm fine." Sharita shook off his hand, angry at herself for appearing so careless and angrier at Rhodan. Did he always have to be right? And worse, play the rescuing knight who rushed to help her without a word of reproach?

Sharita stood, smoothed her uniform, and refastened the collar. The fabric felt like a clamp around her neck. It held her upright, which was good.

She walked slowly around the wreck. On the narrow side, which she assumed was the forward end, bulged a facetted dome that reminded her of an insect's eye. A second dome had burst. Sharita peered inside, but the slushy ice coated everything. Below the bow protruded an ice-covered projection. An antenna? No—it was too short and too thick for that purpose.

She continued around to the rear of the wreck, where she faced a tangle of blasted metal. Using both hands, she grasped one of the struts sticking out of the mass—practically daring Rhodan to make a comment—and pulled at it with all her strength. There was a cracking noise and pieces of ice fell, but the strut wouldn't come loose, and couldn't be used as a lever.

Rhodan said nothing.

"Piece of junk," Sharita murmured in the direction of the wreck. "Give me a break here!"

She stepped back, pulling Rhodan along with her. She drew her beamer and aimed it at the wreck.

"Sharita, no!" Rhodan exclaimed.

Well, how about that, she thought. *Sounded almost human. So you can lose your composure.*

Sharita fired. A green, flickering beam bored into the wreck's hull in a circular pattern.

The metal groaned in protest. Sharita resisted the impulse to dive for cover: she was determined that Rhodan would have to acknowledge her courage. The sound of rapidly cooling metal died away, leaving only the occasional ping and pop of the expanding metal. A hole large enough to let a human pass now gaped in the hull of the wreck.

"You shouldn't have done that," Rhodan said.

Sharita holstered her beamer. She smiled grimly, the first time she'd managed that expression since Crawler Eleven disappeared. "Oh? And why not?"

"You could have set off an explosion!"

"But I didn't, did I?"

"No, but who knows what you destroyed! Maybe the only clue that could have given us information on the origin of this wreck. Why didn't you wait until—"

"Why, why, why?" Sharita mocked.

Because you make me nervous, Immortal! she thought. *Because I feel you watching every step I take! Because I've got this crazy fear that you're comparing me to every commander you've ever flown with, and you're writing me off as an amateur. That's why.*

"Because I'm not some goddamned archaeologist. I'm just the commander of a prospecting ship," she said aloud. "Do you understand what that means? I don't have a flock of robots and scientists at my side giving me advice and getting their hands dirty for me and planning and documenting everything step by step. I don't have a fleet I can just call, and half an hour later a squadron of battleships filled with trained specialists will come flying up. I've only got this"—she tapped the side of her head—"and this!" She tapped the grip of her beamer. "And do you know what? They've never let me down."

Giving Rhodan no chance to answer, Sharita set her left foot on a projecting strut, tested her weight on it and then climbed inside the wreck. Darkness enveloped her. She switched on her picosyn and used it as a makeshift flashlight. Rhodan, who had followed her without a word, was forced to rely on her for illumination: as a passenger on the *Palenque*, he had not been issued a picosyn for his own use, let alone a weapon. Sharita felt fiercely glad that he was dependent on her for as long as they were inside the wreck.

A landscape of ice awaited them, as if they were inside a cave. Sharita's breath came out in clouds of vapor. The crackling, clicking noises of warming metal now surrounded them.

The air temperature had to be well below zero. Sharita shivered, the uniform jacket in which she had been sweating all day now proving to be little protection against the cold. It had to be worse for Rhodan, who was wearing lightweight, casual clothes.

"Let's not waste time." Feeling slightly guilty for her petty anger at Rhodan, she was now determined to keep him from freezing. Her light provided enough illumination to search each room. The barrel of her beamer followed the light.

"Are you afraid that space monsters might be hiding in here, just waiting to pounce and eat us?" Rhodan asked.

Sharita ignored his remark. She felt safer with the beamer in her hand. That was what counted, not what Rhodan thought about it.

Sharita estimated that the ceiling was about ten or fifteen meters above them and was the inner surface of the exterior hull. They were in a large cargo hold or hangar.

What was it used to transport?

To their left and right, a ledge about a meter high ran along the walls that corresponded to the outer hull. A bench for passengers? Possibly. That would mean the wreck was a spacecraft designed for short flights, probably a shuttle. In that case, the wide, empty interior hold would be for planetary-surface vehicles or equipment containers.

But if the wreck really was part of a short-distance shuttle, Sharita asked herself, what was it doing in the Ochent Nebula, far from all galactic civilization? And racing along at near light-speed, to boot?

She and Rhodan reached the end of the hangar. Before them rose a wall that spanned the ship's entire width. The layer of ice hid from their view the hatch that must connect the cargo hold with the shuttle's bow.

Sharita extended her little finger on the hand holding the beamer and tapped the picosyn on the other wrist. A series of diagrams and schematics flashed rapidly across the tiny screen.

She gave a grunt of satisfaction, then aimed her beamer at a point about three meters to the right of where she stood. A wide green beam of energy melted several square meters of ice. When the steam dispersed and condensed somewhere else, Sharita could see a discolored metal surface.

No wonder, she thought. *The builders of this shuttle never dreamed that its interior would be exposed to temperatures near absolute zero. The materials weren't up to the strain.*

"Aha! There's our hatch!"

A rectangle of straight lines had appeared on the wall, wide enough to allow two people to walk through simultaneously.

Sharita fired her beamer.

"No!" Rhodan exclaimed, but it was too late. The disintegrator ray traced the outline of the hatch. The metal didn't offer any significant resistance. Where it was touched by the beam, it dissolved into greenish gas. Along the outline of the hatch the metal suddenly turned black.

A few moments later, deprived of its support, the hatch tipped forward, falling with an echoing impact that must have been heard in the *Palenque*'s control center.

"Now what's bothering you? I suppose I should have waited for a team of specialists to carefully open the hatch so I wouldn't destroy anything valuable?"

"Yes, and—"

"I don't know what's eating you," she interrupted. "Even they couldn't have managed a better cutting job, right?"

"Hardly."

"So what's the problem?"

"I think I saw lettering. Left of the hatch at eye level."

"Intercosmo, maybe? 'Please don't shoot—the key is under the mat!'"

Rhodan didn't answer her sarcasm. "No, not Intercosmo. But a language that seemed familiar to me."

Well, crap. I really messed up that one. If I keep going like this, I'm likely to blow up the whole Palenque *out of pure nervousness.*

"There's no reason to get excited," she said, trying to downplay her mistake. "That can't have been the only lettering in this entire thing."

Rhodan nodded absently. His thoughts were clearly somewhere else.

Another icescape awaited them beyond the hatchway, though on a much smaller scale. They found themselves in a narrow corridor from which other passageways branched off, lined with doors instead of hatches. Sharita decided that they had penetrated the crew quarters. The engine must have been in the stern section, which had collided with the crawler.

For the next few minutes, they traveled through the corridors and climbed up several decks using primitive ladders. The ladders were installed in square shafts and their rungs studded all four walls.

"No antigravity," Rhodan remarked. "I believe this craft is designed for spaceflight without artificial gravity. In weightlessness, you move by pushing off from the rungs and then grabbing on to them again. In acceleration phases or in planetary gravitational fields, they're used like conventional ladders. Primitive, but absolutely maintenance-free."

Sharita hardly noticed her surroundings. Her left-hand little finger—she wasn't letting go of the beamer iin her right hand—raced over her picosyn as she called up data, took measurements and ran scans. She stopped rather suddenly.

"Got something?" Rhodan asked.

"Um ... " Sharita tapped the display again. "There is something that stands out."

"Yes?"

"Over there." She pointed to a section of the wall several meters further on. "It's too warm. It's much too warm behind that."

Sharita was so fascinated by her armband's readings that for a moment she even forgot her resentful feeling of being on trial.

"What's the temperature?"

"Minus one point three centigrade—which means fourteen point eight degrees warmer than in here."

"Energy emissions?"

"None. There aren't any energy-generating devices in this part of the wreck. If there even were any emergency systems, they haven't worked for a long time."

"So the reading must be an error."

"I ran the picosyn's self-diagnostic. The armband is in perfect working order."

They exchanged glances.

"Let's take a look."

Sharita aimed her beamer at the section of the wall where the heat source registered. The disintegration ray made slow progress cutting through the barely visible hatch.

"This hatch is a lot thicker than the first one," she called over the hissing of the melting metal.

"Maybe it's a rescue pod that's designed to be ejected in an emergency."

Sharita's beamer continued to burn through the wall. The loosened hatch fell away, and Sharita stepped first through the opening, her beamer held ready.

She found herself in a tiny room, this one somehow free of the ice that coated the rest of the wreck. In the weak light beam from her armband, Sharita could see several contour seats anchored to the floor, and in front of them instrument panels and dark, dead screens. At the other end of the room, she saw an opening that led into a kind of cockpit. And in front of that opening, on the floor—

"A body!"

Venron hears a noise. A crash that reminds him he is still alive; the cold has not eaten him. Not yet.

Sharita's light hovered on a human form. The body had drawn itself up into the fetal position, with its back turned toward them. One arm was outstretched, as though the being had been trying to reach something. The body was dressed in lightweight trousers and a shirt that appeared colorless and faded.

Light. Not the light of the stars. *This is softer. Venron tries to open eyelids that are frozen together. He manages only a narrow crack. The colors do not seem right. It is as though the cold has frozen even them. He sees the dully colored floor of the shuttle. And an arm. A long moment passes before he recognizes the emaciated limb as his own arm. He had stretched it out. He had thought he could touch her. Grasp her with his hand and cling to her. Who? he wonders. He has forgotten.*

"That … that … "

Sharita's mind told her to run to the figure on the floor, to help him or her, but her body didn't obey. It was as if her body had frozen at the moment of the discovery. She felt ashamed. How could she have been playing games with Rhodan to save her pride when someone lay here dying?

Rhodan pushed past her in one stride and knelt down next to the prone form.

A blur. A voice. It whispers something. Venron does not understand what it says, but that does not matter. It sounds soothing, sincere.

Rhodan carefully took the body by the shoulders and turned it on its back. It yielded only reluctantly, twisting strangely, as though every bit of flexibility that was natural to the human form was gone.

It was a man.

A man. Venron sees him from large, sad eyes. The man's mouth moves unceasingly, whispering a message he cannot understand. Venron wants to say something. But he cannot. His mouth will not obey him. The man in front of him dissolves into a blur.

Sharita and Rhodan looked at the unshaven face. The eyes lay deep in their sockets, the cheeks were sunken. The man's brown skin was waxy, and had a bluish tint. Rhodan slipped one hand behind the man's head, and with the other opened the magnetic fastenings of his jacket and wriggled out of the sleeve. He switched hands behind the man's head and shrugged his arm out of the other sleeve, then bunched the jacket up into a provisional pillow and rested the man's head on it.

A warm hand. It feels good to be touched. This touch reminds Venron of … Denetree. That was who he was reaching out for. He had seen her among the whirling stars. His sister would never abandon him. The shape above him flows into a new form and takes on solid outlines again. Venron sees his sister bending over him. She smiles.

"Is … is he still alive?" Sharita asked. She couldn't shake off her stiffness. Her beamer was aimed at Rhodan and the man. It was completely inappropriate and unnecessary, but she couldn't help it. The fingers of her right hand clutched the pistol grip with the intensity of a drowning man holding a life-saving tree limb.

A second voice. A woman. Venron tries to turn his head. He wants to see her.

"Yes." Rhodan glanced up at Sharita and looked pointedly at the beamer. "Put that thing away. The poor fellow certainly can't hurt us."

"Oh … sure." Sharita deserved the reprimand. But her fingers didn't obey. She had to use her left hand to unbend the obstinate fingers of her right.

Rhodan turned back to the man. "Don't be afraid. It'll be all right. We'll help you. It'll be all right ... "

The man's voice supports Venron. It is all that keeps him from falling into the abyss from which there is no return. The man will not hurt him.

While he spoke, Rhodan held the back of his hand to the man's mouth and nose. He felt a faint movement of air. The man was still breathing. Rhodan took the man's hand and felt for his pulse.

"The pulse is weak," he said, "but stable."

Did he succeed? Had he found the stars? And with them friends, not enemies, like he had been taught all his life?

"What's wrong with him?" Sharita had managed to kneel down next to the man. Her right hand still would not release her weapon, but she had at least succeeded in lowering her arm. The beamer's barrel pointed to the floor.

Again the woman's voice. Venron wants to see her. He exerts all of his remaining strength to turn his head. Reluctantly his chilled, atrophied muscles respond. The man's whispering gives him strength.

Rhodan shrugged. "Hunger. Thirst. Freezing cold. All I really know for sure is that if he doesn't get medical attention in a few minutes, he'll be dead. When we burned a huge hole into this compartment we removed his protection from the cold, and the temperature is sinking fast. I doubt he has the reserves to resist the sudden drop in temperature."

Sharita nodded slowly. A part of her was screaming in her head, trying to shake her awake.

"Sharita!"

A cry. Sharp. Cutting.

Sharita couldn't move.

"Sharita!" Rhodan exclaimed. "You have the armband—call for help now!"

A shout. What is going on? The security he was feeling begins to fade away.

With a mighty mental effort, Sharita pulled herself together. The beamer slid from her hand and fell to the floor with a rattle. She had done it! She hit her armband with her fist. "Pearl!"

Venron completes the movement and sees the shadowy form of the woman. Now she is shouting, too.

"What is it, Sharita?" the response came, long seconds later.

He opens his eyelids just a crack further. Slowly, very slowly, the outline sharpens.

"We need help immediately! Send the Doc and his medbots down to the hangar!"

Then he sees it: a uniform! Black as night on board the Ship.

The man shuddered. He gasped.

He is back. They have brought him back.

"On the way," Pearl Laneaux announced. "What's going on? Is something wrong with Rhodan?"

They will torture him. Execute him. They will extract everything he knows ... .

"No, we have ... "

No!

The man jerked upright, staring at Rhodan from wide-open eyes.

The man. His whispers were a lie!

Rhodan took hold of his shoulders to press him back down to the floor. "Don't be afraid. We are friends. Lie down. Everything will be all—"

Lies, all lies! He wanted to leave them behind him forever!

The man threw himself to the side, away from Rhodan. He grabbed the beamer that had fallen to the floor.

He does not want to hear any more lies. No more, not ever again!

The man aimed and fired.

Venron sees the beam that frees him from all care ... and turns his head into a cloud of plasma.

7

The night was her enemy.

Denetree gasped for breath as she pedaled. She rode in the highest gear, and had switched on the battery that she had planned to turn over to her Metach'ton in a few days. Such a waste, since she had spent weeks charging it on her daily rides. If she had charged it the final three percent, she could have given the Ship a full battery and received extra food rations for a week. She could have avoided the communal kitchen and cooked and eaten her extra rations alone.

Alone with Venron.

But all that was over. Venron was dead. She spelled it out in time with her pumping legs. D-E-A-D. Denetree kept viewing the scene of the shuttle blasting out of the ship over and over in her mind, watching the Tenoy being sucked out into space. She had never before seen anyone die except for old people, when it was time for them to step back and make room for the young. Accidents were practically unheard of. Over the course of centuries, work procedures and tools had been perfected for maximum safety. In order to maim or even kill oneself, it was necessary to possess a considerable amount of stupidity. Or intent. But again, only older people managed that. Not the ones who counted, the metach in Denetree's and Venron's age group.

The Ship took care of its own down to the smallest consideration. For example, balanced nutrition. Sustenance was ideally portioned, because to be overweight was waste and waste was a crime—treason to their mission. Over the following months, the Ship would have made up for the extra rations that she received in exchange for the battery by imperceptibly trimming her rations, or assigning her to the heaviest, most calorie-burning work.

Once or twice Denetree met other riders. She saw their lights approaching from a distance and forced herself to reduce her panic-driven speed to a normal rate, ignore the tempting paths in the fields on either side of the road, and greet the metach in a friendly and ordinary manner as they passed.

Denetree was lucky. She didn't encounter any Tenoy. No one stopped to ask her what she was doing on the Outer Deck in the middle of the night. Denetree suspected this was because the other bicyclists themselves were out with intentions contrary to the rules of the Ship. Meeting with Metachs from other Metach'ton for a night of passion, for example. The Ship did not approve of that. A metach's genes were too important to leave their recombination to the whims of chance, to say nothing of the fact that a lively night resulted in diminished work performance the next day. If the furtive lovers were caught by the Tenoy, they were punished with weeks or even months in one of the Metach'ton that the Tenoy watched most closely, and sometimes even permanent assignment to the Outer Deck.

Another light approached Denetree. She slowed her speed, tried to suppress the hammering of her pulse, and greeted the other rider.

Soon she would be at the elevator.

The hunt had already begun: the Naahk's speech had made that clear. And Denetree knew the Tenoy would look first for the traitor's sister.

In ordinary circumstances, the biological relationship between brother and sister would not be significant. Most siblings rarely saw each other, as the Ship generally assigned them to widely separate sectors. Most siblings didn't care. The personal attachment between metach that came from working together every day went much deeper than an accidental biological connection.

But the Ship knew that Denetree and Venron were close. The Tenoy would get her, interrogate her or worse. And Denetree did not try to deceive herself. She would not be able to endure the questioning. No one would believe her when she said that she had dreamed of the stars, but had known nothing of her brother's plan to see them with his own eyes. Then again, perhaps she would find unsuspected strength within herself and hold up under interrogation. But it wouldn't make any difference. Venron was dead. Nothing worse could happen to her. The Naahk needed guilty parties and he would get them, undeterred by the fine points of guilt or innocence.

Denetree's life was over. Hers, and the lives of the other Star Seekers. What a lovely name; she never would have expected that one day it would stand for death and desperation. Venron had given that name to their group. He did not claim it as his own idea, but she never learned where it came from.

There was one slight hope for Denetree: the mysterious present her brother had given her three days earlier. She realized now that by that point, her brother already had said good-bye to the Ship. This gift must be something more than a memento. Or so Denetree hoped.

In front of her rose an elevator tube. The cabin was at the level of the Outer Deck. This was unusual at this hour, because by now there should be no one left on the Outer Deck. Had the Tenoy discovered where she was already?

An old man sat on a stool in one corner of the cabin. When Denetree pushed her bicycle inside, he rose stiffly, supporting himself on a walking stick.

"Gotten late, hasn't it?" He winked at her.

"Er … yes."

He apparently misinterpreted the reason for her red face. He winked a second time and waggled his hips in a grotesquely awkward, obscene gesture.

The elevator started moving, descending with tortuous slowness. The old man had sunk back on his stool and his eyes were closed. Denetree thought she heard a faint snoring.

Denetree suddenly remembered that as children, she and Venron had annoyed the elevator operators by spraying them with water and running away, or throwing objects onto the guide rails just as the cabin began to move. The Ship only assigned old people to this job, metach whose legs were too slow to keep up with the children. As adolescents, they took to taunting the elevator operators with cruel insults. They were the perfect defenseless victims. What was their real purpose? In emergencies or when they dozed off, the Ship controlled the elevators between the decks, and made them faster and more reliable. The old people were just unnecessary eaters!

Only recently had Denetree understood the Ship's reasoning. It allowed the old people to continue to function as part of the community by giving them a task that didn't overtax them—and wouldn't affect anyone or anything if it did. This kept the old ones out among other people, rather than just sitting around and waiting to die. After all, they had no hope of reaching the destination.

The cabin rose toward the Middle Deck. As she approached the Ship's central axis, the physical weight that pulled at Denetree on the Outer Deck melted away. When the cabin finally glided up through the several meters of the Middle Deck's floor, gravity was half what it had been when she started out.

The release from heavier gravity somehow gave Denetree new determination: she would not give up. She owed it to Venron to keep trying. She owed it to her brother and herself. She would go to her Metach'ton and retrieve Venron's present. If she was lucky, the Tenoy already would have searched for her there and would assume that she would not be stupid enough to return.

The cabin stopped on the Middle Deck. Denetree wished the old man, whose chin was now resting on his chest, a good evening and forced herself to slowly, calmly exit the cabin, like a metach who had put in extra time in the fields out of a sense of duty and was headed toward her well-deserved sleep.

She didn't get far. Several Tenoy had taken up positions on the path that led away from the elevator. They wore body armor and carried hand weapons. Several meters away, two Tenoy lay on the ground behind a gun whose barrel rested on a stand. Denetree hadn't known such heavy weapons even existed on the Ship.

A line of pedestrians and bicyclists had formed at the checkpoint, patiently submitting to questioning and a search. The metach were used to following orders. But Denetree could see an unfamiliar excitement on many faces.

She had no choice but to join the line. Denetree took her place, knowing that she could not escape her fate.

Her heart was pounding. When had she last eaten? She couldn't remember. Her surroundings blurred and spun. As though from far away, she heard the whispered conversations of the metach ahead of her in line.

"I hope they catch them soon!"

"Traitors on the Ship! How can it be?"

"The Naahk was right! We have to wipe them out before they drag us down to destruction!"

The spinning grew faster. The metach around her became dancing blurs who leaped wildly up and down. Their whispering swelled to a roar.

What should she do? The Tenoy would scan her arm chip, and the Ship would know in an instant who she was. The traitor's sister. She had to jump on her bicycle and ride away, pedaling as hard as she could, switch on the battery and pedal, pedal, pedal, onwards, onwards, without letting up … .

Denetree swayed. The voices of the other metach thickened to an angry growling. With both hands, Denetree grabbed the handlebars of her bicycle and held it upright. For a brief moment, the solid metal bars supported her. The spinning stopped. Denetree saw clearly the faces of the other metach: they shrank away from her as though she had a contagious disease.

A Tenoy ran toward her.

Then … blackness. Denetree fell and fell and fell … .

She didn't feel an impact. Light abruptly flooded over her in a harsh wave that threatened to drown her.

"Take that lamp away!" said a voice. "Can't you see you're blinding her?"

The flood of light moved away. Denetree became aware of the outlines of men and women standing over her. They wore black uniforms and helmets with visors that revealed only their mouths and noses.

They've got you!

Strangely, she felt no fear. Her capture was inevitable. What was she thinking, defying the entire Ship by herself?

"Kisame!" There was that voice again. This time it wasn't giving an order. No, it was filled with consternation, overcome with concern.

59

Who was the voice talking to?

"Kisame! Can you hear me? Is everything all right?"

A hand slid under her neck and positioned something soft under her head. As the hand withdrew, fingers pinched her neck.

"Kisame! Can you feel that?"

Y-yes, Denetree thought. She tried to speak the thought out loud. She managed only a gurgle. The man attached to the voice was taking care of her. He had pinched her to see if she was conscious. But she thought he also had clasped her neck for a brief moment, as though he wanted to give her a sign. But what did the man want? And who was Kisame? Had he mistaken her for someone else?

"We should summon a doctor, Tenarch," another voice said. "Something is wrong with this woman."

"No, no, that isn't necessary," declared the man. A Tenarch, one of the Naahk's advisors. There was no way out now. "Kisame is just a little overworked. I know her Metach'ton very well. She is the best worker. Very devoted. Does everything for the Ship. Often too much." She could hear a smile in his voice. "Like now. She must have put in an extra shift. Right, Kisame?" He patted her forehead, as though she were a child, well-meaning but not very bright. "Everything for the Ship, isn't that so?"

Denetree's awareness snapped back to normal. The faces hovering above came into sharp focus. She concentrated on the man kneeling next to her. He was trying to get her out of this situation. Why? Who was he? He was a Tenarch; she could tell that by his plain gray clothing. He represented the Ship, therefore he couldn't be favorably disposed toward her. And if he found out about the Star Seekers, he would … .

The Star Seekers!

Now she remembered the man's face, from Venron's first effort at organizing a meeting about the stars. She and her brother had been barely more than children at the time, inexperienced and naive. Venron had simply approached everyone who seemed likely to share his interest and invited them to a gathering to discuss the stars. The Ship had of course learned of the meeting, and the Naahk personally warned Venron against any more such gatherings. That seemed to be the end of it. Venron was dealt with as a child, and the Ship was wise enough not to expect blind obedience. The warning had been effective for nearly a year, then Venron began to organize the Star Seekers, this time using all the caution he had learned from his first experience.

A metach who must have been in his early twenties had come to that first meeting. With his carefully trimmed goatee, he impressed Denetree as being vastly older and more experienced than everyone else in the group—and very wrapped up in himself. He refused to speak, playing absently with his beard as Venron enthused about the stars and the adventures and challenges awaiting them out there. Venron insisted that they didn't have to live in fear of what lay outside the Ship. Hadn't the Protector himself come from the stars?

Only at the end did the man speak. "You are a dreamer, Venron," he had said, "a dreamer who goes through life with open eyes, but who is blind. You speak of adventures and challenges among the stars, without realizing that adventures await you right here, in front of your nose." The man stood up to leave, but paused at the door. "I hope that one day you will learn how to see. Before it's too late."

Neither Denetree nor Venron ever encountered the man again, but Venron was firmly convinced that metach had betrayed him to the Ship the first time.

So. He had risen to Tenarch. His chin was shaved smooth now, but something about him made him seem old beyond his years. Was it the wrinkles around his eyes? Or the burden she glimpsed in their depths?

"She's coming around," the man said. "Well, Kisame? Are you feeling better now?"

What was the man's name?

"I'll take you home."

She struggled to remember his name. "L ... La ... ."

"Yes, it's me, Launt. Don't worry, Kisame."

Launt. Launt the traitor, Venron had always called him. The traitor! She tried to laugh, but it became a painful spasm of coughing.

"Very good!" Launt encouraged her. "Spit it out!" He turned to the Tenoy. "She was threshing the grain too long again," he explained, shaking his head. "Good old Kisame! She always refuses to use a threshing machine. 'Wastes valuable energy,' she always says. She hates waste. She—"

The woman, apparently the leader of this Tenoy unit, interrupted him. "That's fine. I get it." She pointed to Denetree. "Take your role model of a metach and stop holding up the line. We don't have time for 180-percenters who think they're doing the Ship a favor by working themselves to death."

The Tenoy disappeared from Denetree's field of vision, and her voice faded as she walked away. "You've got three minutes, then I'll call a doctor!" Then they were alone. The line curved around them, the waiting metach at once curious and fearful. Everyone knew that the essence of a waste-free life was indifference. A good metach did not deviate from the prescribed path lest their neighbors notice them—and, of course, the Ship. It was better to stay in one's place.

Launt carefully supported her shoulders. "Can you stand?"

"I … can try. I'm only … "

"Later. You can explain everything to me later, if you wish. Right now, we have to get you away from here."

Launt took her right hand and guided it to a metal rod. Without looking, Denetree recognized the handlebar of her bicycle. Launt had seen to it that no one took her bicycle!

She pulled herself to her feet.

"Are you feeling better?"

"Yes. But I'm still a little shaky."

"May I?" Launt indicated the bicycle. She understood at once what he was suggesting. He was right, but still she hesitated. She hadn't been carried around like that since … . She stopped her thoughts and climbed into the carrier frame installed in front of the handlebar. By the Protector! Venron was dead, the past was dead—and if she stubbornly stuck to old habits, that was what she would soon be herself.

"Good," Launt whispered. He climbed onto the seat and pushed off. "Thank you!" he called to the Tenoy. "It's good to know that the Ship has intelligent guardians who can differentiate between what's important and what isn't!"

Denetree held her breath. She waited for the Tenoy to catch the double meaning of his words and stop them, but the guardians only waved them on. She thought that she might have seen the corners of their mouths turn up just a little. It wasn't every day one was praised by a Tenarch.

Launt was soon gasping from exertion. Apparently, he didn't ride a bicycle very often. But he refused to change places with Denetree. "You have to rest!" he said. "Relax. People should think we're a couple."

People were everywhere. The Middle Deck was the Ship's living area. It offered protection from cosmic rays along with gravity just high enough to keep a metach's muscles strong. metach were born on the Middle Deck; here was where they died, and here was where they spent the largest part of their lives, safe within the shelter of their Metach'ton.

Or trapped.

Denetree had always preferred the Outer Deck, despite the burden of gravity that at the end of the day made even her arms heavy. There, one could be alone now and then, and believe in the illusion of doing things unobserved.

Not so on the Middle Deck. The paths were lined with metach enjoying the evening. Children played with balls they had made themselves. Adults sat or stood together, eating and gossiping. The houses of the Metach'ton stood close to each other and the narrow spaces between them were filled with impenetrable bushes. The plants on the Middle Deck had been bred to provide the highest possible carbon dioxide-to-oxygen conversion rate; food crops were raised on the Outer Deck.

Launt greeted people to the left and the right and smiled happily, as though the Ship had assigned him an especially pretty partner in order to fulfill his reproductive quota, and Denetree did her best to force joyous anticipation onto her face.

At length, Launt stopped in front of a house that stood by itself, surrounded by a high wall.

"What kind of house is that?" Denetree asked. It was too small for a Metach'ton and too large for an individual. Not even the Naahk had such a big house—or so she imagined. No one she knew had ever been to the Naahk's quarters.

"It's mine. Being Tenarch requires much thought and reflection, and thought and reflection require peace and quiet."

The gate opened automatically. Launt rode through and parked the bicycle. "No one can take it from here. That's important to you, yes?"

Denetree nodded.

They went into the house. It was huge. Four rooms for one person! In her excitement, Denetree almost forgot the circumstances that had brought her here.

Launt led her into a room with a single, narrow bed. He smiled kindly. "As I said, thought and reflection require peace and quiet. I'll sleep in another room."

Denetree wanted to protest—she was strong! She didn't anyone to take care of her!—but suddenly she felt terribly tired. She sank onto the bed.

"Sleep," Launt said gently. "Sleep, and tomorrow the world will look completely different."

Denetree sat bolt upright. Launt's words shattered her illusion of safety. "No," she said. "It won't. Unless you can do something for me."

Launt seemed only mildly surprised that she would ask. "And what's that?"

Denetree explained.

8

When Pearl Laneaux arrived in the hangar, less than two minutes after the call for the med-team, she found Sharita, Rhodan and a body missing a head and right shoulder. The body's dead fingers clutched the grip of Sharita's beamer.

The first officer held a primed, heavy beamer. Half the control center crew, also armed to the teeth, crowded the corridor behind her.

"What's going on?" she exclaimed.

"I called for a med-team," Sharita retorted, "not an assault squad." If Pearl didn't know her commanding officer better, she would have guessed Sharita was unaware of the dead body lying on the floor. But Pearl knew Sharita. She saw the minute trembling of her eyelids—and the glaring evidence of her beamer in the dead man's hand. Sharita Coho had never given her beamer to anyone else.

"Doc is at the back of the line," Pearl said in the casual tone she always used in conversations with Sharita. "Your call was interrupted by laser fire, so I assumed that medical help would be a secondary priority." Pearl pointed to the corpse with the hand holding her beamer. "It seems as though I was partly right. He doesn't need a doctor any more."

Sharita and Rhodan didn't repond. An answer seemed superfluous.

"What happened here?"

"That's what we'd like to know," Sharita replied. She knelt next to the dead man, gingerly took the beamer from him, then secured the weapon's safety and holstered it. "This guy did himself in."

"I can see that," Pearl said. "With your beamer."

Sharita rolled her eyes. "Very observant."

Rhodan stepped in. "He killed himself, Pearl. We found the man in this compartment, already half dead. We tried to help him. I spoke to him reassuringly, and though he didn't answer, I got the impression that my words calmed him. And then, suddenly, without any obvious reason, he grabbed Sharita's beamer and turned it on himself. We couldn't have anticipated that. It wasn't Sharita's fault."

Pearl nodded. "I understand." Then she shook her head. "No, no, I don't understand a thing. Here's a man holed up in a wreck going along at nearly light speed through the ... well, the backside of the galaxy without the slightest hope for rescue. But when help does arrive—by some chance with such slight probability I don't even want to try figuring it out—the fellow has nothing better to do when he sees his rescuers than to blow his own head off."

"We're at as much of a loss as you are."

"Well, let's retrace the sequence of events, see if we can figure out what happened. Did you do anything that might have frightened him?"

"Sharita did have her beamer pointed at him, at first," Rhodan said.

"No," Sharita contradicted him. "I had my beamer in my hand. I wasn't aiming at him, or not consciously, anyway. And even if ... look, if he's afraid of a weapon being aimed at him, killing himself with that same weapon isn't exactly a triumph of logic, is it?"

"Fear isn't logical," Rhodan said. "But you're right. It wasn't the beamer. He was only really aware of you after you had dropped the weapon."

For some time, the only sound was the footfalls of the command crew as they swarmed over the wreck to make sure there weren't any other survivors.

What had driven this man to suicide? Pearl looked around the tiny compartment—Lord, it was freezing in here!—then back at Rhodan and Sharita. She cleared her throat. The commander wouldn't like what she had to say, but it was the obvious conclusion. "Sharita, it must have been something to do with you."

"Pearl!"

"It's a statement of fact, not a reproach. But according to what you've said, he reacted positively to Rhodan."

"What's so different about Perry? This guy couldn't possibly tell that he's immor—"

"Sharita, he isn't wearing a uniform."

Sharita looked down at her black uniform, then turned to look at Rhodan's brightly colored slacks and shirt. "All right, I'm wearing a uniform. Since I'm the commander, that isn't so unusual, is it? Anyway, all this is pure speculation that we'll never be able to prove one way or the other."

"I disagree. We do have clues to work from," Rhodan said.

"Oh? Like what? This fellow here can't tell you anything."

"I wouldn't be so sure about that. Pearl, would you be so kind as to bring forward the ship's doctor?"

* * *

Hyman Mahal, the *Palenque*'s medical officer, was a stocky man with a receding hairline. Without a word, he bent down next to the corpse, sparing only a passing glance at the large wound sealed by the beamer's ray.

Mahal was a man of few words, and few of his shipmates knew much about him. Pearl's sympathetic nature invited confidences, however, and in a sentimental moment some months earlier, Mahal had spoken of his early career.

As a young doctor, the medical officer had been stationed on a mining world. There was little competition for such jobs, which was why even a new graduate with average grades could get hired for the position. Mahal believed being stationed even to a mining post would be a great adventure; all he had to do was make the best of it, and sooner or later he would move on to bigger and better things. A mere six months later, he stood on the verge of alcoholism, worn down by his monotonous duties, prodigious amounts of overtime, and loneliness. Comradeship was for those who went into the mines; everyone else lived in safety and isolation.

When he thought it couldn't get any worse, a fully loaded freighter, a steel globe a kilometer and a half in diameter, had crashed into the planet, and the resulting earthquake collapsed every mine. Mahal spent the next six days treating the maimed and dying, then the six months left on his contract recovering horribly mangled corpses.

"One good thing came out of it," Mahal had concluded, as Pearl sat in shaken silence.

"What is that?" the first officer had asked.

"It's all behind me. I've seen enough death for ten lifetimes. What can bother me now?"

Pearl was a long way from such philosophical acceptance. The sight of the headless corpse made her ill. She would have liked nothing better than to run out into the corridor and throw up—and then not come back.

"Doctor Mahal," Rhodan said, "I have two questions that I hope you can answer. The first is: Is this a human being?"

Mahal set to work without acknowledging Rhodan's question. He had his medical kit with him, a mobile, antigrav-supported mini-laboratory. At his direction, the kidney-shaped device lowered itself onto the corpse's chest. Pearl heard a humming and a hissing as the mini-lab extended its nano-feelers and took tiny tissue samples. At the same time, Mahal examined the dead man the old-fashioned way. He felt the corpse, lifted its arms and legs, tapped on the knees and elbows. He spent a particularly long time examining the hands and fingers.

He took a pointed scraper from his pocket and slid it under one thumbnail. When he withdrew it, a tiny black clump clung to the point. Mahal inserted it in an opening on the mini-lab.

"I thought as much," he murmured, more to himself than those waiting. "Soil. Enriched with microorganisms."

"What? That's impossi—"

The mini-lab interrupted Sharita with a sustained buzz. Mahal read the results of the evaluation on a directional display.

"Well?"

"The corpse is definitely human, of Lemurian descent."

"Any unusual characteristics?"

"He is strikingly healthy. He seems to be accustomed to physical labor. He is less than twenty-five years of age, and shows no trace of the deposits typical of an unbalanced diet, even though practically all human beings have them."

"Anything else?"

"He has never been sunburned. The skin samples are definite on that point."

"That doesn't necessarily contradict the dirt under his thumbnail," Sharita said. "Maybe he was really careful about using lots of sunscreen. Why is no sunburn so significant?"

"His genes are severely damaged—to an impossible degree for a planet-dweller, and certainly for someone who has never been exposed to the sun without protection."

"That can be explained, too," Pearl put in. She had been concentrating on the faces of Rhodan, Sharita and Mahal, and so her nausea had decreased to an almost bearable level. "This wreck can't have shielded him very efficiently from cosmic radiation in open space. Thus the genetic damage."

Mahal shook his head. His fingers played absentmindedly with the scraper he had used to sample the dirt from under the dead man's thumbnail. "Not a bad guess, but the nature of the damage is against that explanation. This could only be the result of years worth of exposure to cosmic radiation penetrating through insufficient shielding."

"This compartment was the only section of the wreck that remained airtight. There is no evidence that he had any supply of water or food—no empty containers or scraps—and the air supply had to be limited, as well," Rhodan stated.

"He can't have spent years in this compartment."

"Exactly. And that brings me to my second question. Can you tell us, Mahal, how long he was drifting through the vacuum on this wreck?"

"Hmm." The ship's doctor gave the mini-lab's syntron new commands. New values appeared on the display. "Based on his condition and assuming he didn't have any food or water with him, I'd estimate between thirteen and fifteen days, seventeen at the maximum."

"Thank you, Mahal. That's all I need to know," Rhodan said. He turned to the commander. "Sharita, I suggest we go back to the bridge. There's nothing else to learn here."

Sharita nodded without argument—a telling sign of how deeply the suicide had affected her.

***

The rest was a simple exercise in calculation, some fast talking and a stellar performance by the *Palenque*'s hyperdetection officer.

Rhodan presented his theory to Sharita Coho and Pearl Laneaux at the map table in the control center. The other members of the bridge crew and the crews of the crawlers were connected in real time.

"The calculation isn't difficult," Rhodan began. "We know how long the dead man was confined in the wreck: between thirteen and a maximum of seventeen days. The wreck was traveling at near light-speed, so the point at which the shuttle came apart has to be roughly half a light-month away, plus or minus ten percent."

"Assuming that it didn't change its speed," Sharita interjected. An undertone in her voice hinted that she had regained her self-confidence in the comfortable surroundings of the control center.

"Anything else would be highly unlikely," Rhodan replied mildly. Pearl wondered if the Immortal could be made to lose his composure—and if the sight would be worth being around him in such a moment. "The shuttle broke into two sections. Our half had no means of acceleration."

Sharita grimaced.

Pearl intervened before Sharita could voice the violent retort that surely was on the tip of her tongue. "So, we know where the shuttle broke apart. What do we accomplish by finding that location?"

"We find answers. The shuttle didn't collide with another object. As the fate of the crawler proves, there wouldn't be anything left but a cloud of particles if it had. Someone shot at it."

"The Akonians?" Sharita guessed. "The Ochent Nebula has been swarming with them these past few weeks."

"Probably not," Pearl said. "I've had the techs take a closer look at the wreck, and this shuttle was struck by a conventional warhead—hardly more than an oversized firecracker. Neither we nor the Akonians use anything like that. And it was not an accident.

We've found the entry point."

"All right, so it wasn't the Akonians. Who, then?"

"I don't know." Rhodan shrugged. "In order to find out, we have go where the attack took place."

"And then what?" Sharita balled her hand into a fist and struck her other palm. "Do you think the attackers are just sitting there waiting for someone to bring them to justice? And think about the company you're in. We're prospectors, not saviors of the universe intent on righting every wrong. We're out here to make a profit!"

"The biggest profit waits for those with the courage to step off the beaten path," Rhodan advised. "Executing an ultra-light jump will take only a few minutes, and we won't stay more than a few minutes."

"Then why go there at all?"

"To be certain of what we've found. Maybe to find more information. But definitely to search for the mother ship."

"Mother ship?"

Pearl hoped her mouth wasn't hanging open as unattractively as Sharita's.

"The mother ship. Think about it! We've brought the wreck of a shuttle, a transfer craft, on board. Its engines could not have accelerated it to near light-speed; everything about its design is clearly intended for short-range flights. There's only one explanation: the shuttle must have gotten its velocity from the mother ship. And that ship must still be in the area of impact, unless it has hyperdrive capability. But I consider that extremely unlikely since we haven't found any trace of five-dimensional technology in the wreck."

Pearl and Sharita were silent, then they exchanged a long look. Pearl nodded almost imperceptibly. She hoped Sharita had enough self-control to follow her advice.

"Very well," Sharita said finally. She spoke slowly, as though she had to force out each syllable. "Your logic is convincing. We'll investigate." She looked into the lens of the humming microcamera floating nearby. "You heard me, people! We're going on a treasure hunt!"

She turned to Pearl. "Plot the trajectory of the wreck before we took it on board—we'll follow it. And not half a light-month, but four light-years."

"But that's much too far!" Pearl protested. What had gotten into Sharita this time? "That's almost a—"

"—hundred times. Exactly. Because of the high velocity, time ran a hundred times faster on the shuttle than for us. The fifteen days we're assuming are measured in subjective time on board the wreck."

Pearl felt herself turning red. "Oh. I didn't think of that."

"Don't worry about it," Sharita said. "That's what you have me for."

9

"Lemal?"

The Naahk of the *Nethack Achton* had to force himself to turn his attention away from the screen. He didn't appreciate being disturbed. Especially not when he was working on the Ship's chronicle.

"Yes? What is it?"

"The Tenoy have succeeded in capturing one of the traitors."

"Good."

Lemal Netwar bent over the screen once more. The work on the chronicle was difficult and tiring, but indispensable. Who would record the history of the *Nethack Achton* for future generations if not he? The Net, perhaps, but somehow he doubted a presentation by a group of linked computers would say much to human readers. In an attempt to present an accurate depiction of facts, the Net would support its account with graphs and statistics, possibly even letting the numbers speak for themselves with no text at all.

Lemal Netwar was not interested in that kind of truth. His account was based on human qualities—and for him, chief among them seemed to be forgetfulness. It seemed to him that he found it harder to remember with each passing year.

And to remember, he needed quiet.

"Lemal?"

He suppressed a curse. "Yes, what is it? Have you caught more?"

"No, not yet," the Net replied. "But it won't be much longer. The interrogation will begin very soon."

The interrogation. The Naahk had managed to drive it out of his mind. "I know that."

"Don't you want to be present? The last time ... "

The last time was long ago! he wanted to shout. This interrogation, many other difficult decisions ... they were the price of his rank. He had to pay that price or resign his rank along with everything that came with it. At the thought, his hand went automatically to the chain around his neck, and he knew he could never make that sacrifice. Lemal Netwar had too much to lose.

"I'm coming," he said.

The Naahk left his rooms, something he did more and more infrequently. The older he grew, the more inclined to stay in his quarters he became. The Net took care of most routine business without his participation, and probably did it better than he would have—at least, truer to the spirit of the Ship and less prone to error. For the few critical decisions that required his involvement, he had learned that he could make them just as easily inside his quarters. He had even convinced himself that making judgments from the isolation of his quarters was better. Distance between him and those whose fates he determined allowed him to be more objective.

There was one additional and immediate reason why Netwar left his quarters only reluctantly: it was unbearably painful.

The Naahk's residence was situated near the long axis around which the *Nethack Achton* rotated in order to generate artificial gravity. Gravity increased with distance from the axis. The Inner Deck, which lay closest to the axis, had a third of the Homeland's gravity. In the Naahk's quarters, which hung like a spider's ensnared prey in a web of cable connections almost in the center of the Ship, that level sank to a tenth. Just enough for things to stay in place but exerting no undue pressure on his joints.

The elevator that connected the Naahk's residence with the Inner Deck began moving. Since the cable was seldom used, it now groaned loudly. Netwar idly imagined that the strain of moving affected the cable in the same way moving affected his joints.

Netwar moaned as pain stabbed his knees and hips. He tried to stand perfectly still to deny the pain a target, but either he failed to remain motionless or the disease had reached a new stage of intensity.

As the Naahk, Netwar commanded the skills of the best doctors on the Ship, but they couldn't help him. They could only give a name to his suffering: arthritis. The doctors couldn't prevent the accelerating deterioration of his joints; they couldn't even slow it down. All Netwar could do was accept his disease as a necessary evil that went along with his rank and hope that he would be freed from it sooner rather than later.

Through the transparent plastic floor of the elevator cabin, Netwar saw people waiting for him. Several Tenoy, but no officers—no one from the higher ranks of the administration, not even a Tenarch.

Why get their hands dirty, when others would do it for them?

He pulled himself together as the cabin approached the Inner Deck. Just before the elevator glided to a stop, he injected himself with pain medicine, his hand clenching the injection gun in his pocket.

The pain disappeared at once, replaced by a feeling of elation for which Netwar knew from experience he would pay dearly. The injection freed him from pain for several hours: the problem with eliminating it was that he ordinarily used the pain to regulate his movements. By paying attention to his level of discomfort, he could avoid actions that would aggravate his condition. Without the pain to guide him, he almost certainly gave the deterioration of his joints a push, and in the long term twisted the screw of his pain one turn higher.

The Tenoy bowed to him mutely, their eyes fixed firmly on the chain around his neck. This was perhaps the most significant moment of their lives: they were meeting the Naahk in person! Perhaps their emotion was so great that they would be able to repress the memory of the screams they would soon be hearing. Netwar already knew that he would not be able to do that. These screams would join the many others that tore him out of his sleep at night.

The Tenoy had brought an electric three-wheeled vehicle, and now politely indicated for him to sit on the wide padded seat. The Naahk refused. If he only had a few dearly purchased hours left to use his body, he didn't want to waste them by sitting, even if doing so would have been easier on his joints. More importantly, refusing the ride would reinforce his status. The Tenoy would tell every detail of their meeting with the Naahk, including, of course, his modesty.

They started out. The walk led them through the steel landscape of the Inner Deck. Netwar knew that most metach came to this section of the Ship only reluctantly. They missed the green that defined the Middle and Outer decks, but most of all they felt oppressed by the close quarters. The Inner Deck had such a small diameter that there could be no illusion of a sky. If one raised his head, he saw the opposite side of the deck, on which the machinery complexes and people hung upside down, attached to the floor by centrifugal force. After all these years, even the Naahk found it hard to shake off the feeling of being about to fall toward the ceiling.

But Netwar didn't look up. He concentrated entirely on the miracle of his legs carrying him forward with the effortlessness and strength of a young man.

The walk lasted almost half an hour. Too long for the Tenoy, who felt increasingly uneasy in the presence of the silent, mysterious Naahk; too short for Netwar, who wanted to enjoy his fleeting illusion of health and was reluctant to reach their destination.

It couldn't be avoided. The small group arrived at a low-roofed shed constructed of plastic slats. "Here we are, Naahk," one of the Tenoy said, unnecessarily.

Netwar stared at the shed; there were dozens like it on the Inner Deck. They provided storage for spare parts for the *Nethack Achton*'s machinery, which was concentrated in the protected interior of the Ship. Light shone through the age-deformed slats; one shadow moved slowly, a second lay not moving at all.

They will hear every word, Netwar thought. *Every scream.*

The door of the shed opened. A man with gaunt features stepped out.

"Launt, what are you doing here? There is no need for a Tenarch at this proceeding."

"I want to speak with you, Naahk. Alone."

"Of course." Launt was the most intelligent of the Tenarchs, a capable administrator. And a courageous man. No other would have dared to speak to the Naahk so directly.

Netwar turned to the Tenoy. "Go! You have fulfilled your duty. I no longer require you."

Hesitantly, the Tenoy withdrew. Netwar hoped that they wouldn't linger in the vicinity out of a sense of duty. It was not necessary for them to overhear his conversation with the Tenarch. And certainly not for them to hear the screams.

"Speak!"

"I must make an unusual request, Lemal. Perhaps it is even outrageous. But I am compelled to ask." Launt cleared his throat. "I ask you to release them. The traitors, the woman inside this shed, all the others. They pose no danger to the Ship."

The request was unusual. But outrageous? Netwar considered. Yes, outrageous. The more so because it reflected his own desires. He didn't want to do what lay ahead of him, but that didn't change the fact that he had to do it. For the good of the Ship.

"Not to you, personally," the Naahk said. "And not today or tomorrow, that is true. But what would happen if we let them go unpunished? They would promise never to dream of the stars again. A worthless promise. The traitors can't give up their dreams. When it becomes clear that there is nothing to fear, others would join them. Within decades, order within the Ship would break down. And we can't allow that. We have to think in terms of centuries, even millennia."

Netwar did not speak the name the traitors had given themselves. *Star Seekers*. That name meant something to him a long time ago, so long ago that he often wondered if he had only imagined that time. Perhaps it was only an illusion he had created to justify himself.

Launt's face flushed. "That is easy for you to say! You have—"

"On the contrary. It is an extremely difficult decision, precisely because I know exactly what I am talking about. We must deal with these traitors now."

Launt didn't move.

"Launt, you are one of my best Tenarchs. I don't want to lose you. Go now, and I will forget this incident!"

A vein throbbed in Launt's throat.

"Please go!"

The Tenarch trembled, but stepped out of the way. His head bowed, he disappeared between the machines of the Inner Deck without looking back at the Naahk.

Netwar took a deep breath and went into the shed. A single unshaded bulb threw harsh shadows around the room. The Pekoy greeted him with a silent bow. He wore a mask with slits for the eyes and mouth, and a round hole for the nostrils. Even Netwar didn't know whether the mask concealed a man or a woman. The Pekoy's heavy apron revealed nothing about the wearer's body shape.

The Net would know who was hidden behind the mask. If he asked, the Net would give him the answer: after all, he was the Naahk, but Netwar had never asked the Net for information about the Pekoy. Though he had questions—How did the Net select the Pekoy? Did the Pekoy (Netwar couldn't help it: he always pictured a male) exercise his office voluntarily? Out of a sense of duty toward the Ship and its mission? Or out of greed, for additional rations, his own house? And, perhaps the most important question: was it for the Pekoy as it was for him? Did the screams of his victims pursue him? Or did he go back to his Metach'ton afterward with the satisfied feeling of having done his job well? Some knowledge was easier to live without.

In the middle of the shed, a young woman lay on a work table improvised from a rigid plastic sheet set across two stacks of crates. The traitor. Sweat had clumped her chin-length hair in damp strands. Plastic cords tied her to the table at her ankles and wrists. A wide strap passed around her neck, preventing her from raising her head more than a centimeter or two without choking.

"Y-you're the Naahk?"

Netwar nodded.

"P-please … help me. I didn't do anything bad." She spoke softly, and had to swallow more than once between words.

"I am here to help you."

Her clothes were torn. Not as a result of mistreatment—the Net would have informed him immediately if the Tenoy had overstepped their authority—but of the arrest. The woman had fiercely defended herself.

"Thank you," the woman whispered. "Thank you. Please tell him"—her eyes rolled toward the Pekoy, who stood silently at the head end of the table—"that he should let me go."

"I can't do that. I do not have that power."

"But you're the Naahk!"

"I am the Naahk because I live up to my responsibility."

"We all do that."

"Not you. You betrayed us."

"I didn't!" The woman coughed violently.

"Then why did you try to go around the Tenoy's checkpoint?"

"I wanted to go home. It was a long day in the fields. The Ship needs well-rested metach. And the line was long, so I wanted to avoid it."

Netwar stepped closer to the table and cautiously sat down on the edge next to the woman. As usual, the Pekoy had been thorough: the sheet forming the tabletop was firmly anchored. Netwar studied the woman's features, and admitted to himself that the Net had been right. She was still a child. She didn't know what she had gotten herself into, the danger she was inviting onto the Ship. And now it was too late. She would very quickly become an adult and then die.

"The Net recorded your arrest and your actions during the minutes prior to your capture. You were very nervous for a metach on the way home from work and annoyed by a delay."

"I ... I had some trouble at work. A stupid argument with another metach."

"That happens. But didn't something rather different disturb you as well? The report about the traitor Venron, perhaps?"

The woman swallowed again. "Yes, of course. I was outraged. I was afraid."

"Afraid of the traitors? Or afraid of being exposed as a traitor?"

The woman's body writhed; she coughed and gagged. The Pekoy stepped closer, ready to turn her head in case she had to throw up. She must not choke to death on her own vomit. Not yet.

"I ... had nothing to do with the traitors," she burst out. "I hate them."

"Yes? Then prove it. Tell us the names of the other traitors."

"But how can I know that?"

"You knew Venron, didn't you? Then you know the others, too!"

"That's a lie!"

Netwar shook his head sadly. "I wish it were. The Net has eyes everywhere. It has recorded your encounters with the other traitors."

That was a lie. Once, the Net did have eyes throughout the entire Ship, but most had failed over the centuries and there were no spare parts to repair them. But even if all the cameras had been working, the Ship's memory storage unit capacity had been sufficiently damaged by cosmic radiation that they could not be spared to store the data from the remaining cameras for any significant amount of time. The Net had recorded the activity at each of the Tenoy's checkpoints, but Netwar had made up the rest.

A lie, but it served its purpose. That was what counted.

The woman's pupils went wide as she realized her fate was sealed.

"No," she moaned as she shook her head. "No, no, no!"

"Yes. You have put the Ship in incalculable danger. Did you not listen to your teachers? We must hide; we must never draw attention to ourselves."

"Venron only wanted to see the stars. He didn't want anything bad to happen to anybody. He only wanted ... "

"He very nearly killed us all. Forty-three Tenoy paid for his madness with their lives."

"He didn't want that!"

"Of course not. But he did it. And perhaps it was only the beginning. Perhaps he put our enemies on the trail of the Ship. Perhaps—"

A piercing scream interrupted the Naahk, turning into wailing. The woman shook, then twisted in her bonds. Her face turned red as she cut off her own air.

Netwar took her hand. First she pulled away. Then she felt for his hand and clasped it.

"Calm down," the Naahk said softly. "They aren't here yet. And you can help so it doesn't come to that."

"How ... can I help?"

She was a good metach. She only wanted what was best for the Ship.

"What is your name?" Netwar asked.

"Mika."

"Mika," he repeated softly.

Mika ... why did you let yourself be led astray? Why are you forcing me to do this to you?

"You must tell me their names, Mika."

"Their names?"

"The names of the others. Venron was not alone. Dreamers like him are never alone. They must tell others about their dreams, draw them in as well. You were one. And his sister, certainly. But who were the others?"

It's the best of us. Always the best. The ones who refuse to accept boundaries. The curious who want to know what lies beyond the Ship's wall. The ones we will need someday ... and the ones who until then must be eliminated.

"The ... the ... " The woman gagged.

"Please, Mika. Tell me their names. Surely you don't want the Ship to be destroyed?"

"I ... "

Her fingers, which had closed around his hand, clutched him so tightly that the pain overcame the barrier of the injection. Netwar suppressed a scream. Then her hand dropped back to the table.

"Mika, tell me their names. You—"

It was too late. She had closed her eyes, squeezing them shut with all her strength. Mika had made her decision.

The Pekoy slowly shook his masked head.

"Mika, tell me the names!"

The woman didn't answer. She merely lay there, rigid with fear.

"Mika, you must ... "

The Pekoy set down his leather instrument bag on the work table. It must have been made in the Homeland, because there were no animals on board the Ship from which it could have been made. The thought that someone assumed the necessary equipment for the Ship included a toolbox for torture made Netwar nauseous.

The Naahk stood and took two steps back from the table. He wished that the pain would return to his joints and distract him from the pain that would be soon administered to this human being who lay helpless before him. But that merciful pain didn't come. Netwar saw what happened with absolute clarity.

The Pekoy opened the bag and took out a tray on which had been mounted tools gleaming with clinical sterility. They resembled a surgeon's instruments. The Pekoy selected an instrument and applied it.

Mika was strong. She held back her screams for a long time. But when they came, they came like a wave and swept aside the mental barriers Netwar had built against them.

At last she named names. There were more than two dozen, more than Netwar had expected. Perhaps the corruption had spread further than he suspected, or perhaps Mika had named innocent people in her terror. The Tenoy would arrest them and find out the truth.

With his free hand, the Pekoy entered the names into his pico-syn, which relayed them at once to the Net.

The Naahk left the shed. His task was finished. The Pekoy would do the rest.

He met no one on his way back to the elevator. If the Tenoy or Launt had stayed in the area, they remained hidden.

Just as well. He wanted to be alone with his thoughts. Netwar sensed that he had opened a new chapter in the chronicle of the Ship.

He doubted he would ever find the strength or courage to write it down.

10

Solina Tormas was thoroughly sick of it.

For months, the Akonian research ship *Las-Toór* had been cruising through this cursed nebula on the backside of the galaxy, traveling from one dead world to the next. The only life here, if you could call it that, was prospectors of every kind and affiliation. Akonians, Terrans, Blues, members of races whose names she had never heard and could not pronounce, and whose unappetizing appearance she could have done without.

And what a gang of monomaniacs these prospectors comprised! All they had on their minds was money. Money and still more money. Solina's questions about the origins and fates of their immediate and remote ancestors they answered with, "Oh, I have something to do," then left her standing. A historian! Someone occupied with the past? Their prospecting instincts told them there wasn't any money to be made out of her.

Not that her colleagues treated Solina Tormas any better. No, the ladies and gentlemen of the Yidari were simply more refined. "That is really quite interesting," said these people who called themselves scientists when Solina's area of specialization came up, which it did seldom enough. "We really need to find a quiet moment and give your important work the time for discussion it deserves. Unfortunately, I must go to an important meeting/there's an urgent experiment waiting in the laboratory/I have to write my report at once, you know the bureaucracy. But when we have a chance … "

And that was the end of it. No one was interested in Solina's work. Lemurians! "Aren't they the ones who've been dead for fifty thousand years or so?" her fellow Yidari had asked during the obligatory polite introductions in the first few days after the *Las-Toór*'s departure. "Our ancestors whom those insolent Terrans want to claim for themselves?"

She knew it was not an idle claim. The Lemurians are the common ancestors of Akonians *and* Terrans, Solina wanted to inform them. And of the Arkonides and the Ferronians and probably every other humanoid race in the galaxy! You know that as well as I do! she wanted to shout. You just refuse to accept them as they really were, preferring to venerate them as the glorious founding fathers whose courage you can parade around as if it were your own!

Solina finally snapped. She took out her anger on a fat little geologist, the incomparably untalented offspring of one of the best families of the Blue system, a genuine Vakt'son, who had sympathetically patted her on the hip—he couldn't reach her shoulder—and advised her that she should transfer her field of research to a more useful era, such as the glorious battles against the Terrans after the first contact between the two races, or the underground war of the Condos Vasac against the Terrans' Solar Imperium.

Solina had cursed so violently that the fat geologist had dropped his glass in terror and run off as though pursued by the notorious and deadly Energy Command.

Since that incident, no one had spoken to Solina about her work. Not that it made any difference. *A more useful era.* The stupid little Vakt'son had hit her sore point. All the other Yidari on board were doing useful work. The astrophysicists were cataloging the Ochent Nebula, gaining new knowledge about the life cycles of stars and thus further developing the technology of tapping the energy of suns. The geologists of the *Las-Toór* were discovering planets and moons rich in valuable ores. That pursuit put them in direct competition with the private prospectors, but of course the Yidari were committed to the common good; the rights to their finds went to the Akonian state and so to all Akonians. On the worlds they visited, the metallurgists gained valuable knowledge about new alloys and element combinations that would contribute to keeping Akonian products competitive in galactic markets.

Everyone did something useful. Even the lowest-ranking neelak could claim that his work contributed to keeping the *Las-Toór* operating at peak efficiency.

And what did Solina Tormas contribute?

She stuck her nose in old files and documents, and occupied herself for days at a time coaxing secrets out of ancient data storage crystals. And usually without success: without the appropriate reading devices, her experiments often turned the stored data into a jumble, or worse, destroyed it entirely.

And what was the point of it all? To find out more about the Lemurians! The era when Akonian society collectively refused to recognize its common origin with the Terrans fortunately lay many centuries in the past. People were more enlightened in the Blue system now, or claimed to be. Even if Akonians and Terrans had common ancestors—it wasn't the line of descent that counted, or the genes, but what one did with them. And right now, things didn't look too bad. The Terrans' Solar Imperium, once the greatest power in the galaxy, was almost forgotten. These days, the Terrans set their sights considerably lower. They were an important power, but only one of many in the galaxy at the same level of influence.

The Akonians no longer had reason to fear the Terrans. The more than one hundred systems settled by the Akonians had belonged for several decades to the Forum Raglund, one of the galaxy's most powerful political alliances. Membership in that elite group had allowed a political thaw to take place on the capital planet of Drorah and other Akonian worlds. Foreigners streamed into the Blue system, most only as tourists, but here and there colonies of aliens had established permanent settlements. It was a slow process and not without numerous conflicts, but one thing was indisputable: a fresh wind blew over Drorah.

Solina believed that times had changed. Wasn't she living proof of it? She didn't come from the Blue system, but from one of the most unimportant worlds in the Akonian empire. She knew the nobility, the Vakt'son, only from the series on the tri-vid. Hers was such an undistinguished family tree that she stopped paying attention to it quite early on. It seemed impossible to make a good impression coming from a family of political dissidents, yet Solina had managed to win a place for herself at one of the most important Akonian research institutes on Drorah.

But since she had chosen Lemurian history as the main focus for her research, what had been a stony path had become an obstacle course littered with innumerable hazards. She felt as though someone was just waiting for her to carelessly tangle herself up in one of the subtle traps in order to have her quietly dismissed and packed off back to Shaghomin. Her home world. The Establishment could not have invented a worse exile.

At first, Solina had refused to believe. Could it be that no one was interested in the truth? Did no one else care about the struggle that had reached its shattering climax in the Sol system more than fifty thousand years ago? The Beasts had very nearly exterminated the Lemurians. If the Lemurians had perished in the onslaught, no human beings would exist today—neither Akonians nor Terrans, Arkonides or any of the other humanoids. Billions upon billions had lost their lives in that war. Didn't their descendants owe the dead at least an effort to uncover the truth about their fate? An accounting of the indescribable terror, capturing it in numbers, in the hope of one day being able to comprehend it?

The answer, Solina had quickly discovered, was simple: No one had any interest in learning that truth.

Some avoided that truth because thinking about the catastrophe was depressing. They were afraid that they might fall victim to a similar cataclysm some day. Others, because they sensed that Solina's research could shake the very foundations of their identity. Akonians were Akonians, and for centuries that had been synonymous with aversion, if not outright hatred, for all non-Akonians, especially those upstart Terrans. The old Lemurians were an inconvenient reminder that they all belonged to the same family.

Solina's career ground to a halt. In helpless anger she watched as far less talented historians were promoted and honored. No wonder: they were doing *something useful*. They sang the glory of the Akonian people and of its most excellent and wise nobility, and reinterpreted history to suit their theories. Bitter defeats at the hands of the Terrans were transformed into heroic deeds, in which the vastly outnumbered Akonians were overwhelmed only by the sheer strength of the Terrans. Victories, really.

These historians strengthened the Akonian community, did their part for the success of the whole.

And Solina? Despite her family history, she could not be declared an enemy of the state. The era was fortunately past in which the regime's opponents—genuine or imagined—were poisoned out of hand or exiled to desert planets. Akonian society had discovered subtler ways to rid itself of members who had fallen out of favor.

For example, by sending them on months-long research expeditions to regions where, by virtue of their field of study, they were completely out of place.

The Ochent Nebula was uninhabited. By a whim of chance—as her colleagues in the astrophysics section certainly would have explained to her, had they any inclination to speak with her—there were hardly any worlds that bore life at all, let alone intelligent life. Solina had always been of the opinion that a good historian should be prepared to practice archaeology, and had been ready to continue her research with a folding spade in hand. But even that had been denied her. None of the few life-bearing worlds the *Las-Toór* visited had ever been inhabited by intelligent beings.

This whole trip had been one big miserable disappointment.

But Solina had had to swallow many disappointments throughout her life and had learned to get around them. The trick was being flexible, always ready with an alternative strategy. So they sent her to the backside of the galaxy, to a place where there was guaranteed to be no work for a historian? No problem—she brought some with her!

There was an enormous amount of original documentation in the galaxy on the Lemurians, and the amount grew almost daily, both as the result of dedicated searching by archaeologists and historians and by chance discoveries. This mountain of documents, many in written form and in a widely varying assortment of data-storage media, had to be recorded, evaluated, interpreted and placed within the overall context of all other findings to date—a Sisyphean labor often delegated to assistants or syntrons. Yet this mountain served as the foundation of their historical knowledge.

On board the *Las-Toór*, Solina had the leisure to delve into Lemurian history. Above her desk floated an array of holos. Displayed in the middle was the original document, with which Solina had already struggled for three days. It was a private letter written on a paperlike material. She had never held the original. It was located in a Terran archive to which the Akonian historian had no access. To gain access, her superiors would have had to make an official request to the appropriate Terran authorities. Solina Tormas knew her superiors. The Vakt'son would have sooner pulled out their manicured fingernails with tweezers than ask the filthy Terrans for anything.

Solina had dispensed with the formal request and instead contacted her Terran counterpart directly. Ten minutes later, she had the scan on her syntron and had made a new connection in the galaxy-wide community of historians.

Much to her delight, her colleague had already done much of the preliminary work. He had dated the document, which originated from the time between the years 51,389 and 51,378 before the beginning of the old Terran calendar, the common dating system used by all Lemurian researchers. Solina's superiors would throw a fit if they discovered the historian was working with the Terran calendar, but Solina didn't care. It was necessary to have a common dating system, and any one would do. Why should she ignore the existing one just because the Terrans had founded Lemurian research?

Solina's Terran colleague had also run the document through his institution's syntron. The computer had taken an image of the document, cleaned it up, converted the handwriting to Lemurian standard script and suggested several translations. Though Akonian had evolved from Lemurian, the passing millennia left only rudimentary similarities between the two languages. The results of the syntron's work were incorporated in several holos surrounding the original document.

She couldn't have wished for a better overview—and yet she understood almost nothing. The problem began with the simple challenge of interpreting the handwriting. Several words remained unclear. Did the second sentence of the letter start with "vecktran" or "vecktron"? The difference in the pronunciation and the spelling of the two letters was minimal, but the difference in meaning was huge. The sentence could mean either, "I write these words with a heavy heart" or "The words I write to you should not make your heart heavy." And it was still this difficult when the writer of the letter (it was unclear whether it was a him or a her) had included the vowels in the words. All too often, the Lemurians left out the vowels and simply assumed the recipient would mentally add them in while reading.

In moments like this, she cherished a ludicrous wish that people would be more considerate of the poor historians who would attempt to make sense of original sources tens of thousands of years later. If they thought ahead, they would never again so carelessly scrawl their letters. They would type them and store them in some medium that would still be viable in the future.

But even if that miracle occurred, there would still be the difference in meanings! Almost every word in any language had different meanings depending on context. And that was only the beginning of the problem for historians, because words also changed their meaning over time. "Bailff," for example, meant "fishcatcher" in the oldest surviving texts, but later also came to mean a petty criminal. Then, just before the onslaught of the Beasts, the term referred to a fashion craze among youth for clothes with a herringbone pattern. And those were the meanings that had been identified so far. Bailff might mean a dozen other things according to context.

Solina's Terran colleague had also supplied her with a database of Lemurian terms that he had compiled himself—a favor that she of course had returned by sending her own compilation—but in this case it didn't help. She wasn't going any further with the resources she had at hand.

It was time to ask for help. "Syntron," she said, "connect me to HistNet!"

The holos of the aggravating letter moved to the side and made room for a new one, the trademark for HistNet. For several long seconds, the logo hung over the desk: a pen guided by an invisible hand over the page of a book, leaving behind symbols in a fantasy language. The pen filled the page and then began a second.

Was her access being blocked? Researchers on Drorah—and many other worlds in the galaxy—were discouraged from participating in HistNet. HistNet was, as was immediately apparent from the name, a Terran invention and thus automatically suspect. And HistNet offered unrestricted access. Any inhabitant of the galaxy could use it to exchange views, opinions and knowledge with others. And, of course, anyone could lurk without being noticed, which was precisely the reason why the high Akonian officials didn't like it: The Enemy Could Be Listening.

Why let others have a look at your cards? It was much smarter to listen in anonymously and integrate any useful information into one's own work than to take an active part and reveal your line of research. Accordingly, Solina, like all the other historians in her institution, had received read-only access. Like all the others, she used it aggressively. But unlike all the others, she had hacked it.

It was easy. No one considered historians, who concerned themselves with things as unworldly as the past, to be potential hackers. So the read-only access restriction was relatively poorly secured. It took her less than two weeks of careful work to crack the access block; after that, she made full use of her new freedom.

A good historian was resourceful in any situation.

The pen in the HistNet logo wrote an additional page, leaped up as the page turned by itself, then went back to work.

Still no connection. She hoped it was due only to the *Las-Toôr*'s remote position. The Ochent Nebula was unpredictable in terms of energy transmission, and the ship had just detoured around a hyperstorm raging through the sector. Perhaps a remnant of the storm was affecting her access.

She hoped that's all it was. Life on board the *Las-Toôr* was very different from life at the Institute. With its dozens of departments, the Institute offered anonymity, like a city within a city with no fixed boundaries. There, she could count on being overlooked; the barely noticeable trickle of the data stream that connected her with HistNet traveled from the Institute over a plethora of constantly changing connections and communications channels. By comparison, the *Las-Toór* was a tiny village around which a high-energy fence had been erected. The ship was relatively spacious, but it was a microcosmos nonetheless. Everyone knew everyone else and kept a sharp eye out for peculiarities and odd occurrences. And all the data that reached or left the ship traveled through a single hyperantenna.

Early on, Solina hadn't dared manipulate the *Las-Toór*'s syntron. *Patience!* she admonished herself. *You can live without HistNet for a few months. It isn't worth the risk.*

She hadn't been on the ship even two weeks before Solina felt like a fish stranded on dry land and desperately snapping at the air. She simply couldn't make any progress. None of the documents on which she was working would yield to her efforts, and she felt that she needed only a small hint here and there from a qualified colleague in order break through to her goals. And she missed the company. She often felt that the bodiless beings who populated HistNet were more real to her than the people with whom she was riding through space in this steel cage.

It's for the sake of the work, she had told herself. *Akon needs good work!* Then she had attacked the syntron like her life depended on it. It had taken her several long days to gain access—days in which she went weak in the knees every time she saw the flamboyant figure of Eniva ta Drorar, the *Las-Toór*'s network specialist, even from a distance. But at last she had done it. She was back in HistNet.

She thought.

The stupid logo didn't budge. What was going on here? Solina was tempted to kick the tiny box under her desk in which her personal syntron was housed. She had read in the old documents of many races that in their early periods of technological maturity, this strategy was considered a proven means of getting a balky machine to perform its function. As though there was a universal constant behind it.

Solina pushed back her chair, stood up and aimed her foot at the syntron.

"Solina Tormas!"

The voice issuing from the syntron startled her into missing her target, and she painfully slammed her big toe into the solid material of the desk.

"Ouch! Damn, that hurt!"

"Solina! What are you doing?"

The historian raised her head and faced the image of Jere von Baloy, commander of the *Las-Toór*.

Blast! Does he know? Never mind, just pretend nothing happened!

"I ... I ... uh ... the clasp on my shoe came loose, Maphan. I was about to fasten it when you called, and I was so startled I stubbed my toe."

"I see." Jere von Baloy glanced up for a moment, as though praying to an unseen god to deliver him from the plague of this hopelessly clumsy and incompetent Yidari.

Good! Underestimate me!

"How badly are you injured?" the commander asked.

Solina searched in vain for a trace of irony in his expression. It was convenient for her that the commander considered her impractical, but still ... .

"I'm all right," she replied.

"Can you walk?"

"Of course, Maphan. What—"

"Then proceed at once to the bridge! You are needed."

She continued to stare at the empty space in the air for a moment after the holo dissolved, then shook off her surprise and ran to the nearest teleporter.

The commander had urgently requested her, the useless historian Solina Tormas, to report to the bridge.

She would have given her HistNet access to know what was going on.

11

The position of communications officer was by far the best job on the *Palenque*. Alemaheyu was firmly convinced of that. More than that: communications officer was the best position anyone could have at all.

It didn't bother Alemaheyu that his rank commanded little respect. He even received condescending smiles when he got into conversations with the locals at spaceports during brief layovers.

"Communications officer, eh? Doesn't ... " *Doesn't the syntron take care of that?* was what they meant to say, but most managed to swallow that comment and babble instead, "Oh, communications officer! Interesting. What ... uh ... does a communications officer do, exactly?"

"He communicates," Alemaheyu would answer casually, giving the other person his patented *What a stupid question* look. So far, no one had ever dared ask a follow-up question.

Which was a shame, Alemaheyu thought, since they missed hearing a lecture on the greatest job in the universe. On the wonderful feeling of being a spider in a web, the center of a community. All the *Palenque*'s lines of communication ran through Alemaheyu, both internal and external. Nothing escaped him. He knew about the constantly changing love affairs and relationships on board, about the prospectors' prior lives—usually turbulent and not exactly crowned with success. Alemaheyu knew who was with whom, what for and why, or why not and with whom else. He only had to close

93

his eyes and think of the individual crew members in order to rattle off an exact description of their strengths and weaknesses, their characteristics and moods.

Admittedly, the multiple redundant syntronic systems did relieve him of a large part of his work as comm officer. But any series of redundancies had its limitations, and in such cases human sensitivity was required that not even the most refined personality simulation could replace. And besides, the syntrons performed only the routine tasks—the requirements, so to speak—leaving Alemaheyu the electives: tending the network of relationships between the crew members, strengthening it to withstand the most powerful forces that could be arrayed against it.

Alemaheyu was convinced that he was a good net weaver. Why else would the crawler crews have nicknamed him "Mama?"

No, Alemaheyu never would have traded his job, even though he earned the smallest share of the *Palenque*'s profits. Sharita Coho might earn a hundred times more than he did, but what did the commander get out of it? A podium in the center of the bridge from which she could bark her orders, and a whole lot of aggravation that followed her around like a contagious disease. No thanks. Alemaheyu could do without that. And what did he care that the commander nearly had saved enough capital to buy her own ship? For Sharita it would just mean a new podium that isolated her from her shipmates, and an ulcer when she had to watch some gang of bungling amateurs called a crew mistreat her hard-earned property.

Perhaps she already had the ulcer.

Sharita sat in her seat as stiffly as though she had swallowed one of the *Palenque*'s landing struts, her head rigidly facing forward as she waited for reports from the hyperdetector.

The suicide of the shipwrecked stranger had affected her. Alemaheyu, who just by being the comm officer knew the commander better than anyone else on board—even better than Pearl Laneaux—knew there was a soft core beneath the hard shell. You had to look for it, but it was there.

Sharita was reproaching herself. Rhodan was breathing down her neck, yet she was condemned to inactivity until the hyperdetector came up with something.

"Hyperdetection!" she snapped in the direction of Omer Driscol. "When will I get some results?"

"Soon, Commander," the stocky black man replied with his trademark calmness. "You want me to be thorough, don't you?"

The commander declined to answer.

Alemaheyu kept in constant contact with the eleven remaining crawlers combing the sector in which Crawler Eleven had presumably collided with the shuttle fragment. The reports coming from the crawlers were unusually terse and businesslike, an expression of the pain that the crews felt at the loss of their comrades. Alemaheyu answered in the same tone.

Later he would try to come up with a good joke, but not now. A good mother knew the moods of her children.

"We have the analysis," Driscol announced. "No sign of your hypothetical attacker."

"Are you sure? Not even a cloud of particles coming from impulse drive engines?"

"Yes, I'm sure," Driscol said, louder than necessary. There was only one thing that stung him out of his usual reserve: when someone questioned his ability as a hyperdetection expert.

"Fine, Omer," Sharita quickly reassured him. "That settles that. Maybe the Akonians aren't behind this after all. Increase the hyperdetection radius to five light-years!"

The hyperdetection officer went back to work. Alemaheyu called up Omer's data on his console, aligned it at the edge of his field of vision and looked around the control center. Sharita continued to stare at some point beyond the *Palenque*'s walls, and Pearl was making every effort to look busy.

The other members of the bridge crew bent over their work stations.

And Rhodan ... Rhodan sat in his seat and looked unhappily at the only information Sharita had authorized him to receive: some very general data along with a selection of screen savers. It was clear to Alemaheyu he felt as chafed by this inactivity as did Sharita—except that Rhodan was effectively blocked even from looking on.

Alemaheyu felt sorry for Rhodan. The comm officer knew how it felt to be the object of Sharita Coho's displeasure.

A thought came to him. Why not?

Alemaheyu entered several commands at his console, then looked back in the direction of the inner bridge.

Rhodan was a pro. When the hyperdetection data suddenly flashed across his holo, he merely raised his eyebrows. A moment later, he let his glance sweep with studied casualness across the control center. When he made eye contact with the comm officer, Alemaheyu winked. Rhodan winked back.

All right, then. Alemaheyu wondered why Sharita was so hard on Rhodan. You just had to treat him like a normal person. The rest would take care of itself.

"Hyperdetection!" Omer called out.

"Put it on the bridge holo!" the commander ordered.

"Impossible." The hyperdetection officer shook his head. "The impulses are too weak and indistinct to get a visual."

"Then tell us what you are getting."

"A large object. The syntron might be misinterpreting the data, but it says the object is several kilometers long."

"Several kilometers?"

"Just what I said. But that's only a guess. I can't really get a solid reading on the thing. Don't ask me why—the hyperstorm has long since faded. Maybe it has some kind of anti-detection field."

"Anything else?"

"Yes. The object is moving at nearly light-speed. Distance just about four light-years. Its trajectory deviates only by a few degrees from the piece of debris that we picked up."

Sharita released the air in her lungs with a loud snort. "Well done, Omer. We're on the right track now." She turned to the first officer. "Pearl, take us in!"

Alemaheyu didn't expect any further orders and bent over the console in order to inform the crawlers. Before he got that far, Sharita's voice echoed through the control center once more. In it was a hard note that Alemaheyu had never heard before.

"Harriett," she said, turning to the engineer who handled the *Palenque*'s offensive and defensive systems. "Keep your guns ready! I don't know who's out there, and they probably only have a few firecrackers to shoot off ... but they've shown they're willing to use them!"

***

The *Palenque* went into ultra-light flight, towing its swarm of crawlers.

Alemaheyu was surprised to discover that he was so anxious he was panting. And he wasn't the only one affected by the tension. Everywhere in the control center he saw nervous gestures, clumsy movements, flushed cheeks. Even Rhodan seemed to be clutching the armrest of his seat more tightly than necessary.

Harriett Hewes was calmness personified. With economical movements showing no signs of haste, she checked the *Palenque*'s defense fields and weapon systems. If Alemaheyu hadn't known better, he would have assumed Harriett was working on one of the three-dimensional puzzles with which she passed her time, and which she used to make it almost impossible to enter her cabin unauthorized. Every so often Harriett approached Sharita about using one of the storage rooms for what she called her installations, but her attempts failed with equal regularity.

"This is a prospecting ship," Sharita would explain. "We need the storage rooms for rock and ore samples, not for ju ... well, you know."

Of course Harriett knew. Alemaheyu was fairly certain that she outshone everyone else aboard in terms of intelligence, Perry Rhodan included, but that didn't keep her from being stubborn, with an endless patience that was often painful to see.

In other words: she was the best weapons control officer that Alemaheyu could imagine. Harriett thought first, then pressed the button. Maybe. And when she pressed the button, she used exactly the necessary firepower. Not a watt too much or too little.

"All systems ready," she reported.

"Good. We're about to need them." Sharita didn't take her eyes off her holo. As commander, she was the only one on board with real-time access to all data, with the exception of Alemaheyu, who had hacked his own, as-yet-undiscovered access: as comm officer, he considered it his duty to be completely informed. And Rhodan, whom Alemaheyu had patched in.

The comm officer called up a new holo next to his console. To his relief, all systems on board the *Palenque* showed green. Harriett was stockpiling energy in order to be able to raise the Paratron shield at maximum power immediately after entry into normal space; she was even drawing energy from the weapon systems.

Alemaheyu grinned. What did Harriett always say? "There are only dead heroes."

On a second holo, the comm officer checked to see what data Rhodan was viewing. To his surprise, the Immortal wasn't following the preparations for reemergence from hyperspace, but was working through the video material that had been taken inside the wreck. What was bothering Rhodan? Was he afraid that an unpleasant surprise might be waiting for them at their destination?

Alemaheyu switched to hyperdetection. No major change, still an oscillating gray-toned image that collapsed into a constantly shifting swirl. Now and again, he thought he could see a long, extended cylinder with projections like an insect's antennae at both ends. Omer might be able to make something meaningful out of the image—Alemaheyu could just as easily read the future in the swirls of a newly stirred cup of tea.

The lower edge of the holo showed the estimated length and mass. The numbers wavered between three hundred meters and thirty kilometers. First, the syntron gave the mass as five million tons, then five hundred million. What was going on?

"Ten seconds to reentry into normal space."

Alemaheyu clicked off the hyperdetection holo. It was more confusing than helpful. There was something out there. It was probably fairly gigantic, moving at nearly light-speed and, when it felt like it, cutting innocent little shuttles in two. He didn't need to know any more. The rest would come to light on its own.

"Five more seconds!"

Belts shot from the sides of his seat, automatically united over his stomach and pressed him firmly against the cushion. It was the last resort in case everything else failed: the *Palenque*'s shields, its hull of highly compressed laminated steel, and even the force-field generator built into the contour seat. The safety belt was a strange feature, Alemaheyu had always thought. By the time a space traveler found himself in the embarrassing situation of having to depend on the safety belt, a chaplain or the appropriate holy object of his faith would have been just as much help.

"Three seconds!"

Still, the belt gave him a feeling of security, as though a protective hand rested on him. Man was a strange being.

"Reentry!"

The *Palenque* shuddered as Harriett pulled the Paratron up to one hundred-sixty percent of its normal value. The defense-shield projectors could withstand that level for only a few seconds, but the maneuver was absolutely necessary. Perhaps someone was expecting them, hoping to destroy them as they reentered normal space.

There was no attack.

The shuddering faded to a barely noticeable vibration that spaceship builders never had managed to completely eliminate, despite millennia of experience. The Paratron leveled off at ninety-nine percent capacity.

The crawlers checked in with Alemaheyu as one after the other fell out of hyperspace and crowded closely around the *Palenque*, as though they hoped to be able to use the Paratron to shield themselves.

"Hyperdetection!" Sharita barked. "Is there anything out there that could be a danger to us?"

"I ... don't think so."

"Do you call that a report? Is there something there or not?"

Confused, Omer shook his head almost angrily. Alemaheyu remembered there was one more thing the hyperdetection officer couldn't stand: not knowing.

"There is something. I'll switch it to the bridge holo."

Alemaheyu turned in his chair—the belt yielded but didn't retract—and looked into what resembled a window into space. Stars. And a long shadow that blocked some of them.

"Very enlightening," Sharita said sarcastically. "Can you make that any better?"

Omer bent over his console and punched at the virtual keyboard. Sharita had hit him in his professional honor; Alemaheyu had never seen the stocky black man move so fast.

The shadow in the holo blurred, the blackness of space took on a reddish tint, then the shadow manifested itself. Alemaheyu saw a long, slender cylinder. At either end, metal fingers projected from the hull at regular intervals, reinforced by a ring that connected them about halfway along their length.

Antennae was the first thought that popped into the comm officer's head. *Those guys over there certainly have a big appetite for information.*

But then they should also have been broadcasting. Alemaheyu checked his console again: all systems were in working order. He would have picked up even the weakest comm signal. Only … there was nothing. Was the ship itself a wreck? But then who fired at the shuttle?

"That's better!" Sharita said, satisfied. "That thing out there is obviously a ship. Tell us more about it, Omer!"

"I can't. None of the sensors or hyperdetectors are providing reliable data. What's on the holo is only a depiction based on the optical data, nothing else."

"An improved snapshot, in other words."

"Yes. As for the rest … You know there is no planetary secret in the galaxy I cannot penetrate. But I can't get through to this thing. They've got a damned good hyperdetection shield."

"I consider that unlikely," Rhodan said.

The Immortal spoke just loudly enough to be heard above the excited murmur of the bridge crew. Everyone turned at once to look at him.

The man had a sense of timing. And presence to spare. Even after observing the Immortal for the weeks he'd spent on board the *Palenque*, Alemaheyu still didn't know how Rhodan commanded attention so easily, with so little fuss—but he swore to himself that he would find out. And once he had succeeded, then … then he would more often have the pleasure of people listening to him. He didn't want any more than that. After all, he already had the best job in the universe.

Sharita's expression made it clear that she would like to ignore Rhodan's interjection, but that was impossible.

"And why is that? Would you perhaps be ready to share your Immortal wisdom with us?"

"There's not a great deal to share."

How could he tolerate Sharita's aggressive tone so calmly? Alemaheyu always lost his cool at some point and snapped back.

Rhodan pointed to the holo. "That ship is rotating along the long axis. There is only one explanation for that: the rotation is the source of centrifugal force, which provides gravity to the ship. It's a primitive but foolproof method. But anyone forced to produce artificial gravity by rotation most assuredly isn't capable of the higher-dimensional technology needed to baffle our hyperdetector."

Pearl Laneaux chimed in. "According to my calculations and assuming that the optical data is correct, I estimate a gravitational strength of one and a half gs in the outer sections."

"I guess that sounds reasonable. We'll accept that estimate as a working hypothesis. And how do you explain the failure of the hyperdetector, Perry?"

"I don't have an explanation. At the moment."

"You don't have a—"

Rhodan held Sharita's cutting gaze. "But I can tell you who must be on board on that ship. I took the liberty of going through all the visual data that Pearl's investigation teams transmitted to the ship's syntron from the interior of the wreck."

"How? You don't have any authorized access to the syntron whatsoever!"

"What? I didn't know that." Rhodan's attitude was the ultimate in innocence.

Way to go, buddy! Alemaheyu thought. *Let her have it!*

"I would never attempt to procure unauthorized access to data. You must have made an error in the allocation of access rights."

Sharita began to protest, but Rhodan spoke over the beginning of her diatribe. "But that doesn't matter. Mistakes happen, right? At the moment, the important thing is what I stumbled across. The teams found lettering on the walls in several places where they removed the ice layer, and there was enough to confirm my initial suspicion. The lettering is in Lemurian."

"Lemurian!" Sharita needed a moment to absorb it. "But ... that would mean that thing out there has been under way for fifty thousand years. Or longer!"

"Yes," Rhodan agreed. "We—"

"Hyperdetection!" Omer interrupted him. "Hyperspace exit at ninety light-seconds distance!"

"Put it on the screen!"

The holo of the mysterious cylinder ship collapsed. When it reformed, it showed a different ship: a spherical shape, flattened poles, extended weapon turrets.

Sharita was the first to find her voice again. "Didn't I say it from the start? Akonians!"

12

When Denetree awoke the next morning, she was alone in the house. She went from one room to the next without finding Launt or even a note from him. Denetree tried not to worry—she hoped Launt was out trying to fulfill her request—and to her surprise, she actually succeeded.

Her surroundings were too strange, too unreal. Four rooms! She spent several minutes just going from room to room to room, as if she had to convince herself that the house really existed. Never before had she met anyone who had sole possession of a whole room, to say nothing of an entire house. The houses of the metach'ton belonged to the community. Each room housed three, four, or even five people, and who slept with whom in which room was always changing, depending on personal feelings and the outcomes of the power struggles that constantly seethed under the surface of every Metach'ton.

Now and then she stopped at one of the windows and looked out. A wall surrounded the house and protected its inhabitant from curious glances. Denetree saw her bicycle leaning against the house. She wanted to go outside and check to make sure it was in working order—not because she doubted that it was, but from a need to feel something familiar in her hands. But she resisted; there might be some way she wasn't aware of to see into the courtyard from outside.

She ended her restless wandering in the most wonderful of the rooms: the kitchen. Launt had his own kitchen: he wasn't forced to eat in the Metach'ton's community kitchens! He could be by himself!

She looked through the cabinets and found several doughcakes and some vegetables. She hesitated for a moment: this food wasn't for her! but in the end hunger overpowered her reluctance. She gulped down all six doughcakes and would have eaten more if she could.

It felt good to be full, but an undercurrent of fear mixed quickly with the sense of being pleasantly stuffed: had the condemned prisoner just eaten her last meal?

It was a miracle that Launt had saved her from the Tenoy. A miracle that could not last. Tenarch or no, even Launt's power was limited. Sooner or later, the Ship would track down Denetree, even if she stayed with the Tenarch. Denetree needed another miracle.

She heard the door opening.

"Denetree!" Launt called in a low voice. "Don't be afraid, it's me!"

She ran into the front room. "Where were you so long? Did you find it?"

Launt hung his jacket on a wall hook and pulled a small box from his pocket. "Duties," he said. "And this took me some time. As a Tenarch, it's easy to do most things, but even for me it was hard to just show up at a Metach'ton and tap on the walls looking for hiding places."

She took the box from him. "How did you manage it?"

"The old Respect for Authority routine. The Naahk sent one of his advisers to make sure that the hard-working metach didn't want for anything. To guarantee impartiality, the Tenarch naturally insisted on not being disturbed during his inspection."

"Naturally!" Denetree laughed and hugged the box tightly to her chest. A part of her observed her behavior suspiciously—there wasn't anything to laugh about!—and noticed that Launt's good mood seemed forced. The Tenarch was pale and appeared tired. After he gave her the box, he began to continually rub his hands together.

They went into the kitchen. Denetree put the box down in front of her, picked up a knife and prepared to cut the twine wrapped around the box.

"Denetree," Launt said, "you can't stay here."

"I know." She couldn't stay anywhere on board. That was clear to her. But she wasn't worried. She had her gift from Venron, and her brother would not leave her in the lurch.

"The Tenoy arrested a member of your group."

"Who?" Her confidence had a hole torn in it.

"Mika. She lost her nerve at a checkpoint."

Mika? She had always seemed to Denetree as one of the strongest of the Star Seekers.

"What happened to her?"

"She … " Launt swallowed. "She betrayed the rest of the group."

" I don't believe it! Mika would never—"

Launt shook his head. "She did. Believe me."

Denetree didn't want to accept it. She grasped the knife more tightly in her hand, cut the twine and opened the box.

Surprised, she froze in the middle of the movement.

"What is it? What's in the box?"

She reached in, picked up the tiny item and showed it to Launt.

"An arm chip?"

"He knew that he would put me in danger. His sister Denetree would not be allowed to live. Venron's gift is a new life for me." She stared at the wafer-thin chip that rested on two of her fingertips. *A new identity. Was it possible?*

"May I?" Launt asked. She let him take the arm chip. He disappeared with it into an adjacent room and came back with a hand scanner. "Don't worry," he reassured her when she suddenly stiffened. "It isn't connected to the Net. The computer in this house has … how should I say this … has taken leave from the Ship's Net for a while."

Launt read the chip, whistling appreciatively as he read the data on the display. For the first time since he had come into the house, it seemed to Denetree that he was relaxed.

"Well, it was an honor for me to have had you as a guest, *Danque*," he said to Denetree. "But now it's time that you went on your way. The members of your new Metach'ton are anxiously waiting for the reinforcement they've requested! What are you waiting for, Danque?"

13

When the massive hatch slid to the side and opened the way for Solina Tormas to step into the control center of the *Las-Toór*, the historian had to force her feet to move forward.

It was the first time that she had been allowed to enter the innermost section of the research ship. The other Yidari had made it clear that a person as insignificant as she had no business there. Solina had made the best of the insult, telling herself that she didn't have any reason to go into the control center anyway. What was really there to see? The same people she saw in the mess and in the corridors, except that they would be busy acting important with their instruments.

But when Solina actually saw the control center, she frankly admitted that she had consoled herself with a white lie in order to maintain her otherwise shattered spirits.

The control center was overwhelming.

The historian in her had seldom seen a more meaningful example of the pronounced hierarchical thinking of Akonian society. The control center of the *Las-Toór* had a circular base, over which a domed ceiling arched. In the middle on a raised platform sat the maphan, the commander, Jere von Baloy. At an angle to his left was the place of the Keven, the pilot, and to his right was that of the Ma-Techten, the first officer. The platform was oversized, taking up nearly half the floor space. Around the command platform was a mid-level ring of work stations seating the most important members of the control center crew: the Therso, weapons control officer; the Davron, hyperdetection officer; the Espejel, comm officer; and the Heroth, chief engineer. All stations were circular, but the consoles—and thus the attention of those who worked at them—were directed toward the maphan. Finally, in a third, outer ring on the lowest level of the control center floor, were work stations available to be used by the ship's various Yidari. Solina could see that all but one were all occupied.

The child in Solina, the curious little girl who had made her what she was now, looked past the hierarchy that was literally cast in steel. The walls and dome of the control center were entirely covered by a holo.

It showed hyperspace.

At least Solina thought that was what she was looking at. There were no stars, none of the unrelenting blackness that for her defined space. Instead, she saw a rainbow of sluggishly intertwining colors. It was as though hyperdimensional space consisted of heavy, multi-colored sand that under the influence of an invisible force twisted, mixed, swirled—and somehow continuously escaped her. Each time Solina focused on a single point she lost her perception, and when she squinted to compensate for the effect the point vanished. She could have spent days hypnotized by the spell of hyperspace.

"Solina!" the maphan called from his platform. "Instead of standing there like you've never seen hyperspace before, why don't you report?"

"I ... uh ... was just about to."

"Very good."

The screens and instruments of the only empty work station in the lower ring woke to life, and the blue glow of the indicators mixed with the iridescence of hyperspace.

"There is your work station," Jere von Baloy pointed. "Please sit down."

Solina did as he told her, then looked at the maphan. Looked up at him, since the arrangement of the control center did not allow otherwise.

Jere von Baloy turned away and exchanged some words with the Keven, who accordingly adjusted the course vector. What could he want from her? Solina had difficulty judging him. Just the "von" in his name and the fact that he was the commander of the *Las-Toór* should have created an unbridgeable gulf between him and Solina. But somehow, it didn't. Since their departure from Drorah, the maphan had not worn his uniform even once. Mostly he went around in dirty overalls that could have belonged to any neelak maintaining the smallest auxiliary craft.

The maphan wasn't particularly concerned about rank, even though he had spent his entire adult life working within a ranked system—and successfully, too, as his position showed.

According to everything she knew about him, Jere von Baloy was closer to her mental outlook than anyone else on board the *Las-Toór*. Or was that just wishful thinking? The maphan had yet to indicate by a single syllable or gesture that there was any special understanding between them.

"Take a look at this," Jere's voice said from her console. A holo took shape in front of her. It showed a pixilated, gray-toned flickering. By making an effort, Solina thought she could make out a cylinder-shaped form that seemed to appear for just a moment.

"What is that?" she asked. "And what should I do with it?"

"The hyperdetector picked up that image, but that's the best resolution it can give us," the commander explained to her. "It's the destination of our ultra-light jump. And I believe this object will be of interest to you."

"Why? What makes you think that?"

She didn't get an answer. Solina looked up. Jere von Baloy had turned away and was now speaking with the Therso, who with the ease of long practice was checking the readiness of the ship's weaponry. The maphan appeared disinclined to waste another moment of his valuable time on Solina.

So. A good historian was resourceful in any situation. Solina called up all the available data on the mysterious object. The numbers relating to its size were extremely vague; the only thing certain was that it was quite large. Such a large object in space was most likely a ship. Did Jere von Baloy hope that she would recognize the type? If so, that was either a very stupid or a very clever test, depending on what he intended by it. If he hoped that she would recognize the type, he was stupid. There were literally billions of spaceship types that had seen use in the galaxy over the preceding tens of thousands of years. The chance that Solina would recognize one that wasn't listed in the ship's memory was nearly zero. If he hoped to show her up with her failure, he was fiendishly cunning.

Whatever. Solina had no choice but to play along. The historian called up ship types from the *Las-Toór*'s database and started with the most obvious comparison: the cylindrical ships used by the Springers in all eras.

But Solina wouldn't have been Solina if she hadn't kept an ear open to what was going on in the control center. The dome-shaped room was filled with the oppressive silence of enormous tension.

"Entry into normal space in ninety seconds," the Keven announced.

No one commented on his report.

"Sixty seconds to go."

Another voice spoke up. "Hyperdetection! A second object has emerged from hyperspace in the vicinity of the destination point!"

Jere von Baloy swore. "Wonderful! Someone has gotten there ahead of us!"

"That's not all!" exclaimed the Davron. "Ten, correction, eleven other objects, considerably smaller, are grouped around the first object."

The commander took a deep breath. His gaze covered the control center, passed over Solina, who made a quick effort to look occupied by staring at the holo in front of her, and finally landed on Oe ta Acenusk, the Therso.

"Ready, Oe?"

The weapons control officer grinned wolfishly. "Have been for a while now."

"Entry!" called the pilot.

The muffled roar of the ultra-light engines faded away, and the flickering of hyperspace suddenly gave way to the blackness of normal space.

"Hyperdetection?"

"It's Terran!"

An angry groan went through the control center. It *would* have to be Terrans!

"Signature resembles that of a heavy cruiser."

"But is it?"

Solina was not a military expert, but she knew they didn't have a chance against a warship.

"It appears not. The radiation scatter from its energy emissions is too small. Possibly built on a heavy cruiser frame. But the small escort ships could be fighters of some unknown type."

Solina knew that the *Las-Toór* had four fighters of its own on board. Four against eleven; that didn't sound good.

Jere von Baloy was about to turn away from the Davron. "But there's something else, Maphan. The Terran has its Paratron up and the gun turrets extended!"

The maphan hesitated for a brief moment. "Oe, shields up to battle load. Target acquired?"

"Already done. Attack?"

"What are our chances?"

"Fifty-fifty. But they won't get any better if we wait. If we launch the fighters now and—"

"We'll wait."

"But Maphan, the Terrans will claim that they found this thing first and it's theirs by right!"

"I said we'll wait. We don't even know yet if that thing, as you call it, is worth anything, and before we do I'm not prepared to sacrifice even a single life for it. Not even that of a Terran, understand? Put it on the main holo!"

The visual pickup of the object was now perfectly clear, but when Solina tried to call up data on her console, the hyperdetector seemed unable to register it as a scan.

Echkal cer Lethir spoke up, the Ma-Techten of the *Las-Toór*,. He was small, stocky and a Terran-hater of the first water; in the officers' mess, he proclaimed at every suitable and even unsuitable opportunity that the Akonians should teach those Terran upstarts a lesson they'd never forget, with the help of the Arkonides if necessary. More than once Solina wondered what he was doing on a research ship. Lethir belonged on a warship—or perhaps on a psychiatric ward for aggression reduction treatment. Solina had overheard that Lethir had once served in the fleet. Given his attitude it was probably true, and his martial posturing was an attempt to compensate for the shame of failing to meet the requirements of the Akonian fleet.

"Let's call the fleet for help," the Ma-Techten urged. "I happen to know that a squadron is operating in the immediate vicinity of the Ochent Nebula. In an hour, this Terran pest will be a bad memory!"

Jere von Baloy didn't reply to the suggestion. He turned to the historian. "Solina, have you gotten any further?"

"Ship type comparison negative," Solina reported, finding herself infected by the clipped military-style speech pattern used in the control center.

"Is that all?" Jere von Baloy's disappointment was unmistakable.

"At the moment … "

"That isn't enough. Use your brain, Solina!"

Solina would have taken anyone else to task for the public insult, but Jere von Baloy was the maphan. And the truth was that the comment sounded more like a plea for help than an insult.

For some reason she couldn't figure out, Jere von Baloy seemed to be pinning his hopes on her.

All right, she told herself. *Use your brain!*

"Maphan, as Therso of the *Las-Toór,* I must concur with the judgment of the Ma-Techten," Oe ta Acenusk said. "We are in contact with an artificial object of unknown origin. Its builders are potential allies—or enemies, if we leave the field to the Terrans!"

Solina feverishly reviewed the existing data on the object. Here—it was moving at near light-speed. She'd overlooked that before.

Why did Jere von Baloy call me? she asked herself. *What can I do that others can't?* The answer was obvious: She knew more about Lemurian history than anyone else on board. But by all the stinking glowfish of Shaghomin, how did that knowledge apply?

"It is our duty to secure this object for the Akonian Empire," Echkal cer Lethir urged the maphan. "It could contain advanced technology that we must not allow to fall into other hands!"

Lemurians, Lemurians, Lemurians … that had to be the key. But Lemurian artifacts were being found practically every day somewhere in the galaxy. Assuming that this was an artifact, what made it so special?

Well, it was gigantic, but that didn't necessarily mean anything. It was located in a barren region of the galaxy known to be uninhabited by intelligent beings, friendly or otherwise. It was moving at nearly light-speed.

Why was it moving at light-speed?

Was it about to make the jump into hyperspace? Or were its ultra-light engines broken down? Or ... or perhaps it didn't have ultra-light engines at all?

"Maphan, what are we waiting for? Let's call the fleet!"

Aha! Solina used the syntron to make a quick calculation, then cried out, "Maphan!"

She practically screamed. All heads turned toward her, disapproval writ large on most of them. What did she, the superfluous historian, have to report in a situation like this?

"Yes, Solina?"

"I believe this object is Lemurian!"

"And how do you know that?" snapped the Ma-Techten.

"I traced its flight path to the point of origin. Assuming that this object hasn't changed its course and speed significantly, it started out fifty-five thousand Terran years ago—in what was then the Lemurian system!"

"A Lemurian generation ship? I've never heard of such a thing."

"Nor have I," Solina replied. "But the earliest period of Lemurian history has been researched only sketchily. The fact that we have no knowledge of Lemurian generation ships doesn't argue against one existing. If my calculations are confirmed, then this is a discovery of enormous importance."

Jere von Baloy said nothing. But she saw in his eyes a gleam of acknowledgment and recognition for the value of her work that Solina had never seen in anyone's eyes before now.

Echkal cer Lethir spoke up. "Very well. If it's a Lemurian generation ship, that's all the more reason for us to call the fleet. It's a matter of security for the Akonian Empire!"

"You are mistaken, Echkal," the maphan declared. "This is not a matter of security but of research. If this ship really has been under way at sub-light speed for more than fifty thousand years, no technology it carries on board would interest us. But it would be a huge research bonanza for all the scientists on the *Las-Toór*. From the historian"—he smiled in Solina's direction—"to the metallurgists to the planetary ecologists. I see no reason to call the fleet. The Lemurian ship is no threat, and even the Terran ship has shown no aggression as yet."

"And what about the activated Paratron and its fire-ready status?"

"The Terrans are just being cautious. They can't know what might be hiding behind the object on their hyperdetectors."

"That means we won't chase them off?" Sounding disappointed, Oe ta Acenusk withdrew his finger from the sensor fields of the automatic gun control, over which it had been hovering since their entry into normal space.

"We'll see. Launch the fighters to patrol the immediate area. Perhaps our Terran friends are timid and will withdraw."

"And if not?"

"Let's wait. Perhaps they are in a mood to talk instead."

***

"They're launching fighters!" Sharita Coho exclaimed. "Harriett, can you blow them away?"

The weapons control officer thought before answering. The circular holo of the offensive and defensive systems had formed around her like a barricade. "The fighters, yes," she said at length. "But the Akonian mother ship? I doubt it."

"Why not? It isn't a battle cruiser."

"That's correct. Judging by the energy signature, it's probably an Explorer. But that isn't the point. *We* aren't a battle cruiser either. Our systems are designed for defense—and right now, that's a good thing."

Right you are! thought Alemaheyu Kossa, who had been observing events from the comm console with increasing concern. What had gotten into Sharita? The control crew was familiar with her outbursts against the Akonians, and quite rightly refused to take them seriously. It was like the ancient Terrans expressing their opinion about the weather. The meteorologists always got the weather wrong, but no one thought to punish them with transform cannons and heavy disintegrators.

"Thank you for the reminder, Harriet," Sharita snapped. "As it happens, I am thinking about defense. If what those fighters are doing just now isn't an attack, then—"

"—it's a transparent attempt to scare us off."

Sharita gave up. If Harriett didn't want to fire a weapon then she wouldn't, and even the commander had to accept it.

"Very well, then we won't attack. But I won't allow them to get hold of that Lemurian thing out there. We were here first, so it's ours."

"Should I contact them?" Alemaheyu asked. "Then you can tell them that to their faces."

And you'd forget about the idea of turning them into a particle cloud! the comm officer added to himself. People generally found violent acts more difficult once they had looked their opponent in the eye.

"Good idea, Alemaheyu. And what do we do when they claim they picked up the thing on their hyperdetectors first?"

"Then … there's the Law of Space Travel, which the Akonians are bound to as well!"

"Law of Space Travel! Right, we'll drag them in front of a galactic court. The lawyers will put a big 'Keep Out' tape around the thing until all the arguments have been presented, and if we're lucky, our grandchildren will be able to set foot on board. Or those of the Akonians. If the thing hasn't run into a star in the meantime!" Sharita slammed her fist onto her console. "No, I won't let it happen! This thing belongs to us! Rhodan was right. We had the courage to take a risk, and the reward is right in front of us!"

Now Alemaheyu understood which way the wind was blowing. With the discovery of the gigantic Lemurian spacecraft to her credit, the commander saw her chance to finally get her own ship. The comm officer's eyes were drawn back to the flattened sphere of the Akonian ship that hung over them in the main holo. Suddenly he felt sorry for the Akonians. They had no idea with whom they were dealing. Once Sharita set her mind on something, only people tired of life got in her way.

Why didn't Perry Rhodan do something? The Immortal sat in his chair and called up syntron data as though nothing happening in the control center was any concern of his. Rhodan had to realize that Sharita was threatening to spin out of control.

But the Immortal continued his work of analyzing the hyperdetector data. And then something happened that the comm officer never would have anticipated: Sharita asked Rhodan for help.

"Perry ... " she began in what for her passed as a sugar-sweet voice, at the same time stepping down from the command post.

Pearl Laneaux, as surprised as the rest of the bridge crew by Sharita's apparent transformation, leaped from her contour chair and followed right behind the commander.

"Perry!" Sharita stopped one step in front of Rhodan.

The Immortal deactivated the data holos. "Yes?"

"I need your advice as a strategist. Our situation seems muddled. In terms of weaponry, we're in a stalemate with these Akonians. How should we proceed?"

It seemed to Alemaheyu that the commander's equivalent of a quadruple backward somersault actually disconcerted the Immortal. In any event, Rhodan took a few seconds to come up with a reply.

"Well, I think—"

"Yes, so do I!" Sharita interrupted him. "We need reinforcements, right? An LFT squadron—a small one, let's say a battleship and a handful of cruisers—would show the Akonians who's boss around here."

"Sharita!" the first officer exclaimed from behind her back. "You—"

"Can't you see I'm talking with Perry?"

"You can't do th—"

"Go back to your console! We need to be ready to defend against an attack at any moment!"

Pearl didn't move.

"That's an order."

Murmuring French-sounding curses, the first officer threw herself into the seat at her console. As a child, Pearl had learned that there had once been French-speaking inhabitants in the Province of Quebec, her family's country of origin. Their reputation had been a little quirky, but Pearl had liked that and as a teenager, she had learned a few fragments of the now extinct language. Mainly curses and salty expressions she could use as an officer on a prospecting ship.

"Now where were we?" Sharita asked, turning back to Rhodan. "Oh yes, the reinforcements. Alone, we don't have enough firepower. But we can fix that. One comm call from you and half the fleet of the League of Free Terrans will be here within a day."

Sharita was just over a meter-seventy tall and usually looked up at the other members of the crew. But now she was looking down on the seated Rhodan. *And she's enjoying it,* Alemaheyu thought. *Every second of it. She's got him right where she wants him.*

"That's correct," Rhodan confirmed. "A comm call would be enough."

"Then what are you waiting for? We don't want to let our Akonian friends cherish their false hopes for too long."

Rhodan rose easily from the contour seat and said in a friendly tone, "You can wait for that comm message until the universe dies of entropy."

"What? But—"

"Have you forgotten why I'm on board? To make friendly contacts with the Akonians through unofficial channels."

Sharita stepped back. "But no one bought that line of bull you were spreading! That can't be the real reason you're with us!"

"I'm not the one spreading bull here!"

Alemaheyu could swear he saw Rhodan's eyes flash. Was the Immortal angry? The comm officer wouldn't have blamed him. He always maintained that anyone who didn't blow up at Sharita now and then couldn't be human.

"Let's assume I give in to your pressure," Rhodan went on, "and call in a fleet squadron. What would happen? The Akonians would slink away with their tail between their legs? I don't think so. We wouldn't do that even if an Akonian squadron materialized here a second from now, would we? If we left, it would only be to get backup. And it would go on like that. Each side would bring in more and more reinforcements until someone lost his nerve and fired." Rhodan took a step toward the commander. She didn't move, either from consternation or because she had decided to go through with what she had started. "Is that what you want, Sharita? A few thousand dead, political disavowals, and hatred that will take centuries to heal? And along with it the risk that this valuable Lemurian ship might be turned into a gas cloud in the heat of the battle?"

"No, no," Sharita shook her head vigorously. "I—"

It's consternation, Alemaheyu decided.

"Dammit, all I want is for us to get what we're entitled to!"

"That's what I want, too."

"So why can't you think of anything better than to sit there and disagree with my suggestions?"

"Perhaps because you sat me down in this guest chair." Rhodan smiled. Conciliatory? Dangerous? "But that's in the past, right? I do have an idea how we can get what we're entitled to."

"Well, what are you waiting for? Out with it!"

Rhodan explained his idea.

"Hmm. I don't think they'll go for it … " Lost in thought, the commander tugged down her uniform jacket out of habit. "But it's worth trying. Alemaheyu, connect me with the Akonian commander! I—"

"One moment," Rhodan interrupted her. "You are known as a woman with a pronounced sense of fairness. And as such, you would surely admit that I deserve a reward for my suggestion if it's successful. Right?"

"Well … yes." Sharita sounded like a woman at the foot of a mountain watching an avalanche that she couldn't outrun rolling toward her.

"Don't worry. I'm a man of modest tastes. If this discovery results in financial gain, I'll divide my share among the crew of the *Palenque*. No, I'm only asking for one very small favor: I want to be on the team that's first to board the Lemurian ship."

Sharita's assent was drowned out by the crew's cheers for their generous benefactor.

What a sly fox! Alemaheyu thought. *If I were an Akonian and found out who I was up against, I'd make sure I got out of here while I still could!*

14

"Hurry up, Danque! Can't you move any faster, girl?" The voice came from all sides and echoed like thunder.

Denetree needed a few seconds to realize the voice was talking to her.

You fuzzbrain! she admonished herself. *You've been here almost two weeks and you still haven't gotten used to your new name!*

"Be right there!" she called. She crawled more quickly through the narrow air shaft. Behind her scraped the tool and replacement parts that she pulled along on a cord fastened to her belt. She had left behind at a branching of the main shaft the backpack that the Kalpen, the "airmakers," normally used to carry their gear. This shaft was too narrow for her to crawl through with a pack on her back, even though it fit to her body like a second skin. Sometimes, when Denetree became careless and failed to maintain the discipline that the Kalpen had taught her, the feeling that there wasn't even enough room to breathe overwhelmed her.

At times like that, only one thing helped: stay calm and breathe shallow and quick, so that her ribcage didn't press against the air shaft walls, and think of other things so that she was transported far away in her mind.

Denetree sometimes thought of Venron and the gleam in his eyes, and of the gleam of the stars and the endless space between them. That frightened her.

But she also sometimes thought of her camp bed—the Kalpen didn't have permanent quarters, instead moving continuously through the Ship, always following their never-ending work—and of simply dropping down and going to sleep, and not wasting any more thoughts on yesterday or tomorrow. That frightened her even more.

At times like that, the best thing was to close her eyes and crawl on. Feeling her way to the next leak in the airshafts or to the defective sensor that was denying critical air supply to a sector, concentrating on the task in front of her.

Denetree's searching fingers found an uneven area, then she was reaching into emptiness. In the weak light of the lamp on her forehead, she saw the dim outline of a hole. The batteries in the lamps had long exceeded their life expectancy, so the old-timers among the Kalpen had given up struggling with them. They didn't really need the lights anymore; the required hand movements had long become second nature for them.

"Tekker!" she called. "I think I've found the spot! A hole!"

"Very good, girl! There's a Metach'ton of fieldswine depending on that conduit. We don't want your old comrades to slog away at half strength, do we, girl?" Tekker's cackling echoed through the shafts.

Girl this and girl that. It had been like that since she arrived in the Kalpen Metach'ton. The metach barely had been able to hide their disappointment with the newcomer. A beginner—and they could hardly keep up with the emergencies as it was! That accursed traitor had thoroughly disrupted the Ship's oxygen balance. And now the newcomer turned out to be a fieldswine! Working in the fields had given Denetree a powerful body, which was the last thing she needed for working with the Kalpen. The airmakers were slim and sinewy, agile human snakes able to make repairs in the narrowest shafts.

Denetree pulled on the plastic cord and drew up the slender bag of parts to between her legs. When she stretched out her arms to their limits, she could barely touch it. The bag had twisted; the sealant she needed was between her feet.

Swearing, Denetree worked at turning the bundle centimeter by centimeter.

She heard Tekker's cackling again. "Very good, girl! Music makes work easier! You've learning something from old Tekker, haven't you?"

And then there was Tekker. He was by far the oldest member of the Metach'ton. How old he was, no one knew, but he looked so wrinkled and shaky that it seemed reasonable to fear that he might fall over at any moment and only a bag of rattling bones would remain.

Tekker practically never spoke Denetree's new name. For him she was only the girl. Period. Her demands that he call her by name didn't move him. "Get as old as I am first and then we'll see," was all he told her, and then disappeared into an airshaft with the agility of a monkey.

Denetree finally managed to reach the screen she needed and pulled it out. Her arms ached; she wished she could fall sleep right then and there, but it was impossible. Tekker wouldn't give her any peace. She unrolled the screen and tore off a piece to cover the hole. "Much too big," Tekker would have griped. "You're wasting supplies!" But she was a beginner! She pressed the piece against the shaft. As the materials comprising the shaft and the screen reacted to each other and melted together, a pungent smell hit her nose. She was in luck; often the screens were too old or not made to spec and the chemical reaction didn't work. In those cases, Denetree had to attach the screen by hand.

Tekker had driven her close to madness. "Do this, girl! Do that, girl! Aren't you good for anything, girl?" Never had he left her in peace, never had he been satisfied with anything she had done. Here the adhesive seam wasn't right, there a repair didn't look good. And if the visual appearance was fine, something else didn't suit him: the newly installed sensor was too loose or she had used the wrong component. After a week she was ready to turn herself in to the Ship voluntarily. Nothing, nothing could be worse than this hell, this endless squirming around in the guts of the Ship, eternally being ordered around and yelled at.

And then had come the day when she nearly died.

The pungent smell dissipated quickly, carried away by the constant air current that blew through the narrow gaps around Denetree's body. She stowed the rest of the screen and pulled out the spray sealant. The pressure gauge was low. Denetree swallowed a curse with some effort—not Tekker's cackle again!—and applied herself to building up the pressure with the mechanical pump unit.

On that day she had been on her way through the Middle Deck, deep within its twenty-meter thickness of steel. It was an emergency, Tekker had barked, as though there were anything for the Kalpen but emergencies. But this time, it probably really was. The Kalpen had abandoned their deliberate, relaxed approach to their work. Rather than working at their individual discretion, they followed Tekker's instructions without the usual chatter.

The general excitement had infected Denetree. She had enjoyed the change from the routine, even though that routine was barely a week old, as well as the fact that Tekker hardly had time to "girl" her. As a newcomer she was marginally useful in a situation like this, and when Tekker finally gave her an assignment, she suspected he was just making sure she wasn't in the way. That suspicion had hurt her pride a little, but she decided to make the best of it, crawled into the shaft Tekker had assigned to her, and tried to catch up on a little sleep.

Finally the indicator on the spray sealant showed sufficient pressure. Denetree allowed herself—and in particular her right arm, which throbbed painfully after the pumping—a little rest, then she held the spray nozzle over the screen. The spray caught in the screen and quickly thickened to a solid layer that sealed the leak. Until the next repair, as the Kalpen told each other with a wink, and then burst out laughing and enjoyed another glass of the illicit alcohol slipped to them by grateful metach—often as a gift even before they made the repair.

A sound had awakened Denetree. Not the pounding by the Kalpen that came from a distance, but a kind of pattering. As though tiny paws flitted along the shaft wall. Denetree raised herself and listened attentively. Were there really shaft rats, then? Denetree had thought the Kalpen were pulling her leg when they told her of the pests that nested in the shafts and how tasty they were when roasted over an illegal fire.

She had decided to lay back down when she caught a glimpse of a shadowy form. There really were shaft rats! What if she caught one? She, the slow, clumsy fieldswine! That would bring her respect and glory. Maybe Tekker would even stop calling her "girl!"

Denetree waited a few minutes, then she went over the connecting shaft with the material strength tester. In two places, the measuring device sounded. Denetree sprayed a second spurt of sealant on those spots.

The rat had been nimble. Denetree had difficulty tracking it. But in the brief time that she had been with the Kalpen, her hearing already had grown sharper. The pattering gave the rat away. Denetree had quickly forgotten everything around her. The emergency. The sharp-tongued Tekker, yes, even her brother. She had thought only *about the rat and the triumph she would achieve in presenting it to the others. That she hadn't caught it yet didn't mean anything.* Who knows, *she had thought*, maybe the rat will lead me to its nest. Then we'll have a banquet!

She went over the connecting shaft with the strength tester. This time it didn't sound. The weak spot had been patched.

"Tekker!" Denetree called. "The leak is sealed!"

"Took long enough, girl!" came the answer. "I was starting to think the Ship would run into the end of the universe first. Now get your bottom back down here—we're waiting for you!"

As though insane, she had bent over and run through the main ventilation shafts of the Middle Deck, and then, when the rat turned off into a side shaft, she crawled. If only Tekker could see me now, she had thought. He would be proud of me!

Then the shaft suddenly angled downwards. Denetree gave a wild cry of jubilation. That was even better! She would catch up with the rat by sliding without having to exert herself! Almost immediately she slid out of control, and in a second her slide had become a fall. Denetree screamed.

She crawled back. That was actually the hardest part in the narrow shafts. You could always get in somehow. But going back … you were exhausted, and the supply sack blocked the way. You had to push it through the shaft centimeter by centimeter.

She fell. She could see a bright light below her. She had stretched out her arms and legs in an attempt to brake her plunge, but in vain. Then she was on top of the light, and there was a narrow black shadow. She grasped at it and felt a cold metal bar between her fingers, and her fall had come to an abrupt end nearly two hundred and fifty meters above the surface of the Outer Deck.

Denetree screamed again and again, louder and louder. Hoping for a miracle.

Only a few more meters separated her from the other Kalpen. Denetree heard their grumbling conversation. She turned on her forehead lamp and checked her arm chip. Launt had been able to help her remove her original arm chip, but they had not been able to fasten the new one securely. When she was hanging on for dear life above the Outer Deck, it had nearly come loose. Without the arm chip she was lost.

The chip held in place, though one edge stuck out just a little.

And then the miracle had happened. Something had seized her by the wrist and pulled her up. Not with the even movement of a winch, but in jerks. Denetree had looked up and saw a thin human shape, its legs braced against the step-grooves in the walls of the shaft.

Gasping, Tekker had dragged her upward. And when they had reached the slanted shaft where they could finally collapse without sliding back down, the Kalpen had not chewed her out. Tekker had merely taken her into his arms and held her until the shaking that gripped her body stopped and she could crawl again.

Tekker had never mentioned the incident. Neither to her nor to any of the other Kalpen.

"Here's our fieldswine at last!" Tekker greeted Denetree as she crawled through the main shaft. "Can we finally go? I'm hungry!"

The other Kalpen laughed dutifully.

Denetree stowed her tools in her backpack and the Metach'ton headed for its night quarters. She suspected they could get there over the surface of the Middle Deck, but the Kalpen preferred to travel in one of the roomy main shafts.

As if reading her mind, one of the men said, "Down here, at least we aren't knocked over by one of those blasted bicycle riders!" with a side glance at Denetree, who insisted on taking her bicycle from one job to the next. To the amazement of the Kalpen, she managed to prevent any other metach from riding off with it. The others, Tekker most of all, laughed loudly at this comment. Denetree didn't care. She had learned that the Kalpen expressed their feelings differently than the metach in her previous Metach'ton. The best difference was how quickly they accepted the newcomer as one of them: Denetree found herself automatically in the middle of the line, as a part of the company.

They camped under the "open sky." The Kalpen made it a rule to ignore the shelters assigned to them; perhaps because they spent their days in the cramped shafts, perhaps as a sign of their independence. Denetree was still trying to figure it out. What she was certain of was that she liked at least this part of her new existence. Camping gave her a feeling of freedom that she had never known before.

That evening, some metach came from the Metach'ton whose air supply they had brought back to standard pressure, bringing gifts. Food and some alcohol that had been distilled on the sly. Tekker accepted them, but when the metach politely tried to start a conversation, he quickly drove them off with his rude remarks and cackling. All Denetree heard before they left was that the Tenoy had caught another traitor.

Then they were alone. Tekker lit a small fire. "We make the air, so we can use it, too!" he declared as he built it, and the others agreed. Soon they were roasting the protein plants they had received as gifts, along with the standard rations that the Ship had allotted them. The bottles were passed around. The first time one came to her, Denetree passed it on without drinking, and just stared into the flames.

Someone held a plate with a large protein plant on it under her nose. It was Tekker. She took the plate. A young Kalpen had sat down next to her, but Tekker sent him away with a disapproving look and sat next to her himself.

"Everything all right, girl?"

"Yes, of course. Why do you ask?"

"You often seem like you're somewhere else in your thoughts."

"Maybe I am," Denetree admitted.

"That isn't good. You're here with us, and your thoughts should be with us too."

The bottle came to Tekker. He took a long swallow and held it out to her.

"Thanks, but none for me."

"It would do you good." Tekker continued to offer her the bottle as though he hadn't heard what she said.

Denetree took the bottle and weighed it in her hand. Tekker meant her well. She gave in and took a swallow. The alcohol burned her throat and stomach.

"Better?"

She raised the bottle again and forced down several more swallows. The burning sensation became a pleasant warmth.

"Yes, I think so,"

A tear ran down her cheek.

"You're crying."

"Yes."

"But why? You're here with us. With Tekker."

"I know."

More tears came. The flames in front her blurred. The sparks flying from the wood shone like stars.

"I know," said Denetree.

15

What a day.

First, the maphan called her into the holy sanctuary of the control center, then they stumbled on a gigantic Lemurian ship—the largest artifact found in centuries from the time of the First Humanity!—and finally, Jere von Baloy let her stay in the control center, at her own console, quite as though she belonged there.

Solina Tormas wondered what further wonders awaited her.

She did not have to wait long.

Hardly a quarter hour after the *Palenque* had launched its peculiar fighters, the Espejel announced, "Maphan, the Terrans are calling. Their commander wants to speak with you!"

Jere von Baloy sent the faintest hint of an all-knowing smile in Echkal cer Lethir's direction and said, "Put them through, Netkim. We don't want to waste any more time here."

Solina understood the underlying meaning of his remark. The *Las-Toór* had matched its speed with the Lemurian ship. At just below light-speed, each minute on board the Lemurian ship corresponded to one hundred minutes in the Blue system—so time was passing quite quickly. It was regrettable, but there was nothing to be done at the moment if they didn't want to give up their claim to the discovery. And no one on board would consider that, certainly not Solina.

Floating above her in the holo, the huge cylinder with its long, antennae-like feelers filled her with a powerful yearning. There, the early history of her people waited for her—and possibly even *living* history.

The head of the Terran commander displaced the image of the Lemurian ship. She had an angular face set in a military-neutral expression, an effect that was not softened by almond-colored eyes and a smooth fall of shining hair. The holo showed her body only to just below her shoulders, but it was enough to see that she wore a black, tightly fitting uniform that reminded Solina unpleasantly of the security forces on Drorah.

"Sharita Coho, commander of the Terran prospecting ship *Palenque*," she introduced herself, speaking the intergalactic language of Intercosmo.

"Jere von Baloy, Maphan of the Akonian explorer ship *Las-Toór*," came the reply, also in Intercosmo.

For a moment there was silence as the two tried to size each other up.

The Terran's expression gave nothing away, but Solina wondered what was going through her head at the sight of Jere von Baloy in his dirty overalls. This was supposed to be a starship commander? On the other hand … Solina had never before looked a Terran commander in the face, but somehow the Akonian had pictured it differently: more relaxed, certainly not in uniform. But as a historian, Solina knew that when one looked more closely, things were always different than one imagined them.

"You look like a man who appreciates frankness," the Terran said. "Therefore I won't waste any time: you're wasting *your* time. We were here first, so just go away!"

"Not so fast," Jere von Baloy replied, giving the Terran his most radiant smile. "Isn't there an old Terran proverb, 'Good things take time'? We are ready and willing to compare the log data in our syntrons with yours. As you certainly know, hyperdetection alone is decisive for ownership priority, as has been repeatedly affirmed by galactic courts for centuries now, and—"

"Keep the lawyers away from me! I'd sooner—" She broke off.

"You'd sooner what … ?"

"Never mind! The ship belongs to us and you might as well leave. Anyway,"—the Terran's voice changed to a sticky-sweet chirping—"that thing is just a low-tech tin can. Flying scrap metal. It isn't worth fighting over."

"A Lemurian tin can," Jere von Baloy said simply.

"What? How do you know?"

"We are a research ship. It's our mission to ask questions and find answers."

"Then go look for them somewhere else. You've got the whole goddammed galaxy for that! Or do you want to force me to request the assistance of the LFT fleet?"

Jere von Baloy did his job well. Very well. Solina knew there were some on board who were not satisfied with his leadership. "A maphan who dresses like a simple neelak! It's a scandal!" they whispered, though only behind his back. But others often underestimated Jere von Baloy. In moments like this, he showed one of his greatest strengths: grace under pressure. Whether it was an emergency on board the ship, quarrelsome Yidari, or impertinent Terran starship commanders, he did not let himself get excited. Another man might have exploded under the hail of insults and presumptions. Not only did the maphan remain calm; Solina had the impression he actually enjoyed the battle of words with the Terran.

"Do what you must," he said and spread his arms in a gesture of generosity. "I will not, however, conceal from you the fact that cruising in the immediate vicinity of the Ochent Nebula there happens to be an Akonian squadron under the command of Gartor von Taklir, a most unpleasant and short-tempered character, or so I've heard. He has a reputation for shooting before getting around to asking questions."

The Terran seemed ready to explode. Her deep frown wrinkled her forehead and a thick vein bulged angrily. She opened her mouth. Solina instinctively ducked behind her console.

But the fit of rage never came. The Terran's face remained rigidly fixed toward the camera, but her glance wandered to the side, as though she was concentrating on a director just out of camera range. And he seemed to be giving her new instructions.

When the Terran continued speaking, all the anger had vanished from her voice.

"It's good that we spoke of that, Maphan. Now we both know where we stand." The Terran allowed herself a moment of silent triumph as she sensed that she had caught Jere von Baloy off guard for the first time with her surprising change of tactic. "Now that the lines have been drawn, I can get down to my actual purpose in making contact with you."

"And that would be?"

"I want to make you an offer. In consideration of the fact that we're dealing with a Lemurian artifact, I see a special responsibility for both parties. After all, it's a matter of our common ancestors."

Solina wouldn't have been surprised if the Terran had choked on the syrup in her own voice. But Sharita Coho was made of stern stuff. She held on, breathing deeply and evenly.

"Why don't we investigate the Lemurian ship together? It would be childish to let petty jealousy get the better of us, right?"

"How very true."

Sharita Coho lowered her head. "I can understand that you're not ready to trust us whole-heartedly. Terran-Akonian history is unfortunately filled with regrettable ... um ... misunderstandings. Therefore, I suggest a trust-building measure. Why don't we exchange guests? It would be a wonderful opportunity for each side to get to know the other while the joint exploration team goes about its work."

"An interesting suggestion." Jere von Baloy gave the ship's syntron a hand signal outside camera range and turned to the control center crew. "The cards are on the table. What do you think of the offer?"

The Terran would not be aware of the small council of war: the ship's syntron had seamlessly inserted a simulation of the maphan into the conversation. Jere von Baloy's digital doppelgänger would answer her remarks as long as necessary with banalities meant to delay making any meaningful response.

"This is a trap!" exclaimed Echkal cer Lethir, not surprisingly the first to be heard from. "You can't trust Terrans. Call the fleet! That's even what the *Las-Toór*'s regulations say: In a hopeless situation, the fleet is to be called upon for assistance!"

Other crew members expressed themselves in turn. Their opinions were divided: half agreed with Echkal cer Lethir, the other half felt negotiations should continue.

This was a quirk of Jere von Baloy's that Solina had only heard about prior to this moment: before an important decision, he often solicited advice from the crew. Though such collaboration might be considered a sign of weakness—a maphan didn't discuss, he decided—Solina saw it as just the opposite. It was a sign of strength: this way, he made his decisions the decisions of the entire crew. And—

"Solina, your opinion?"

She gave a start. All others present had voiced their opinions, but she didn't expect to be asked. She wasn't part of the inner circle.

"Solina, we're listening!"

"Well ... I ... " Redness flushed her cheeks. "I think we should accept the offer. The Terran commander may rant and rave, but we have a proverb on my home world: 'A glowshark that beats its fins doesn't bite.' The Terrans won't do anything to us as long as we have their hostages on board. "

"And you believe the Terrans have no ulterior motive?"

Solina nearly burst out laughing. "Of course they have! They consider themselves smarter, and think that sooner or later they can kick us out—but we'll see who kicks out whom!" Without realizing it, Solina had stood up from her seat and cried out the last few words.

Jere von Baloy's gaze locked on her. "You would pay any price to go aboard that Lemurian ship, wouldn't you?"

"Yes."

"Then we don't want to disappoint you." The maphan gave the syntron a sign again and said to Sharita Coho: "That is a very wise and sensible suggestion. We accept."

Solina collapsed in her chair. Her knees trembled. She would board the Lemurian ship!

What a day.

16

If it just wasn't so blasted cramped!

Pearl Laneaux was convinced she would cease being able to breathe at any moment. The air in the crawler was hot. It stank horribly. Of the sweat of her companions, of course, from their excitement and anticipation, but there was also a smell that Pearl had trouble placing at first, then identified as mold. That was the legacy of the crawler's regular crew, who had cleared out of their beloved vehicle for this mission only under protest.

There you are! she thought. *You've always wondered what being in a crawler felt like. Now you know.*

The crawlers were purely utility vehicles, equipped to take read-ings in life-hostile environments, collect samples and analyze both. Pearl had the impression that it had only occurred to the builders of the crawlers at the last minute, just before delivering the first model, that they had to accommodate three people somewhere. *Nothing could be easier,* they must have thought. *We'll just bolt a cabin on underneath!*

A cabin large enough for three people who must be prepared to live for weeks or months in a kind of symbiosis that would trans-form them into a conjoined entity, not a collective being but no longer individuals.

Three people. For months. Pearl had been on board for less than half an hour.

She only had to shift her weight to the left and pull her head back slightly in order to find her nose between Perry Rhodan's shoulder blades. She wondered how the Immortal would react to that. Rhodan would probably make a polite remark, or a joke. That might not be so bad, and who could claim to have ever been so close to an Immortal? Pearl cautiously shifted her weight, and her nose came within a couple of centimeters of Rhodan's back. No, better not.

She stretched out her right leg, folded it again and felt it rest against something solid. She quickly shifted back, but too late. Hayden Norwell gave her a sharp glance. *Sharita, what were you thinking?* she mentally demanded of her commander, who had assembled the team. *Did you want to punish Rhodan for being smarter than you? Or me because I was on his side?*

Hayden was one of the prospectors. Crawler Twelve was his normal assignment—she had no idea how the other two on board with him could stand it—and so most of the time he was out of sight and out of mind. Pearl had once tried to find out what tasks Norwell actually performed on the crawler, but his comrades had nothing to say. The first officer, whose curiosity had now been properly spurred, turned instead to Alemaheyu Kossa. The comm officer knew everything about everybody on board the *Palenque*. But even Alemaheyu had passed on her question. Norwell had no identifiable qualifications that explained his presence: not professionally, and not personally.

And on top of all that he was ugly. Incredibly ugly. Pearl considered herself a sensitive person. Even though she loved to vent her anger now and then with French curses that no one on board understood, she appreciated a minimum standard in the matter of conduct and grooming. Norwell was a failure in both categories. His dark eyes were always outlined by faint shadows, as though he'd had too little sleep. His eyebrows were bushy, seeming to cry out for scissors to trim back their rank growth. Then there was the scar over the right eye, which seemed to have slipped. That part of his face, including his eyebrow, must have been torn off and then crudely sewn back on again. The injury probably had the same cause as his nose with its impossible bump. When and how he had been injured, no one could say. Here, too, Alemaheyu had had to pass.

Why is he in our team, for God's sake? Is he supposed to keep the inhabitants of that Lemurian crate—if there are any—at a distance by the sheer sight of him?

That Norwell was in so-so physical shape hardly mattered. They weren't going on board the Lemurian ship to do gymnastics. And besides, Pearl, Perry Rhodan, and the prospector wore protective suits equipped with antigrav propulsion systems.

"Crawler Twelve, are you ready?" Alemaheyu's voice asked from an acoustic field.

"Couldn't be better," Pearl answered bravely. She gasped for air, being careful to breathe through her mouth so she didn't have to tolerate even more smells. "How much longer … Mama?"

Pearl could just about hear Alemaheyu's satisfied grin through the acoustic field. He loved being called "Mama" even though he indignantly denied it when anyone suggested that might be true.

"I see you've made yourself at home," the comm officer said.

"It's not bad," Pearl coughed. "How much longer, Mama?"

The crawler was under the control of the mother ship's syntron, which guided its course. Pearl and the others were only passengers. She hated having no control, but it was the most reasonable solution. If the Akonians or the presumed Lemurian ship decided to open fire in a surprise attack, any human reaction would come too late. The *Palenque*'s syntron gave them the best advantage here. It also had an overview of everything that was happening and so could coordinate the actions of the prospector ship and all the crawlers.

"Eleven minutes, forty-three seconds," Alemaheyu replied.

"Good," Pearl said succinctly. "How are things with the Akonians?"

"They're holding to the deal. Their fighters have withdrawn to the specified distance and they've launched two objects that we think are Shifts. One will dock with the *Palenque*, and the other is on course for the rendezvous point."

"What about us?"

"Of course we're keeping our word," Alemaheyu laughed. "Did you expect anything else?"

"Certainly not," Pearl replied, knowing that the commander could tap into the *Palenque*'s entire communications traffic at any time. Sharita was considered capable of anything, even an attempt to dupe the Akonians at the cost of the special team.

"The hostage is—" The impulse engines came to life in order to brake the crawler and drowned out the comm officer. The builders of the vehicle had skipped the acoustic shielding. At that moment, Pearl wished she could get her hands on one of them and lock him into one of his vehicles for a three-week test flight at full thrust. She would have gladly listened to what he had to say afterwards—if he could manage to string together a coherent sentence.

She deactivated the acoustic field, hoped that the vibration of the crawler didn't make her lose her balance, and shut her eyes.

She tried to imagine what awaited her on board the Lemurian ship. A paradise, perhaps? If her calculations were correct and the ship had been under way for tens of thousands of years—and for centuries for those currently on board—it must amount to its own little world inside. A utopia in which there was no crime and no violence, no cares, only simple people who contentedly went about their work, and the stars that surrounded them, stars that … .

A holo appeared above the heads of the crawler's crew. It showed space and in its center a massive shadow that rapidly grew larger. The shadow's outlines took shape, revealing it to be the widely-used all-purpose transport vehicle called a Shift.

The Akonians' Shift.

The Akonians. Pearl wondered what to expect from them. "Don't trust any Akonian!" Sharita had advised her, but Pearl had dismissed the idea almost immediately. The Akonians were human beings like them, weren't they?

She would soon find out.

***

Solina Tormas wondered what the Terrans would be like. She had never met one in the flesh. Not that she hadn't dealt with them. As a historian, she regularly took part in conferences that included Terrans, but for reasons of cost, or perhaps because her superiors were afraid of what direct contact with Terrans and other aliens might stir up in her, such meetings had been strictly virtual—up to now. Admittedly, in the thirteenth century of the New Galactic Era, a virtual conference was recognizable as such only on the third look and then by careful observers. An academic institution's syntron projected simulations of the participants in the lecture hall and placed them in the seats. When a participant spoke, his digital avatar stood up and talked and gestured exactly like a being of flesh and blood.

And yet … something was lacking. Was it some last gap in the behavioral model the syntron used to animate the avatars? Or the uniformity of the model that could never imitate the diversity of actual living beings? What Solina missed was somewhat more concrete: odors. Avatars were bodiless, didn't smell, and even when the entire lecture hall was fully packed with them, Solina's nose perceived only the sharp odor of the cleaning fluid that the robots used on the floor every night.

What did a Terran smell like?

She would soon know the answer, and much more as well.

"Everything all right, Robol?" She turned in her seat in the direction of the logistics officer, who had taken over guidance of the Shift.

The man, unusually brawny for an Akonian, gestured in the affirmative. "The Terrans are right in front of us. Strange looking crate."

He pointed to the hyperdetector holo showing the Terran ship. No, not a ship. *Vehicle.* Solina had the impression that someone had pounded on a Terran spacesphere with a colossal sledgehammer until it was as flat as one of the predatory fish that pressed themselves into the seafloor along the shallow coastlines of Shaghomin, except that the giant hadn't stopped until he had beaten a hollow into the center. And the Terrans didn't seem to care much about their engineering; it was surrounded by a simple High-energy Overload (HO) shield, scant protection that the Shift's on-board gun could have blown away at any time.

"What do you expect, Robol?" replied Hevror ta Gosz. "They're Terrans!" The two men laughed. Solina hesitated, then joined in. It felt good to relieve the tension a bit, and she didn't have to worry on Hevror's account. He wasn't a Terran-hater, but simply carried on Akon's sacred tradition of making fun of the Terrans. It felt good to always have someone to blame or to sneer at. Solina often thought that if the Terrans didn't already exist, her people would have had to invent them.

Hevror adjusted the quiver-like bag he carried slung over his back. More than two meters in height, he was tall even for an Akonian. His skin was weather-beaten and wrinkled, and occasional bright spots of pigment stood out from the otherwise velvety brown of his skin, a souvenir of the uncounted suns Hevror had walked under without protection.

Most of the crew members of the *Las-Toór* considered Hevror ta Gosz a little crazy. For Solina, he was the closest thing she had to a friend. Hevror had called her as soon as the expedition was a go.

"Solina, I've got to come along!" was all he had said.

"You?" she had asked.

"I'm a specialist in planetary ecologies."

"True."

"That thing on the screens may be a metal cylinder, but I swear that you can use somebody like me there. Care to bet that thing has its own ecosystem?"

"That could be," Solina had said simply, but in her heart she had already decided to bring Hevror. It would be good to have a friend along, even if he was a bit crazy. To her surprise, Jere von Baloy supported her choice.

When Hevror had arrived at the Shift, the long, leather bag was dangling on his back.

Solina had frowned. "What do you want with that?"

"The same as always?"

"In the Lemurian ship?"

"We'll see," Hevror had answered and disappeared into the Shift.

Solina had let it go. What did she care if Hevror dragged along his bag? The thing was light. It wouldn't get in his way. And hadn't she railed against conformity all her life?

In front of the Terran vehicle, a huge dark shape emerged from the blackness.

The Lemurian ship.

They approached it near the bow. The gigantic ship—now that they had the thing right in front of their noses, the hyperdetector was finally delivering consistent data—had a length of some five kilometers. The diameter of the hull was nearly five hundred meters. At that size, it was bigger than any of the ships ever built in Akonian shipyards. Now, size meant little by itself. Solina was certain that viewed through the eyes of a technician, this ship represented an anachronistic scrapheap. But that wasn't the point. What was critically important was understanding the effort behind building the ship. Building such a massive artificial structure would have required considerable financial means, persistence and an iron will. Solina could hardly believe that the construction and launch of such a ship had been forgotten, but that exact possibility was the fascination of her profession: the past held mysteries and wonders without end, and every answer one found led to a dozen new questions.

And they still knew so little about the Lemurians!

The onslaught of the Beasts had destroyed the Great Tamanium of the Lemurians, nearly wiping out the human race. Only by escaping to Andromeda was humanity's survival ensured. Those who remained behind eked out a miserable existence in the ruins of their once-glorious civilization. The Akonians had been the one major exception. Once, they had comprised the Eighty-seventh Tamanium of the Lemurian Imperium, in which separatist tendencies had been evident even before the Beasts attacked. The later Akonians managed to seal themselves off so far from the outer universe that they had been left untouched by the great cataclysm that struck the Lemurians.

But the Lemurians' knowledge had been lost. What hadn't been consumed in the firestorms launched by the Beasts was eaten away by the simple passage of time. The tens of millennia had hit even the highly advanced Lemurian technology so hard that only a very few of the data storage units that researchers found were still readable, let alone intact. Even in the Blue system, where the flow of civilization had never been interrupted, the legacy of the Lemurians had been forgotten.

It was just human nature. Each new generation saw the world in its own terms, interpreted it according to its own ideas—and gave little thought to what had gone before. Computer nets were remodeled; in the passing millennia cities were rebuilt many times over until their origins were erased.

So they actually knew very little about their ancestors. So many surprises lay hidden in Lemurian history. And some of them, as

Solina was now seeing with her own eyes, could be big enough to equal the mass of multiple Akonian battle cruisers.

The Lemurian ship lay directly before them. Its "antennae" stuck out from all sides like a wreath. About halfway along their length they supported a ring. The other Yidari on board the *Las-Toôr* had unhesitatingly identified the projections as antennae, but Solina had her doubts. Since their emergence into normal space in the vicinity of the ship, the presumed antennae had not emitted a single comm signal. Well, they might be defective, or the Lemurian crew—if there was one—might be trying to hide their existence, but that last seemed illogical to her. Why build such colossal antennae if they weren't used?

"Robol, can you get anything more about those antennae?" she asked, turning to the logistics officer. In their team of historian, planetary ecologies specialist and logistics officer, he served as technician.

"Let's see." Robol von Sarwar busied himself for a moment with the hyperdetector data. He was so deeply absorbed in his work that he unconsciously grinned when he found something. It wasn't a pretty sight. His teeth were black, the result of a childhood accident. The progress of the poison was stopped and even the stimulus for growing new teeth had functioned. But the new ones grew in pitch black.

Along with his dark eyes, the teeth gave people the impression he was a robot, so Robol generally avoided showing them.

Robol raised his head and looked at Solina. "I've found *something*," he said, speaking in his usual fashion by barely moving his lips. "Between some of those antennae are neutrino-capturing fields."

"Energy fields? That sounds like five-dimensional technology!"

"Could be. It could also be coincidence. The fields come and go in a rapid rhythm. There can't be much getting caught."

"Neutrinos ... " Solina thought out loud. "Assuming that they're trying to capture them intentionally ... what for?"

At that point she was distracted. The Terran craft had reached the level of the antennae. Since the entire Lemurian ship turned along its long axis, the antennae spun like the spokes of a wheel. It took the ship just forty Terran seconds per single rotation.

"What's he trying to do?" Robol exclaimed. "Has he gone crazy?"

Solina saw what he meant. The Terran craft was not trying to avoid the spinning antennae. Just the opposite: the pilot was heading straight toward them, traveling along the ship's hull to where the distance between the antennae was only a few dozen meters. With awe-inspiring precision, the craft slipped between two antennae.

The pilot must have nerves of steel.

Solina watched as the Terran craft slowed its speed and paused a few meters above the spinning hull, apparently looking for an appropriate docking point. Then she noticed how the Lemurian ship's antennae were growing larger, the slender masts turning into massive towers.

"Robol, have you lost your mind?"

The pilot of the Shift kept his eyes on the instruments. "On the contrary. The Terrans are trying to humiliate us. They want to prove that they're braver than we are. I'll show them!"

The gigantic cylinder of the Lemurian ship suddenly expanded, filling the entire view from the Shift's forward window, rising before them like a wall of steel.

Robol clearly wasn't worried about it. With his pitch-black teeth bared—was he whistling a tune or did Solina only imagine it?—he fixed his gaze on the steel colossus ahead, and at the last second, when Solina was convinced they were about to crash, he gave the impulse jets a precisely calculated energy thrust. The Lemurian ship seemed to jump. Out the corner of her eye, Solina saw the base of a massive tower racing toward them, and then they were past it.

The Shift glided barely above the spinning hull.

Jere von Baloy's worried voice came from the acoustic field. "Solina, is everything all right with you three?"

"Of course, Maphan," she replied serenely. "What shouldn't be all right?"

She did not suspect that more than just discoveries about Terrans and Lemurians awaited her.

17

Launt seldom returned to the house which more than one metach secretly envied him. The spacious rooms, whose sheer emptiness soothed him and allowed him to find some distance from the innumerable duties of a Tenarch, now seemed deserted, almost silently accusing, since the day Denetree had mounted her bicycle and rode off to begin her new life.

He had not seen her since and hopefully never would. If he met her again, it would in all probability be as a result of the new duty the Naahk had assigned him. That thought robbed him of the few hours of sleep remaining in this rest period.

The problem was not that Launt was in love with Denetree. During the first few days after her departure, he had carefully listened to his inner voice, but had found no evidence of such a feeling. He did not even feel physically attracted to her. As a Tenarch, he had virtually free choice of partners for coupling among the metach. It was not a right provided for in the Ship's code, but few women would refuse a Tenarch, whether out of awe for what he represented, or out of fear of his influence. In fact, Launt recently had accepted a woman who had come to him on her own. That night also was sleepless, but at least Denetree and the other traitors were not preying on his mind.

During the day, Launt had no such convenient distraction from his troubled thoughts. Even as a young man, he had always relied on his work to divert his mind, and his fervor was rewarded. Practically from the moment of finishing his obligatory service in the fields the young, intelligent man, bursting with enthusiasm for the Ship's mission, had attracted attention. He climbed the Metach'rath with uncanny speed until he reached the top of the Ladder of Life and became a Tenarch.

Never in the history of the Ship had such a young metach been appointed Tenarch.

Launt had achieved what others only dreamed of—but it was then that his problems really began.

As a Tenarch he had access to nearly all information available on the Ship and its inhabitants, information only slightly less complete than that available to the Naahk himself. The Tenarchs were where all the threads of life aboard the Ship came together, more obviously so as the Naahk retreated further into the background. Rumors claimed he was afflicted by a disease that robbed him of his strength and decisiveness: this did not concern the older Tenarchs. During the decades in which they had occupied their positions, they had experienced many highs and lows in the life of the Naahk. "It's only a phase," they said. "A new upswing will follow the decline."

Launt accepted that the Naahk might regain his old energy and authority and return to lead them all as strongly as in the past, but the curse of his intelligence and knowledge also forced him to accept that even an all-powerful and robust Naahk would be helpless to stop the Ship's decay. Here a shelter collapsed because the plastic it was made from had reached the end of its lifespan. There, an important machine failed after centuries of continuous use, or—and it happened more and more often—work stopped because a single moving part wore out. The spare parts bins grew emptier and the ability to make new replacement parts dwindled.

It wasn't the fault of the metach; they were bright and dedicated. The problem was that the Ship itself bent under the burden of age. Most worrying was the ongoing and ever more rapid loss of memory storage units. The memory storage specialists long had been waging a discouraging rearguard battle against the decay. They erased less important data to allocate room for more life-critical information, and to back up that information. The end of this downward spiral could be foreseen, and the angle of the decline became increasingly steeper when more data storage units failed, necessitating more erasures, and what had been assumed to be unimportant knowledge turned out in hindsight to be indispensable.

Another decade, maybe two, and the metach community would be in free fall.

The end might come quickly if the hull of the Ship collapsed and the vacuum suffocated the metach, the way it had the forty-three Tenoy Venron dragged along in his flight into space. Or it might come gradually if the Kalpen could no longer accomplish their makeshift repairs of the air supply system.

Launt hoped for the first alternative. He saw no higher, hidden purpose in suffering. Suffering was simply suffering, and anyone who was intelligent avoided it.

Sometimes Launt dreamed that he could still avert disaster. He dreamed of refuge for the metach—on a planet.

His privileged status gave Launt access to data about the home world of Lemur. Their forefathers had fled that planet for reasons he didn't question. But Lemur had provided its inhabitants with everything naturally that on board the Ship they maintained artificially with constantly decreasing success: a stable ecosphere with environmental conditions that were beneficial for a metach.

Launt gradually became convinced of a singular fact. For the Ship's community to survive, they must find a Lemur-like planet and leave the Ship. Launt believed this plan supported their forefathers' intentions. The forefathers had placed survival of their race ahead of all other considerations, and had left everything behind that was familiar in the certain knowledge they would never see it again.

It was time to follow their example.

Launt had investigated, so he knew the Ship possessed the means. Besides the shuttle that was destroyed in Venron's attempt to escape, there were another forty-seven shuttles of the same design waiting to be used.

Why, Launt asked himself, would the forefathers have put shuttles on board if they hadn't planned for their descendants to leave the Ship someday?

It was a revolutionary, outrageous thought—and an unspeakable one.

Launt's tentative attempts to touch on his idea in conversation ran into utter lack of understanding. Either literally—the mental horizon of most metach was simply not wide enough to imagine life outside the Ship—or, with the more intelligent of the metach, figuratively, as they tried to guess at his motives. Just to think of leaving the Ship seemed to them like treason. It bordered on a miracle that none of the metach had reported Launt to the Ship.

Launt had retreated to the luxury of his house, to the soothing monotony of the Ship's daily routine, and waited for the thoughts that haunted his mind to die. But he was the one dying. Day by day, even while he continued on as though his efforts had a point, as though there were a goal they could reach, as though destruction did not await the Ship.

On the evening he watched Denetree lose consciousness at the Tenoy checkpoint, he had acted so decisively that it seemed as though he had been waiting his entire life for this moment. It wasn't that Denetrée herself mattered to him—he would have rushed to the aid of any of the traitors—it was what she represented. He simply couldn't watch and do nothing while the only metach able to consider the future of their community were eliminated, even if that outlook was naive and unrealistic.

Launt had saved Denetree, at least for the time being. For the others, he had failed.

And matters would get even worse.

The day after Mika's interrogation, which Launt had tried in vain to prevent, the Naahk had called him. It was not unusual for the Naahk to request a conference with Launt. He generally called to discuss minor details that Lemal Netwar had chosen from the daily reports he received. Netwar dragged out these discussions almost beyond reason, all the while looking at Launt almost pleadingly from the display screen. Launt puzzled over the Naahk's actions for a long time.

What is on his mind? he had often wondered. *What does he want from me?* And sometimes, when his work had piled so high that any interruption angered him, he thought, *How did you get to be Naahk if you can't tell the difference between what's important and what isn't?*

At first, Launt tried to be polite. The Naahk was not like typical metach. Even Launt's considerable powers of imagination could not see them developing a relationship that would allow Launt to ask these questions directly. Later, when the calls had turned into a constant disturbance, Launt had become downright abrupt.

Launt's attitude made no difference. The Naahk refused to give him any peace, and the look of pleading Launt saw in his eyes became increasingly urgent.

Then, quite suddenly one day, Launt understood. The Naahk wasn't calling him to discuss trivial administrative questions. Those issues interested him as little as they did his Tenarchs. Whatever topic of discussion the Naahk chose, it was simply an excuse for human contact. His quarters lay in the center of the Ship, yet separate from its life. From that moment on, Launt had made all other duties a secondary priority and patiently took time for the Naahk when he called.

Launt pitied the master of the Ship.

He also had an ulterior motive. From the very slowly and carefully growing relationship between him and Lemal Netwar, perhaps something good would develop. The prospect for reform, a new direction for their mission. A chance for survival.

One such discussion on the day after Mika's torture began like any other. Without warning or transition, the Naahk's face appeared on Launt's display screen, replacing the meeting minutes on which the Tenarch had been working.

"Launt, I don't want to bother you for long," Lemal began. "I just want to be certain that we correctly understood each other in our last … encounter."

Even after all this time, Launt was still faintly amazed that he was on such familiar terms with the Naahk, even though their discussions were now his normal routine. Since his attempt yesterday to save Mika and the other traitors, however, he had been feeling sad about their relationship.

"Yes, of course," Launt replied. The Tenarch had understood. His choice was between obedience and dismissal, perhaps even death. Lemal Netwar might hesitate to give the appropriate instructions, as in the case of the traitors. But he was the Naahk, and he would force himself to perform his duty. "I'm just now working on the minutes of the most recent Tenarchs meeting. You'll have it shortly. But I can tell you now that the functional deterioration of the neutrino catcher was the main topic. The be'ketren have no idea as to the cause. Before much longer, the engineers say, we'll be forced to shut down additional systems. The energy we produce and gather isn't sufficient any more."

"I'll read the minutes carefully," the Naahk promised, looking past Launt at some point in the distance. He held his head absolutely rigid when he talked, never making the slightest movement, as though it were tightly screwed onto his backbone. He never shook his head nor did he nod. It had taken Launt a long time to get used to it. It was such a small thing, but it made the Naahk seem less than human.

Launt waited for the Naahk to continue. Lemal Netwar cleared his throat, then began to talk about optimized harvest rotation in a certain sector of the Outer Deck, saying that he expected an increase in yield from the system that would allow them to feed nearly a hundred additional metach over the long term.

Launt resisted the urge to explain to the Naahk that neither the air nor energy supply was up to the demands of additional bodies, and that they must raise fewer children. There was no point to initiating such a discussion, because when confronted with such realities, Lemal Netwar retreated into indignation. It was one respect in which the old man was losing his touch.

In other respects, his mental grasp was laser-sharp.

Lemal cleared his throat again. "Launt, I've thought about our conversation from yesterday."

Launt couldn't speak; irrational hope squeezed his chest.

" You know that I think very highly of you. You are the youngest of the Tenarchs, and by far the most capable. Yours is an intelligent, independent mind. We have too few metach like you."

No wonder, Launt thought, *when the Ship does everything possible to suppress independent thinking!*

"I don't want to lose you, Launt," the Naahk continued. "The Ship needs you." His eyes remained focused on the unknown distant point. He did not look at Launt's face. "Therefore, I have decided to confer on you a task of extreme importance: you will direct and supervise the apprehension of the traitors. It will be your responsibility to see that they receive justice."

"Naahk, that is ... is ... "

"No one is better suited for this task. You are not a fanatic who will condemn innocents in your zeal. You are competent! You will find and punish the guilty, and all metach will know that justice was done with complete impartiality."

"Naahk, I ... "

"I'm counting on you, Launt." Now the Naahk looked directly at his Tenarch, and Launt was frightened by the intensity of the plea in his eyes. "Don't disappoint me."

Lemal Netwar's image disappeared, but the meeting minutes had now lost all meaning. Launt finished them as though in a trance, his thoughts on the terrible choice that lay before him. He could murder the "traitors"—or sacrifice his own life. There was no real choice; if he died, someone else would take over his assignment.

Since that day, many new pictures had appeared on his display. These were the traitors. They were arrested one after the other. Under torture, Mika had named several dozen names. Some of them were completely fictional. There were no metach with those names. Others had turned out to be obviously innocent. Mika must have named them in an attempt to protect the rest. But still others quickly proved to be part of the group led by Venron. They were interrogated and taken to the Pekoy. That was enough to break their resistance. They had seen what had happened to Mika. In less than a week, the entire group of fourteen metach had been apprehended. With the exception of Denetree, who seemed to have disappeared from the face of the Ship.

Launt had followed events like a spectator, simultaneously powerless and all-knowing. The Tenoy performed their duties out of sincere concern for the Ship; they did not need any incentive. Launt stood by simply to make sure that individuals arrested out of over-zealousness were released—exactly as the Naahk had predicted.

Once the machinery had been set in motion, nothing could stop it.

Freme was the first to fall into their clutches. The Tenoy had seized him in his metach'ton, sitting in a circle of his comrades as they shared the smoke of the vakrin plant. He offered no resistance. Had he resigned himself to his fate? Or had he realized that there was only one chance of survival for the members of the Star Seekers: remain silent and hope that the storm blew over them? Probably the latter. Freme had not been intimidated by the sight of the Pekoy. He would have become too well acquainted with the Pekoy's instruments if Launt hadn't used his power as Tenarch to delay Freme's torture long enough for the Tenoy to seize other traitors who proved to be weaker willed.

Freme was a gaunt man with an unusually furrowed face, like that of a metach past the middle of his life. If he hadn't made the mistake of attaching himself to Venron, Freme would have joined the Tenoy and provided great service to the Ship. There were too few metach who shared with him the mix of enthusiasm, good judgment and strong nerves that made for a good Tenoy.

After Freme, the Tenoy arrested other metach with frightening speed. Most they let go after forcing them to spend the night in a dark, unheated cell barely large enough to stand in upright. It was a valuable lesson, the Tenoy and the other Tenarchs assured each other, but an appalling injustice in Launt's view, and utter stupidity besides. Who could believe that loyalty to the Ship would be fostered this way?

Launt called up the pictures of the traitors and created a gallery of all fourteen on his display. They were pictures from happier days, taken before their arrest. The men and women laughed, and in their eyes shone expectation, not the tired hopelessness of the Naahk.

Launt stared into the faces for a long time, as though expecting them to speak.

Then a precisely modulated voice came from all around him. It could have belonged to either a woman or a man.

"Launt," said the Net, "what are you waiting for?"

The Tenarch gave a start. He erased the picture gallery from the display as if by doing so he could hide his thoughts and actions from the Net.

"What do you mean by that? I'm not waiting. I'm working."

"Not very efficiently. Why are you putting off what must be done?"

"We have yet to capture Venron's sister, Denetree," he replied quickly.

"What difference does that make?"

"The more intelligent among the metach will wonder what became of her. They might get the idea the Ship allowed mercy over justice. That would certainly not be your intention, correct?"

The Net didn't answer for several minutes. For a moment, Launt hoped he had overpowered its logic, but then he heard a sound that reminded him of a sigh and it said, "The more intelligent among the metach are intelligent enough to know that is not the case. They know there is no escape from the Ship's justice. Denetree is almost certainly dead. She might have found an unsecured hatch and followed her brother to the stars. Or she threw herself into a composter and suffocated. There is no place on the Ship where a metach can hide for two weeks."

"You're are right, of course," Launt said, wondering how well the Net could read human facial expressions. It had had more than five hundred years to analyze them.

"The metach are waiting. The Naahk warned them of the traitors' existence. He has described the danger that threatens the Ship because of them. And he has announced their punishment. If there is no punishment, the metach will doubt him and the order of things. Is that what you want?"

"*No!* Of course not."

"And do you doubt the order of things?"

Launt forced himself to express honest indignation. "Of course not! Who has served the Ship more loyally than I?"

"Then I fail to understand your hesitation."

"This … this is not easy. It's a question of human life."

"That, on the other hand, I do understand," the Net replied. "But it is necessary to sacrifice their lives in order to prevent the loss of many others. Give the order."

Again, he was trapped. If he refused to give the command, he would die with the others. Nothing would be accomplished.

"Arrange the execution," Launt whispered. "The traitors will die tomorrow night."

"As you command," replied the Net.

18

The Akonian Shift closed to within a few meters of the crawler and matched its speed.

"Man, what kind of junk are the Akonians using for syntrons, anyway?" Hayden Norwell exclaimed. He played the hyperdetector recordings of the approach maneuver on a holo. The Akonian craft had missed colliding with one of the Lemurian ship's antennae by a hair. "They desperately need to install a few updates—and I'd suggest Terran ones, at that!"

"Perhaps they're flying their Shift manually?" Rhodan suggested.

"You aren't serious, are you? Even Akonians can't be that dumb!"

"No dumber than we Terrans, but certainly as proud. Why should they leave to a machine what they can do themselves?"

Norwell grunted something and dropped the subject, so Rhodan made no further comment. The immortal Terran had often encountered Akonians: as enemies, then at a cool distance and now, as he hoped, in mutual respect. For the prospectors, dealing with the Akonians was a new situation. They didn't know what to expect, and they dealt with their uncertainty in their own ways: Hayden Norwell swore; Pearl Laneaux chatted with "Mama" Kossa as though the fate and well-being of the crawler depended solely on the stream of conversation between them remaining unbroken, rather than on the syntronic umbilical cord that connected them with the *Palenque*.

"We're throwing out the anchor now, okay?" said the comm officer.

"Okay."

The tractor beam guided the crawler to a place on the gigantic hull where several main struts of its framework came together. In the next moment, the ship's body beneath them came to a stop and the stars spun wildly. A jolt indicated that the crawler had set down.

Pearl took a deep breath. "Here we are. Check your suits, then get out there!" She didn't speak to Alemaheyu separately; the comm officer was listening to every word spoken on board the crawler.

Rhodan had already checked out his suit during the approach and shifted to give the others as much room as possible. The two prospectors bumped into each other in the cramped confines, swore and fumbled with the beamers that, per the agreement with the Akonians, they were allowed to carry.

They left the crawler cabin. The Akonian Shift had landed on the Lemurian ship a few meters away and figures in spacesuits were just emerging. Rhodan waved to them and one of the Akonians waved back.

The two groups met in the pale light that shone from their respective airlocks. The Akonians' suits seemed brand new and custom-tailored, as they fit perfectly and emphasized their wearers' considerable height. The Terrans' suits, on the other hand, showed the wear and tear of the hundreds of worlds where they had seen use. Rhodan heard Norwell muttering indignantly; the prospector apparently had picked up on the contrast in their equipment and he didn't like it. Rhodan wasn't bothered by the inequality. Experience had taught him to rely on proven technology for critical missions rather than on the latest high-tech gadgets, which tended to fail the user just when they were needed most.

Pearl Laneaux, by far the smallest person in either group, pointed to a spot on the hull in the near distance. Without a word, the Terrans and Akonians started toward it. No one spoke, even though both sides had agreed on a frequency for communication and they also had a common language available with Intercosmo. It was just the awkwardness of the situation. Besides, they had no faces; the material comprising the helmet visors functioned like a one-way mirror. Looking at the person opposite you was merely to look at yourself.

They came to a stop. Two of the Akonians took a massive object from an antigrav platform that had followed them automatically, and began working with it. A large tarpaulin unfolded and formed itself into a kind of tent that sealed off the Akonians and Terrans from the spinning stars. Rhodan was glad to have it, because the swift movement was making him nauseous. The Akonians set their beamers to low intensity and welded the edge of the tent to the hull of the Lemurian ship. Apparently satisfied, they nodded to each other, then adjusted their beamers again and burned a circular hole in the hull about a meter and a half in diameter.

Rhodan would have preferred to not cut their way into the Lemurian ship with beamers, but the hyperdetectors had failed to find a hatch anywhere that they would be able to open. They couldn't even find the lock through which the shuttle had left the mother ship.

The cut-out section of the hull floated upward. The spinning of the Lemurian ship created an outward-directed artificial gravity that would have thrown the Terrans and the Akonians out into space if they hadn't been using their antigravs. One of the Akonians caught the steel disk with a tractor beam before it could tear through the tent and anchored it with a magnetic mounting to the surface of the hull. The tent walls stretched taut with the sudden air pressure but held.

Pearl Laneaux was apparently determined to show from the start who was in command and led the way down through the opening into darkness. Akonians and Terrans followed her in alternating order. When everyone was inside, the Akonians welded the loose section back into the hull. It would hinder an emergency retreat, but they owed it to whatever remained of the ship's crew to repair the damage caused by their entrance.

They opened their helmets.

***

The first encounter with the Terrans shook Solina Tormas' assumptions. These were the prodigies of the galaxy? The sight of their pathetic spacesuits—they looked as though the Terrans hung them out to dry on the outer hull of their ship, and were obviously of advanced age—made it painfully clear to the historian that the golden age of the Solar Imperium was long over. These people did not represent the supermen who, under the leadership of their ultra-superman Perry Rhodan, had once brought nearly the entire galaxy under their influence. Back then, it would have been unthinkable that the Terrans would use anything but the latest and best equipment.

The second encounter gave her a prodigious shock.

When they had entered the Lemurian ship and made certain that no immediate danger threatened them, they opened their helmets.

Curious, she took stock of the Terrans. Their leader, who introduced herself as Pearl Laneaux, would have been considered a beauty even by Akonian standards if she hadn't been so short. Hayden Norwell, who introduced himself second, was somewhat taller, but even if he had been a two-meter giant his attractiveness would have been only slightly improved. His face was simply ugly; hairy and scarred and attached—or so it appeared to Solina—to a body that preferred to experience adventure from the comfort of a tri-vid couch, not a prospector who allegedly loved risks and privations.

Solina's gaze lingered longer on the last of the Terrans. He was tall, about Solina's height, and slender. He hung back, as though he didn't quite belong to the prospectors, and followed the introductions with gray-blue eyes that seemed somehow familiar to Solina. Solina and her companions had already introduced themselves, which took some amount of time since custom required that they give their full names, amounting to family trees reaching many generations back, when the tall Terran stepped forward to speak.

He said simply, "I am Perry Rhodan."

Solina was grateful that Robol openly lost his composure before she did.

"You're ... who?" the logistics officer stammered.

"Perry Rhodan," the Terran repeated and smiled. "Is something wrong?"

Robol gasped for breath. Ignoring the fact that she found her own mouth gaping, Solina sneered at Robol's behavior, which was certainly unworthy of an Akonian.

"Robol is occasionally hard of hearing," Solina offered, stepping in before the logistics officer made all three of them look ridiculous. "But I have to admit that I'm a little surprised to find you here. Why didn't Commander Coho advise us of your presence?"

"Does my presence make a difference?"

Solina stared at him. "No," she finally shrugged. "Of course not. You're a man like any other."

Pearl Laneaux chose a direction, and they began moving. Solina voluntarily let Pearl take the lead and made an effort to stay close to Rhodan.

Did his presence make any difference? What a question. Everything was the same as it had been, except that the universe had been turned upside down. Yesterday she had been stagnating in her cabin on the *Las-Toôr* and counting the minutes until her return to the Blue system. Now she was walking with a fire-ready beamer and a group of Terrans through the largest Lemurian artifact ever discovered, and at her side was a living legend—Perry Rhodan! And the Immortal had asked her if it made any difference.

Yes, one difference. Never before had she felt so alive.

19

They made slow progress. With literally each meter they traveled, one member of the two teams exclaimed, "Stop!", having discovered something that required thorough investigation.

The pace was fine with Pearl Laneaux. She didn't feel comfortable holding a beamer with the safety off. She knew what to do with a weapon, and more than once in her life she'd had to make use of one, but she preferred to find other ways to reach her goals.

The Lemurians on board this ship—if they existed—were not their enemies, even if the man who had flown the shuttle away from this ship had preferred suicide over returning on board. She knew nothing about him and it was perfectly possible that the reason for his flight was purely private: a deadly feud between enemy families, or perhaps he was a criminal who had anticipated just punishment for what he did.

Literally anything was possible.

Their path led them from the room into which they had burned their way and out into a long, narrow corridor. It was almost completely dark; as they went along, a solitary light ahead of them would flicker to life, then go out after they'd passed it and the next one came on. It smelled strange. Pearl claimed to have a sensitive nose, but she could find no words to describe the odor.

Robol von Sarwar, an atypically brawny specimen of Akonian, had no difficulty articulating his perceptions. "It stinks in here," he said with a closed mouth, a trick that intrigued Pearl. Only later would she learn the explanation for it.

The Akonian, packed like a mule with his team's equipment, had nailed it exactly. It stank on board the Lemurian ship. And now that she had been given a word, Pearl could also say of what: decay. She glanced at her multi-function armband. The air's oxygen content was unusually low—not life-threatening, but still below the mix that had been declared physiologically optimal on board Terran ships.

Perry Rhodan fell into step next to her. "I feel like holding my nose, don't you?"

She nodded, wishing she possessed Alemaheyu Kossa's unshakable calm. Rhodan behaved unnervingly like a perfectly normal person—and even so, she found it impossible to respond in kind to his casually friendly tone.

"Yes," she managed to mutter. Suddenly, she better understood Sharita's resistance to Rhodan. It was unpleasant to be always uncertain how much one's opinion counted against that of an Immortal. "I wonder where it comes from."

"From the inhabited parts of the ship," Hevror ta Gosz answered.

Pearl gave the Akonian a confused look. She suddenly felt like she'd missed something in Xenology class. Her instructor had taught that Akonian society was subject to a complicated system of etiquette that choked off any spontaneity in conversation, and by Terran standards Akonians expressed enormous circumspection in conversation with each other. Joining in a conversation uninvited did not match Pearl's conception of "enormous circumspection." Was it a mark of respect that the Akonian spoke with her so familiarly? Or a sign of his contempt for Terrans, that he did not consider them worthy of even basic courtesy?

"I've given the ship's internal atmosphere a more precise analysis," the Akonian continued, apparently oblivious to Pearl's expression. His skin was weather-beaten and wrinkled, as though he had spent his entire life out in the open without skin cream or sun protection. His velvet-brown skin, typical for Akonians, was marred by numerous light spots. Pearl couldn't begin to estimate his age. Hevror ta Gosz might be fifty, one hundred, or one hundred-fifty years old. All she could tell for certain was that he was used to physical activity. He was lean and sinewy, and carried an unfamiliar piece of equipment—a long, slender bag made from something that resembled warty leather—without any visible effort.

"The composition of the air on board is surprisingly like that of an earthlike planet," the Akonian reported. Above his raised wrist appeared a series of holos that showed various graphs and tables. "I've established traces of more than four dozen different species of plants, along with a large quantity of skin flakes and hair, and have taken samples of both."

"Animal hair?" Rhodan asked.

Hevror ta Gosz shook his head in a gesture that seemed so astonishingly Terran that Pearl forgot for a moment with whom she was dealing. "Practically none. The inhabitants of this ship seem to have done without animals almost entirely. Not surprising, if you ask me. Protein can be raised much more simply with plants than with animals, and with considerably less expenditure of energy and labor."

Perry Rhodan smiled. "So much for the idea that we might meet Noah himself on this ark."

<u>Noah? Who the hell is Noah?</u> Pearl wanted to ask, but Perry Rhodan must have noticed the inquiring looks on his companions' faces.

"An old Terran legend," Rhodan explained. "Well, not as old as the Lemurians. Noah built a ship in order to survive a great catastrophe, what we call the Flood. No one would believe him when he said it was coming, and when it did come, only he and his family were aboard the ark along with a pair of every animal there was, in order to repopulate the world after the Flood. Apparently nobody thought of plants. Or they were so obvious that they didn't have to be mentioned."

"Interesting," Solina Tormas said, and the wide eyes with which she was looking at Rhodan showed that her remark was more than a gesture of politeness. "And was there a basis for this legend?"

Rhodan shrugged. "One, certainly, but no one knows which. The Flood is a catastrophe that appears in the traditions of many of the Earth's ancient cultures. There's some suspicion that they all refer to the same disaster. There are many scholars who believe that the memory of the sinking of Atlantis fifteen thousand years ago survives in the legend of Noah's Ark. In a way, a world was destroyed then."

"Do you believe it, too?"

"Well, I'm at least skeptical. To my knowledge, there was only one survivor of the sinking of Atlantis: my friend Atlan. And he didn't survive in an ark, but in much less romantic circumstances in an undersea dome."

During their conversation, they had made their way further down the corridor and reached an open hatchway. Solina paused for a moment to read the faded writing above it. "Sector XV or XXI, Emergency Chamber," the historian murmured. "I can't identify the number any more exactly. In any case it's Lemurian, at a very early stage in the development of the written language."

They went through the hatchway. The corridor on the other side narrowed. Along both walls, primitive spacesuits that looked essentially like bags waited for their users. The material they were made of was less resiliant than expected. It would be difficult to put on such a suit in the few moments that an emergency would allow. When she pressed her finger with her full strength into a suit, cracks appeared that exposed a shiny orange color underneath. The pale yellow of the surface was evidently the result of the aging process.

Pearl wondered what Alemaheyu thought of her discoveries, and in particular of Rhodan's story, but the comm officer, who was patched in as before to their conversations and their suit cameras, didn't comment.

They proceeded still further down the corridor. Pearl felt uncomfortable in the narrow passage. With each step she brushed against the spacesuits hanging on the walls. What would happen if they met the inhabitants of the ship now? The narrowness of the corridor would make an encounter unavoidable. A fast escape would be impossible even with the help of their antigrav units. They would offer an easy target for long seconds. If the encounter turned hostile, Pearl would be forced to open fire. The thought was not comforting.

But Pearl's gloomy fears failed to materialize. They walked onward without encountering any Lemurians.

Just when Pearl wanted to call for a stop to rest, a closed hatch blocked their path.

"What now?" she asked. The Akonians had not officially granted her leadership of the mixed team. Since she had led the way, she had assumed de facto leadership, but it wasn't something she wanted to put to the test. She raised her beamer and indicated the hatch. "Should we burn our way through again?"

"No, not that!" came an outraged cry from the rear. Then Solina Tormas squeezed her way past the other members of the expedition. "You can't be serious!" she exclaimed. "Do you really intend to vaporize this unique artifact?"

"Me?" Pearl needed a moment to regain her composure. "Who burned an entrance into the hull?" she responded indignantly. "I certainly didn't. You—"

But Solina Tormas was no longer listening to her. The Akonian efficiently shoved her aside to clear the space she needed and began running her hands over and around the hatch.

A few moments later, Pearl heard a triumphant, "Aha!"

She saw a small display set in the wall. It was dim and blurred, so she could only discern a few washed-out letters that she assumed were Lemurian.

Using a virtual keyboard, Solina slowly input commands. Pearl had the impression that the Akonian had to spell out the Lemurian words exactly in her head before pressing the keys. Pearl was forced to look at the historian with new respect; who would have expected she could hack computer systems?

But when minutes passed without the hatch budging, Pearl wondered if she was giving the Akonian too much credit. Her impatience finally got the better of her.

She cleared her throat. "If that hatch is too much for you ... " She raised her beamer, its safety off.

Solina rolled her eyes. "I figured out the hatch ages ago. I'm checking out the ship's computer."

"I'm glad you decided to inform us! And what have you found out?"

"A great deal. This is the most fascinating system I've ever laid hands on. As a historian, I stumble across old computer systems now and then, but it usually takes years to get them running again, and even then they're rarely intact. But this ... actually, to call it a ship's computer is a misnomer. It's more like a decentralized network of computers connected entirely by wires. Imagine that: by wires! That's why we didn't detect any communications signals from the ship."

"Wires? I can hardly think of anything that would take more time, effort and energy. But why use such a system? To prevent hyperdetection?"

"Possibly. But I suspect other reasons." As she spoke, the historian took a bag of tools from her backpack and spread it out in front of her. "First, robustness. Well-shielded cable connections aren't vulnerable to external interference, like stars active in radio frequencies." Solina reached for a tool that resembled a combination of a screwdriver and a crowbar, and removed the wall-display's cover, exposing a tangle of wires. "Ah, here we are. A second reason is power. In order to maintain uninterrupted wireless connections, you need relatively high transmission strength. I can only guess how they produce energy here on board, but from everything I've seen, it can't be advanced much beyond primitive nuclear fission. The inhabitants of the ship would need their energy more urgently for other things."

Solina pulled one of the wires out of the wall and attached a comm-plug. A holo formed in front of her and began showing alternating columns of numbers and structural diagrams. "I can hardly believe it! It's packet-based!"

"Packet-what?" Pearl asked.

"Based. The data is broken down by the transmitter into small packets that carry with them information as to where they belong in the larger packet and sent on their way. The path they take isn't determined beforehand. They seek it out on their own. At the destination, the packets reassemble themselves. Such a system will survive almost anything ... "

"Even atomic bombs," Rhodan said, completing her sentence.

"Yes, that's true." Solina seemed pleasantly surprised that the Immortal had found her explanation worthy of elaboration.

"I learned about such a network just before my flight to the Moon," Rhodan said. "It's been a few years. At the time, computers on Earth filled whole rooms. The Defense Department had a project to network them. It was called ARPANET, if I remember correctly."

The historian shook her head. "I've never heard that name."

"It stands for Advanced Research Projects Agency Network. I'll be glad to tell you more about it when we have an opportunity," Rhodan said. "But right now you should open this hatch for us. Remember: every minute we spend here corresponds to a hundred minutes on our home worlds. We don't want anyone to miss us, do we?"

"All right." The historian clearly would have preferred to spend the next few hours examining the computer network with Rhodan. "Just one more thing," she murmured, "and then you can have your open hatch." The holo showed a new menu. Pearl watched as Solina quickly worked through a series of symbols, finally chose one, and deactivated the holo.

"What was that you just did?" Pearl asked.

The Akonian waved dismissively. "Just a small security measure, so the network doesn't spoil our fun. And now here's your open hatch." She made a bow like a magician performing before an astonished audience.

The hatch slid squeaking to the side and revealed a view of a steep stairway. Warm sunlight played on the steps and blinded the first officer of the Palenque. She smelled flowers.

"Mama!" Pearl exclaimed into her suit's microphone. "See that? We're here! You won't believe what it smells like!"

Alemaheyu didn't reply.

20

As Dr. Hartich van Kuespert, the *Palenque*'s hyperphysicist and a willing volunteer for the Terran-Akonian "guest exchange," exited the crawler into one of the *Las-Toór*'s hangars, he met with a disappointment.

No one was waiting for him.

The hangar was deserted. No Akonian, not even a robot, had appeared to greet the Terran guest. Hartich tugged irresolutely at the collar of his old-fashioned pullover, from which he was never separated, and looked around. The Akonians knew very well that he had arrived! The *Las-Toór*'s hangar doors had opened for his crawler, the ship's comm officer had given him authorization to enter. What was the meaning of this little game?

Hartich had to admit to himself that he was baffled. Everyone knew how obsessed the Akonians were with rituals and official ceremonies, how much they loved to march in wearing colorful, shining uniforms and to declaim in their own brand of Intercosmo with its nasally arrogant tone that generations of Terran comedians had specialized in parodying.

Was he so unimportant to them that they would pass up this opportunity?

As though in answer to his question, a small personnel hatch opened in the wall at the rear of the hangar. An Akonian stepped through. He was tall and slender, in keeping with a member of his race, and wore his black hair short—at which the agreement with the image of a typical Akonian in Hartich's mind came to an end.

The Akonian wore overalls studded with pockets, similar to that commonly worn by a maintenance technician on a Terran starship. Objects protruded from some pockets. Not tools, as Hartich would have expected, but odds and ends: a pen, a handkerchief, a sheet of writing paper. Or was it a piece of packing material?

The man stopped in front of him and held out his hand in an astonishingly Terran-like gesture.

"Welcome on board the *Las-Toór*," he said. "I'm Jere."

Hartich stared at the hand offered to him for several seconds before he overcame his surprise and clasped it. The Akonian's hand was huge, with long, slender fingers that firmly gripped Hartich's own right hand.

"Uh ... thank you," the Terran replied. "I am Hartich van Kuespert. *Dr.* Hartich van Kuespert." The Akonian released his hand. "Jere ... *just* Jere?"

"No, no ... Jere von Baloy and a thousand other things, too many to waste time listing them all."

Jere von Baloy ... von Baloy ... Hartich had heard the name before. He wished he had listened to the communications with the Akonians, but he had been working with the chief technician of the *Palenque*, Kurt Brodbeck, and his colleague, Huang Lee, on the phenomenon of the Lemurian ship's hyperdetection shield. They had believed they were on the brink of a breakthrough and, their minds dedicated to the task, had blocked themselves almost completely from the outside world. The chatter around him seemed peripheral in that stage of investigating a problem, which always put him in a state of ecstasy. Only when they had failed to prove their theory of the hyperdetection shield did he find an interest in the Akonian ship awakening within him. And then with such intensity that he had been able to get a ticket to that ship for himself—a round-trip ticket, he firmly believed. The Akonians were too intelligent and cultivated to deny a highly regarded scientist like him the respect he deserved.

Perhaps he had been wrong about that last, Hartich admitted to himself. And who, blast it all, had been that Jere von Baloy? The communications officer? No, he didn't look like one. But then you could say that about Alemaheyu ... .

"We have prepared quarters for you, Dr. Hartich van Kuespert," the Akonian said. "If you like, I can take you there and show you the ship on the way. You must be very curious."

Am I ever! thought Hartich, the idea of a tour very nearly overcoming his disappointment at his minimal reception. "Well," he said, "I certainly wouldn't be opposed to a little tour."

"Excellent! Baggage?"

Hartich shook his head and raised the small bag in his left hand. "This is all."

Jere led him out of the hangar to an antigrav shaft and graciously let his guest take the lead. The two men floated up several decks and then left the lift in the sector of the ship apparently reserved for crew quarters. The *Las-Toór* proved to be a thoroughly clean ship, as spotless as though it had just left the construction yards. Hartich inquired as to the ship's age.

Jere laughed politely. "A flattering question. But no, the *Las-Toór* is not fresh from the factory. The Akonian government has realized in recent years that while military strength is certainly necessary in order to hold our own in the galaxy, scientific know-how must accompany it as well. The *Las-Toór* is the expression of that view made steel. It was completely refitted before our departure."

That's certainly a deep analysis for a simple technician! thought Hartich, but since they had reached his quarters just then, he couldn't pursue the thought any further.

The door slid to one side and revealed a series of sparsely but tastefully furnished rooms. Crystal mobiles glittered in the shine of hidden lamps and filled the rooms with a soft light.

"This ... this ... " Hartich was at a loss for words.

"Do you like it?" Jere asked with a satisfied smile that showed he already knew the answer.

"Yes, very much!" Hartich had barely managed to avoid being assigned to a crawler when he joined the *Palenque*. Instead, he had been allotted a cabin that was so tiny and stank so overpoweringly that he preferred to spend all his time in the laboratory.

"Are all the crew quarters on the *Las-Toór* so spacious?" he asked.

"Naturally, not. This is the cabin of the first officer, who insisted that it be made available to our Terran guest." Jere's smile had changed. Was it now … mischievous? Hartich found it difficult to read his facial expressions, even though the Akonians were just as human as the Terrans.

Hartich laid down his bag—right by the entrance, since he feared not being able to find it again elsewhere in the wide-ranging rooms—and Jere guided him through the ship. The engine rooms were of slightly less interest to Hartich, as his curiosity concerned the principles on which the engines were based, not on the machinery itself, but his ears pricked when Jere recited their performance data. The *Las-Toór* was considerably superior to the *Palenque* when it came to acceleration and ultra-light capabilities. After that, Jere showed him the life-support and secondary systems, and finally the scientific sections.

Here it became quite interesting. Hartich finally met other Akonians. Scientists, called Yidari in Akonian, and very much in keeping with his mental image of Akonians. Tall and slender with the velvet brown skin that made most Terrans look pale, and manners that in their perfection were worthy of a high culture tens of thousands of years old.

And tiresome. During their introductions, it was clear that none of the Akonians wanted to forego presenting their privileged family trees in the proper light. If Jere hadn't firmly intervened—and why did the Yidari permit this?—every single introduction would have taken half an hour or more. Jere was Hartich's salvation, especially when one of the Yidari decided to ask him about his own family tree. The "van" indicated a title of nobility, didn't it? Not for him. It was simply the result of parents who were enthusiastic about early Terran history and reflected their enthusiasm when naming their child—a freedom of choice unimaginable in the Blue system. It was certainly not the answer the Akonians wanted to hear, and a white lie would have quickly collapsed under the detailed follow-up questioning.

When they left the scientific sections, which he could see were equipped with the best money could buy, Hartich wished for nothing more than to return to his palace of a cabin, take a deep breath and put up his feet.

Jere had other plans.

"All right, now let's go to the control center!" he announced.

"The control center?" Hartich couldn't hide his surprise. Sharita would be damned if she would allow a guest on her bridge; even Perry Rhodan had been permitted entry only after a loud hypercom discussion with the owners of the *Palenque*. And the Akonian would lead him into the ship's holiest of holies just like that? Jere didn't even look as though *he* would be allowed in.

"Yes, of course. No tour would be complete without it."

Curious glances met Hartich as the door to the domed control center slid open. The Akonian officers sat at their consoles on three levels—no, on two, Hartich corrected himself. The uppermost level, which must be reserved for the commander, was unoccupied.

As they entered the control center, the officers bowed. A man stepped up to them, ignoring the Terran, and reported, "We've received a query from Fleet Command, Maphan. They want to know why we've been in dilation flight for so long. They've determined from our standard tracking signals that we're moving at relativistic velocity."

"I expected that, Netkim," Jere said. "Answer them by saying that dilation flight is necessary for the moment in connection with hyperphysical experiments. As commander, I am not happy about it, but my task at present is to satisfy the ladies and gentlemen of the Yidari. And we all know what an incorrigible lot they are, don't we?"

The officer saluted. Jere—Jere von Baloy, commander of the *Las-Toór*—turned one last time to Hartich. "Do you see over there on the second level, that short officer with the reddish brown hair who is staring rather intently at his console?"

"Y-yes," Hartich stuttered, mortified by the faux pas he had committed. He had mistaken the commander for a technician! The status-obsessed Akonians would never forgive him for that!

"That is Echkal cer Lethir, my first officer, and the man who insisted on letting you have his quarters. You should thank him." He winked at Hartich as though they were old friends. "Echkal is often somewhat shy in social situations. Don't let it bother you if he seems a little out of sorts. Just go on talking. At the bottom of his heart, he likes Terrans."

With those words, Jere von Baloy left his guest and resumed his station as the commander of the *Las-Toór.*

***

"Be careful that you don't catch any infectious diseases!" her colleagues had joked when Eniva ta Drorar climbed aboard the Shift that would take her to the Terran ship, and Eniva had laughed heartily together with the other Yidari.

That had been less than an hour ago, and already her time on the *Las-Toór* seemed to Eniva like an eternity in the past. She no longer felt in the least like laughing. The Terrans' ship was thick with dirt. If Eniva had even suspected what awaited her, she would have boarded the *Palenque* in a special spacesuit designed for extreme planetary environments, not in a simple leisure outfit chosen to complement the allegedly so-casual Terrans. Well, she had brought along a few suitcases with more appropriate clothing ... .

The commander had met her right in the hangar. Sharita Coho wore a starkly tailored black uniform that no Akonian would ever have worn, even in the old days when the Energy Command constituted the secret government, and escorted her to her cabin.

Her "cabin."

Even murderers and those making fraudulent claims to noble titles were confined in better quarters on Drorah. The cabin was a rectangular space just big enough to contain a narrow bed. To the side of the bed, a passageway led to a hygiene cubicle. The door separating them didn't close properly, so there was a moldy smell in the air. Or perhaps there was another source of the stench: when Eniva had arranged her suitcases along the wall, she had discovered a dirty pair of men's underwear.

Eniva had been too surprised to protest, and by the time she recovered, the Terran commander had already disappeared—though not without reminding her that as a "guest" on the *Palenque* she only had limited freedom, and she was best advised to remain in her cabin and keep quiet.

Eniva understood what was meant by "best advised" as soon as she attempted to leave the cabin. A massive cleaning robot blocked the way. It was coincidentally occupied with cleaning her door, which in its opinion urgently needed a thorough scrubbing, since the scraping of its brushes simply wouldn't stop.

I'll just try something else! Eniva decided, and occupied herself with the cabin's computer terminal. The Terrans had no idea who they had caught. Eniva was the *Las-Toôr*'s computer network expert and as such she was used to stretching out her feelers in a syntronic way. The *Palenque*'s computer network had been the reason she had volunteered to be a hostage. When else would she ever have the opportunity to give a Terran network a thorough going over?

Eniva sat upright on the too-soft bed, took a deep breath—through her mouth, in order to avoid the mold smell—and went to work. Five minutes. She didn't give the Terran computer more than that before it surrendered to her.

Five minutes became fifteen, then half an hour. Eniva cursed to herself, at first in a low voice, then loudly, but it didn't help. Either the Terrans had guessed who they were dealing with after all or they were cautious sorts. In any case, the cabin syntron had been cut off from the ship's systems, not just on the software side—Eniva could have hacked a block like that—but physically.

The cabin syntron was a self-contained system, and not a very intelligent one.

It was essentially an improved tri-vid that offered her only two choices: unimportant tourist information about various LFT worlds or tri-vid films. In her desperation—Eniva had the feeling that she would die of boredom even before the mold fungus had poisoned her lungs if she didn't occupy herself with *something*—she surfed through the films. Without exception, they turned out to be cheap trash. Tales of secret agents in which heroic Terrans foiled the sinister plans of Akonians who were out to subvert Terran supremacy, or comedies in which Akonians were caricatured as horribly nasal Intercosmo-speaking fops who were just as vain as they were stupid.

Is this what they really think of us? Eniva thought angrily. *Why did I vote against blasting them out of space? We could have easily pulverized this garbage can, and I could now be investigating the Lemurian ship instead of rotting away here!*

Eniva turned off the syntron. Tears of rage and disappointment welled in her eyes. How could she have been so naive as to come here expecting to learn something? She would *die* here! The Terran commander had imprisoned her. If only something would happen that she—

A buzzer sounded.

Eniva jerked up, not certain if she had only imagined the noise. Now she noticed that the scraping of the brushes on the door had stopped.

The buzzer sounded again.

Eniva stood up, adjusted her clothes as well as the limp material would allow, rubbed the tears from the corners of her eyes and activated the door opening.

The door slid to the side. In front of her stood a Terran who was uglier than anything she could have imagined in her worst fantasies.

It was a man—or maybe a troll. The Terran was only as tall as her chest and was so thin that it was a miracle he hadn't snapped in half long ago. His skin was blacker than space, and his curly hair had grown out to a mane that made his head seem oversized. Two big, bright eyes looked at Eniva.

"Hello," the troll said. "I'm Alemaheyu Kossa, the communications officer for this outfit. Sharita sent me." He bared two rows of shining white teeth as he smiled.

"Sharita … the commander?"

"The one and only," the little man confirmed, smiling all the more brightly.

"But why would she send you? She stuck me here with complete satisfaction."

"Oh, she played her little game with you, did she?" The troll shook his mane reproachfully, as though they were talking about a misbehaving child. "Don't let it bother you. She does that to everyone. But afterwards she feels sorry about it. That's why she sent me. I'm supposed to look after you."

Again the troll smiled.

"And why you in particular?"

"Oh, because I don't have anything to do at the moment. Communication with the exploration team has been broken off, and—"

"Broken off?" Eniva interrupted him, horrified. "What happened?"

"It's nothing to get excited about. I expected this would happen. Probably has to do with that Lemurian ship's hyperdetection shield. We haven't detected any energy emissions, and we certainly would have if there had been a fight or an accident." The troll pulled at the headband that kept his hair from falling over his eyes and blocking his vision. "So I'm at loose ends right now, and besides, I'm the most charming host you could find on the *Palenque*."

"You're *what?*"

"Still skeptical?" the troll asked and smiled again. "Come with me, you lucky stiff. You'll see!"

Hesitantly, Eniva ta Drorar followed the Terran, suddenly wishing for nothing so fervently as to remain in her stinking cabin and watch wretched Terran movies.

21

The light caressed her face, beckoning her.

Solina Tormas ignored Pearl Laneaux's cry of warning and climbed up the steep stairway toward the light. Her beamer hung in its holster, where she had stuck it to leave both hands free for her work on the Lemurian ship's computer network terminal.

The stairs ended in a shelter whose roof had fallen away and blocked the view to one side. Solina blinked in the light. She couldn't make out a single source, no equivalent of a sun. The light shone evenly from the "sky" above her, a gentle reddish tone that was very different from the cold blue light she knew from Shaghomin or Drorah.

And anyway, that "sky" ... Solina knew she was inside a gigantic cylinder, and stood on the inner surface of its hull. When she lifted her head, she really had to be seeing the opposite side. Instead, her searching gaze was lost in an intangible haze of the reddish light.

"I think the builders put in several decks," Rhodan said. There was no reproach in his voice for her incautious plunge ahead. No criticism; the light of the ark seemed to soften even the immortal Terran's mood. Solina wondered why the Terrans seemed so nervous. Did they know something dangerous about the ark that they had kept to themselves? Solina couldn't imagine anything that would pose a danger. The ark's inhabitants lived at a low technology level; their spacesuits' defense screens would protect the visitors from any potential attack.

"Possibly," Solina replied. "But perhaps we're simply looking at the center of the ark. I can't make out any details."

"Nor can I. But there are at least three reasons that argue for several decks. First, if there weren't any, it would be an inexcusable waste of space, an enormous unused volume. I can't believe people who could construct such a ship would allow that inefficiency."

"Sounds logical. And the other reasons?"

"Another would be gravity. On this deck, the gravity is one and a half times that of Earth's. If they're trying to preserve the heritage of their home world, that isn't a very good solution. The ship's inhabitants would be forced to develop a new culture within a few generations in reaction to the changed environmental conditions." Rhodan looked down from the "sky" and at his multi-function armband. "And third is the radiation level. It wouldn't be dangerous to stay here, even for weeks. But over a span of years and decades, the effect of cosmic rays would be enormous, leading to an increased rate of genetic damage. If the ark's inhabitants lived continuously on this deck, they would be facing extinction before many generations."

Solina had been listening to Rhodan's explanation with only half an ear. What he said sounded valid, but the next hour or two would show whether it was actually correct. People, whether they called themselves Akonians, Terrans, or even Lemurians, were not logical beings. Quite the opposite: the more Solina delved into history, the more her conviction grew that human societies based on logic were the exceptions. A certain amount of logic was to be found in all human societies that endured for any length of time, but only a certain amount. Often the seed of destruction lay in the premises on which a society was based. When those premises were erroneous, that society headed inevitably toward its downfall.

What judgment could be made of the ark's society, they would find out as soon as they came across the first Lemurians. The ship was huge, but still too small for any such encounter to be long in coming. And Solina wanted to use the time until that happened to investigate the ship in a way that no encounter with the inhabitants, no instruments, however refined, could substitute for: she wanted to feel out the ship herself.

Solina lowered her eyes from the sky and looked to either side. To her right and left, the ground rose evenly, as though she were in a valley. In a manner of speaking, she was: the ark's outer hull presented an evenly curved surface. No matter where she was on the ark, she would always find herself at the bottom of a valley. Like the bow and the stern, the evenly rising "cliffs" were lost in a haze.

Was the haze an accident, an unintended side effect of the ark's ecosystem? Or had the builders planned it in order to give the inhabitants the feeling of distance they would have otherwise done without?

The rest of the team had reached the surface of the deck. The hatch had closed behind them, but there was no cause for concern; it was an automatic security function. Pearl Laneaux and Hayden Norwell had drawn their beamers in order to protect the group. Pearl's face had turned red as she whispered constantly into her spacesuit's microphone. She didn't want to accept what had become obvious in the lower corridor: comm contact with the *Palenque* had broken off. Solina had a certain amount of sympathy for her anxiety; it could be disturbing to be on one's own in unfamiliar surroundings. But it did not escape her professional ear, which didn't miss a word spoken around her, that the Terran was, in all seriousness, addressing the person with whom she was trying to communicate as "Mama."

Rhodan had closed his eyes and was breathing deeply. He seemed to be following an exploration strategy similar to her own. Hevror ta Gosz had gone several steps further and was kneeling in the grass surrounding the collapsed shelter. His long bag stood out on his back like the quiver of an ancient bowman.

Solina walked over to see what he was doing.

Hevror had dug a hole in the ground with a collapsible spade. Next to the hole lay the clump of grass he had pulled out. Solina fingered the stalks; they were markedly softer than the grass on Shaghomin, and felt like a comfortable carpet. Then she felt the roots—or rather she tried: the roots recoiled from her touch as though they were independently alive.

She cried out in surprise.

Hevror grinned crookedly as he pulled out of the soil one of the measuring instruments that he always wore on his belt. "In case you're doubting your senses, the roots really did twitch."

"You can't be serious! These are plants."

Hevror nodded. "It's true. But plants can move independently. Consider flowers that open and close."

"Yes, but that process happens in relatively slow motion, and this ... "

" ... is the same process, just a bit faster." Hevror took a soil sample from the tip of his probe and placed it in an analyzing instrument.

"How do you explain it? Spontaneous mutation as a result of centuries of exposure to cosmic rays?"

Hevror glanced up. "No, it's a deliberate genetic alteration. This soil ... " He reached into the dislodged dirt. The dark, damp soil crumbled into small pieces as he rubbed it with his fingers. "This soil feels like soil from an Akonian world, but it lacks something very critical."

Solina reached into the dirt. It was warm and damp and reminded her of the garden at her family's big round house on Shaghomin. What was so special about it, other than the fact that she had found it in a steel tube that had been racing through space at near light-speed for more than fifty thousand years?

"I'll tell you," Hevror went on, reading the puzzlement on her face. "There aren't any animals. The tiny insects and worms that normally live in soil and loosen it by their movements. In their absence, the grass has been altered to perform the same function with its movable roots. I don't think that's by chance."

"How long are you going to dig around in the dirt?" Pearl demanded. She waved her beamer vaguely forward. "Let's get going."

Solina chose to agree with the Terran's wishes and signaled Hevror to gather up his equipment. Pearl Laneaux seemed convinced she was in command of the group, and Solina preferred to let her believe it. It kept the Terran woman occupied and reduced the risk of her acting on any really stupid ideas.

They walked on. The two teams had agreed to not use their suits' flight systems for the moment. Despite its impressive size, the ark was a small world; it would not be long before they met its inhabitants. How that encounter would play out, no one could predict. So it was best to keep a card up their sleeves. The ark's inhabitants didn't have artificial gravity; they would not anticipate their visitors having antigrav capability.

As expected, Pearl took the lead. Solina walked next to Rhodan and devoted her attention to their surroundings.

Walking through the ark gave her a strange feeling. Part of it had a simple explanation: They were moving through an unknown environment, and didn't know what they would meet. The rest Solina grasped only after a few moments of hard thought: the Lemurian ship simply didn't feel like a ship. The narrow path that they were taking between fields wasn't paved. In some places it was soft; in others, hard stones pressed unpleasantly through the soles of their boots. The air carried a spicy scent that occasionally gave way to a distinct stench. The haze that blocked their view of the distance suggested an endless vista that didn't exist, and gave them the deceptive feeling of being able to walk forever without reaching the end of the ark or meeting another human being.

At the same time, the results of human labor were unmistakable. The outer deck was an intensively farmed area. One field followed another. Irrigation channels separated the fields, so narrow that a person could jump over them even in the increased gravity. The scale of the landscape was small; it was divided into manageable units that could be tended without the help of machines, reminding Solina more of a garden than of serious agriculture. And that was another thing lacking: robots. On the galaxy's civilized worlds, robots had long performed physical labor. Farmers limited themselves to supervising the machinery and to making work processes more efficient in order to survive in the fiercely competitive galaxy-wide agricultural market.

No machines were in evidence here, only their tracks. On the path and between the fields Solina saw wheel ruts, some as wide as a person's thigh, others surprisingly narrow, perhaps two or three centimeters wide.

"No antigrav," Rhodan commented when he noticed Solina was examining the wheel tracks. "The ark's inhabitants don't seem to be able to neutralize gravity at all, or else they wouldn't waste precious farmland on access paths."

"That goes without saying," Solina agreed. "Either they haven't mastered the principle at all, or they lack the required energy."

Solina turned her attention to the plants. As was to be expected under the influence of the high gravity, they had thick stems and grew very close to the ground. Solina couldn't see any trees; the largest plants seemed to be bushes with heart-shaped leaves, which grew to about the height of a man.

The ark's flora and fauna was actually Hevror's department, and the planetary ecologies specialist was avidly at work collecting plant samples and shoving them into the analysis chambers on his instrument belt. Already Hevror would be able to provide the outline of a descriptive model of the ark's ecosystem and a table of the relationships and non-relationships of the various plant species on board, but Solina wasn't interested in that. Her attention was on the plants' cultural history.

After they had discovered faster-than-light space travel, the Lemurians had spread almost explosively across the galaxy. It was estimated that at the high point of the Great Tamanium, about fifty thousand years BC in the old Terran time reckoning, the Lemurian realm had comprised more than one hundred thousand settled worlds. But estimates were all there were. The records were incomplete, partly because in the end stages of the war the Lemurians had begun to destroy them deliberately. With defeat staring them in the face, they had attempted to hide their colonies from the Beasts.

Despite that precaution, thousands of worlds were discovered and their populations wiped out. Many colonies had joined the exodus to Andromeda, and many more—far more than had been estimated—had escaped annihilation by the Beasts, but died out nonetheless. Without the support of the Great Tamanium and its seemingly inexhaustible resources, the colonies had disappeared almost without a trace.

However, it was extremely difficult for a race to leave no evidence of its presence. A planet's ecology always retained some trace, as some animals and plants imported intentionally or unintentionally always managed to adapt to the new environment and survive.

For historians, this was a lucky break. By examining the plant and animal species, it was possible to determine that many planets considered to be virginal were in fact forgotten Lemurian colonies. And more than that; by studying the changes in the plants and animals, it was even possible to map out a picture of the Lemurians' great wave of colonization with ever-increasing exactness.

Solina was not an expert in Lemurian species genealogy, but from what she'd seen so far there weren't any species on board that had originated or been developed on a colony world; another indication that the ark must have set out before the founding of the Tamanium.

"What's that up ahead?"

Pearl had stopped. Solina looked over her shoulder at a thick, dark shape that loomed out of the haze in front of them. It stood at a slight angle and reached into the deck's sky.

"Perhaps an elevator, or some other connection to the inner deck?" Rhodan guessed. "We should take a closer look at it. Our chances of meeting natives there are considerably greater than out here in the fields."

No one objected to this plan. The group set off again, more quickly this time, spurred on by the prospect of encountering the ark's inhabitants. *How much easier it would be then to get the answers to the thousand questions crowding her mind!* Solina thought. *They would—*

A cry tore her out of her thoughts. It came from the right, out in the fields. Solina whipped her head around to find the source of the noise, but only saw bushes the height of a man waving wildly back and forth. Only when she looked more closely did she see movement between the bushes. An arm was visible for a moment, then a leg. Solina heard more shouts, then she briefly looked into the face of an ark inhabitant. The eyes of the man—he wore short pants and a kind of T-shirt, and was barefoot—widened as their gazes met. He cried out once more, then he and his companions vanished.

"What's wrong with them?" Pearl asked, bewildered. "Why did they run away?"

"Out of fear," Rhodan replied.

"But why? They have to see that we're human beings just like them."

"I doubt it. I doubt they've ever seen a Terran in a spacesuit carrying a hand weapon before. Even if they recognized us as human beings, that does not suggest that we mean them no harm. Human beings can be extremely cruel to each other."

The Akonians and Terrans stood there a little embarrassed. Each of them had imagined the first meeting with the Lemurians, but no one had imagined it quite this way.

"Let's take a look at what our timid friends were doing when we disturbed them," Rhodan said. Solina had the impression the Immortal suggested it mainly to keep them from getting hung up on the Lemurians' reaction to their presence. "I saw something flash when they ran away. Perhaps one of them left something behind that we'll find informative."

His guess turned out to be accurate. Between the bushes they found a metal framework mounted on two wheels. Over one wheel was a bar at a right angle to the rest of the frame, and over the other a long plastic bowl.

"What in the name of the star gods is that?" asked Robol.

"Oh, that's easy," Rhodan said. "It's a bicycle. I had one as a boy." The Terran pulled it upright by its forward bar.

"And what do you do with a bicycle?" In Intercosmo, the term translated literally to "riding wheel."

"Ride on it, of course." Rhodan couldn't suppress a smile.

"But how?" Robol persisted. "Does it have an antigrav field or something like that to keep it upright? And I don't see any means of propulsion!"

"It doesn't have any. You provide it yourself!" Rhodan slapped his thigh. "It's so obvious! Bicycles are the ideal transport for the ark. Distances are short and there aren't any slopes. And a bike needs only minimal maintenance, doesn't use precious energy and doesn't give off any emissions."

"That sounds too good to be true," Hayden said, agreeing with Robol. The two seemed to have reached an understanding, made visible by the fact that they were standing next to each other. "I'll believe it when I see it."

"That's easy enough … "

With a practiced movement, Rhodan slid onto the bicycle and pushed off. His thighs moved up and down as he swiftly rode away. Solina waited for him to fall over, but though he wobbled considerably, the Terran kept his balance.

Then Rhodan went around a curve and was lost from their view. Almost at the same moment, Solina heard a loud scraping followed by a louder exclamation.

"What is it, Rhodan? Are you all right?"

"Yes, I'm fine," came the reply. "But you've got to see this! You won't believe it!"

22

The Kalpen were jubilant at the news. They leapt out of their beds, from which they ordinarily rose slowly and with obvious reluctance to begin their daily work; they ran to each other and fell into each other's arms.

"The time has come! The time has finally come!" they exclaimed, faster and louder, until their shouts became a chorus, so loud that it could be heard for many metach'tons around.

Tekker, of course, was in the middle of it all, inventing new cheers in his high falsetto voice that were taken up in turn by the other Kalpen.

Denetree would have preferred to pull her thin blanket over her head, squeeze her eyelids shut, and hold both hands over her ears. But it wouldn't have helped: the stamping dance steps of the Kalpen made the ground tremble, and would not let her forget what had happened.

She was saved.

The others would die.

The two sentences echoed through her thoughts, chased by the sing-song chanting of the Kalpen. The Net had broadcast its news over all terminals this morning The portable terminal that the Kalpen carried like an unloved, useless piece of baggage from one campsite to another, and whose announcements they distrusted on principle, this morning brought joy to their lives.

The announcement had come directly from the Net. In the name of the Naahk, of course, whose obedient tool it claimed to be. In its melodious, neutral voice, it had thanked the Tenarch Launt who had distinguished himself through his unmatched dedication in the hunt for the traitors.

Launt ... Denetree hadn't wanted to believe it. Something terrible must have happened. Launt would have rather died than persecute the Star Seekers. Hadn't he rescued her at the risk of his own life?

The Net didn't dwell on Launt. Mentioning him by name was merely a means to increase the tension by putting off the actual news, which was unbelievable and at the same time inevitable. The Tenoy, the Net had proclaimed, had smoked out the traitors, had dragged them from their shabby hiding places in which they had falsely believed they could conceal themselves from the Ship—an error in judgment barely less traitorous than believing that there could be another life for the metach outside the Ship. Beyond the Ship, there was only death. Only the Ship could guarantee the survival of the metach.

Now that all the traitors had been captured, there was no reason to waste any more precious air and food on them. This evening, at nightfall, the Net had continued, the Star Seekers would be gathered at the Ship's stern and given over to the stars they had sought. They would die the same death that their leader had inflicted on the brave Tenoy who had tried to turn him away from his act of madness. Only when the traitors were dead would peace be restored on board and the community of all metach renewed.

Peace restored on board ... The hunt had ended. Denetree looked at the dancing Kalpen. They waved their arms and legs wildly, holding their breath until their faces turned red and their eyes bulged from their sockets. "Help! Help! I can't breathe any more! Pull me in! Pull me back in the Ship!" Tekker cackled. He wasn't the loudest, but his falsetto voice rang out the clearest.

Denetree was safe. The Ship wouldn't search for her any longer, probably assuming that she had voluntarily followed her brother into death and her corpse floated alongside the ship, headed toward eternity. Launt, who had been put forward by the Ship as the one responsible for the traitors' capture and execution—surely only as a cover for the Net and not by his choice—would not betray her. She just had to keep quiet, go with the Kalpen through the Ship and patch the life-support systems, answer the rude remarks of the Kalpen with equally rude replies, put up with Tekker's "girl," and make sure that she always responded when someone called, "Danque, come here!" or "Danque, bring me some rope!"

She had to become Danque. Forget Denetree, bury her so deep that she never came out again. Some of the men—most of them, actually—had already given her to understand that they were interested in her. She only had to choose one—which one didn't matter, since they were all equally dirty, equally awkward and at the same time foolishly affectionate—and she would have peace. Until the end of her days.

"Come on, Danque! Dance with me!" One of the men had whirled to a stop in front of her, grabbed her with his sinewy Kalpen arms, and was about to pull her to her feet. "What's with that look on your face? Today is a day of joy!"

"No, Mehiu, I don't feel well." She became as much like a dead weight as possible.

"Come on, dance with me!" The Kalpen pulled at her, as though he hadn't heard her refusal. Perhaps he really hadn't. Denetree had learned that the Kalpen had exceptionally sensitive hearing. They heard everything they wanted to, but nothing of what they didn't like.

"Mehiu, please … " It was no use. The Kalpen pulled Denetree upright—and a moment later Denetree fell back on her blanket.

"You heard what she said, Mehiu," came Tekker's high voice. "She doesn't feel good."

"But … "

"She's new in our group. Don't you get it? She's tired because the work in the air shafts makes her weak. She isn't used to the air currents. Wait a few weeks and then she'll dance with you."

Mehiu sank his head in shame and rejoined the dancers. No one contradicted Tekker.

He turned to Denetree. "And see to it that you get better soon, understand?"

Denetree nodded.

The dance of the Kalpen finally came to an end. As with every other day, the work had to be done. The Ship expected all metach, even the Kalpen who considered themselves to be independent, to do their duty. If they didn't, it would cut off their rations.

Denetree went to work on this day, like all the others, with a growling stomach. The dance had cost the Kalpen valuable time that they had to make up. Tekken assigned them their tasks and spurred them on with cackling cries. He gave Denetree something to do at the edge of their working area, far from the others. So far that their calls and the hammering of their tools, along with the thumps of their elbows and knees against the narrow shafts, blended with the normal background sounds of the Ship and gave Denetree the illusion of being alone.

Did Tekker somehow guess at the turmoil inside her? Every moment since she had assumed her new identity, Denetree had been nearly paralyzed by the fear of being discovered and losing it all. All *what*? a low voice within her asked, while the tears ran down her cheeks and dripped onto the worn-out shaft that she was supposed to be repairing. She didn't care. Let the Kalpen or even the Ship punish her for her carelessness. She could survive a few days without eating!

The hours passed. Denetree's tears dried up, and the constant airflow through the shafts evaporated the teardrops that had fallen. The growling in her stomach increased to an ache. There was food at the supply tent that the Kalpen set up each morning, but in order to eat she would have to mingle with the others and listen to their coarse talk. No, it was better to endure the hunger.

After a while, Denetree found herself reaching for her tool, taking it out, and beginning to patch the leaks she had been assigned. Already during the two weeks that she had been with the Kalpen, she had developed a certain routine. It wasn't especially difficult to patch a leak once you got the hang of it. There were different sizes of leaks, but in the end they were all alike. The pipes and shafts consisted of the same metals and Denetree only had one set of tools and materials. Once you had patched one leak, you had patched them all.

Her hands cut screens and put them in place; she sprayed them with sealant, checked her work and felt for the next leak, constantly increasing her speed. Denetree sweated, her breath and her pulse came faster. All she saw were the shaft, the leaks and her job. What did she care about the stars, the Seekers, or her dead brother? They weren't important. The Kalpen weren't important—yes, the entire Ship and its mission weren't important. What mattered was that she found all the leaks. That evening she would fall into her cot exhausted and satisfied, fall asleep on the spot and after a dreamless night look for new leaks, and go to sleep again, and again … .

In the strange enthusiasm for work that had overcome her, it took a long time for the change to penetrate Denetree's consciousness. She finally noticed it after her rapid breathing had calmed somewhat. She was reaching for a new screen and suddenly recognized a unique level of noise outside. It was louder than she'd ever heard it.

The airshafts crisscrossed all the decks on the Ship. If someone had drawn a diagram of them, it would have resembled one of the screens they used to patch leaks, a fine-meshed network of twisting pipes. This network let the Ship's air circulate, along with sound. But Denetree was only beginning to be able to clearly pick out individual sounds from the background noises of metach in the fields, the many thousands of conversations going on at any given moment on the Ship, or the operating sounds of the Ship's systems. The Kalpen, who spent their lives in the shafts, quickly developed the ability to split the cacophony into its individual components. They often sat in front of their forbidden fires in the evening and spoke of what they had overheard during the day. The Kalpen knew everything, knew even that side of a story that the Ship withheld from the metach. Except … there was no other side for the Star Seekers.

Denetree knew how to gauge the overall mood from what she heard. It was generally muted, a reflection of the stoic mental attitude expected of every good metach. Several times during her time with the Kalpen, Denetree thought she had detected traces of fear, when terror of the traitors and what doom they might bring to the Ship won the upper hand. Sometimes the mood was triumphant—when another traitor was apprehended.

Now she sensed something new: panic. The Ship trembled beneath the hurried steps of metach who left behind everything and ran away, their loud cries echoing and infecting other metach with their fright.

Denetree listened helplessly to what was going on. What had happened?

The vibration and the cries faded out, lost in the distance. And then Denetree heard a new sound, one that frightened her: the scraping of the Kalpen sliding through the narrow shafts.

The Kalpen were fleeing!

Had the Ship been right? Were they being attacked? Had Venron brought disaster down on them?

Denetree heard thumps coming closer, underscored by a hectic scraping. Someone was coming toward her! She took the heaviest of her tools and clutched it, ready to defend her miserable existence. A pale light emerged from the darkness, then a wrinkled face became visible in the beam of a forehead lamp. She saw it was Tekker.

"Tekker!" she called out to him. "What's going on? Why is everyone running away?"

"I'll tell you in a moment," he replied. "You don't have time now. Come with me."

Tekker turned around smoothly in the cramped shaft and crawled away. Denetree crawled after him as fast as she could, leaving her tool behind. She had a feeling that she wouldn't need it again.

After a few meters, Tekker turned to the right, into a larger shaft, then made another right turn, so that they had made a complete 180-degree arc.

"Tekker!" Denetree gasped. "This isn't the direction they're all going!"

Without a word, the Kalpen crawled onward.

Finally they reached one of the large main shafts that cut through the Ship's decks like an underground highway system. Denetree's bicycle was leaning against the wall.

"My bicycle! How did it get here?"

"I brought it."

"But why?"

"Because you'll need it. You've got to be fast, girl."

Denetree ran to the bicycle and snapped down the front carrier frame. "Jump on, Tekker!" she exclaimed. "We can get out of here faster than the air blows through the shafts!" She motioned for the Kalpen to get on the carrier.

Tekker shook his head. "No, I'm not going with you."

"But why not? Something terrible is happening. Everyone is fleeing, even the Kalpen! You can't expect me to leave you behind. You saved my life!"

"Let them run." Tekker didn't move. "They don't know any better. The metach are dumb. All they know is their own Metach'ton and the scary stories the Ship tells them. They chew on those stories until they believe that's all there is. Anything that's strange scares them so much they lose their heads."

Denetree leaned against the handlebars. "And the Kalpen? They're running away, too!"

"The Kalpens' mouths are bigger than their brains." Tekker cackled. "Believe me, I ought to know. They think they're different, but in the end they're just plain metach. But you, girl, you're different, and your path leads somewhere else." He stepped close to Denetree and seized her wrist. The pressure of his fingers was painful. "Listen to me, girl. Strangers are on board! I don't know who they are or what they want, not even what they look like. I just know you've got to go to them. Right now. They're your one chance. You don't belong to us."

"But ... but you said yourself that I belonged to you, at the campfire!"

"It was a lie. I lied to you. To you and myself. You want to get out of here, girl. I can sense it. You've got to get out of here or you'll die. Go to the strangers! Go!" Tekker released her wrist and slapped her so hard on the back that she stumbled forward. She lost her balance. The handlebars drove into her hips. She suppressed a cry of pain, fought her way back upright, and turned to the Kalpen.

"What are you waiting for, girl? Do I have to beat you black and blue before you obey?"

"You ... you said this is my chance," Denetree stammered. "But it's yours, too. If the strangers won't do anything to me, they won't do anything to you, either! Come with me, Tekker!"

The Kalpen stepped toward her without speaking. Denetree ducked in anticipation of the blows. Tekker didn't hesitate to use force to get his way. She had witnessed it more than once.

But Tekker didn't strike her. "Look at me, girl," he said. "Look at me real good. Look at the wrinkles that forty years in the shafts have dug into my face. For forty years I've crawled through the Ship's guts. Do you think that's what I dreamed of doing all my life? What I was looking for? I took this life because it was the best that I could get, one that I could stand—and now it's the only one that's possible for me. Without the Kalpen and the shafts I'm just an ugly old man with a shrill laugh who nobody would want to have anything to do with. But you're still young. Find yourself a better life!"

Tekker grabbed her by the shoulders and pushed her with all his strength. This time, Denetree was prepared and caught herself. He feet found the pedals and her legs began to pump. Tekker remained behind.

"Now pedal as fast as you can!" was the last thing she heard him say. "Pedal, *Denetree!*"

23

The welcome daily routine had been restored. Lemal Netwar, who had no reason to doubt that peace on board would soon be reestablished—the elimination of the traitors was imminent—enjoyed occupying himself once more with trivial daily business.

On the display in front of him was collected all the Ship's vital statistics: energy production and consumption, birth and death rates, agricultural and manufacturing figures.

Over the years, he had become increasingly convinced that while the Ship may have been built of steel and plastic, it now functioned more like a living organism. Like a person getting on in years, it showed signs of aging and had good and bad days for which Lemal was unable to determine the causes.

And like a person, it often took only a slight nudge for a complete turnaround in its physical constitution. A rearranged distribution of energy to the various sectors, a targeted spurt of energy or oxygen here or there could work wonders. Over the years, Lemal had developed a sense of what was required, and increasingly he spent his mornings giving the Ship what it needed, what he called "stroking" it. The Naahk's electronic feelers were free from the disease that otherwise made every movement a torment.

Nothing was more satisfying than the interplay of the various numbers on his display. If he changed one variable, it affected all the others. And often, on good days, he even managed to elicit performance levels from the Ship that were close to the maximums envisioned by its builders.

This day was an average one for the Ship, which was welcome to the Naahk. It tickled his ambition, and it would divert his thoughts, which kept returning to the traitors who were even now living their last hours. He resolved to achieve a good day for the Ship.

He checked over the individual performance data. Energy production was exceptionally good. The number of be'ketren had plummeted by a dangerous percentage in recent years, but the remaining engineers performed their duties with nearly superhuman self-sacrifice. Today they were producing so much energy that he could foresee a surplus in the Ship's storage banks by day's end. Lemal called up the data on the various Metach'ton. Here, too, in the figures reflecting the situation of an hour earlier, all the values were above average. The metach were healthy, their motivation extraordinarily high, surely the beneficial result of the events of recent weeks. The Ship's community had passed with flying colors the test put to it by the traitors. The metach had been brought even closer to each other.

Lemal looked at the data with satisfaction. Only after a while did he wonder, why was it just an average day if all the most important figures were well above average?

Now feeling uneasy, he called up more data, and after a while he found the problem: the oxygen supply.

"What is it? Are the Kalpen doing shoddy work again?" he asked out loud. He didn't need to address the Net directly; it was always present.

"Their work performance is precisely in accordance with their assigned goals," the Net answered.

That was good. The Kalpen had a tendency to take liberties to which they weren't entitled. The Naahk would have liked to do without their services, but all his attempts to replace them with typical metach had failed. Either the metach achieved even less satisfactory results or within an extremely short time they turned into rebellious and stubborn Kalpen themselves, and the Naahk was right back where he started.

"Are the assignments insufficient?"

"No. You approved them yourself in the framework of the last ten-year plan. Since then, the Tenarchs have continued to monitor them in accordance with your projections."

Lemal called up additional data without taking the trouble to answer. The Net, never lacking for a reply, was a demanding conversational partner, but it had one indisputable advantage: it was not a human being. Unlike with the Tenarchs, he didn't have to think about whether he offended the Net or behaved impolitely.

A schematic diagram of the Ship appeared on the display. Sectors where the oxygen supply met or exceeded the required amount were shown in green; sectors in which it was below the optimal amount but still within the acceptable range, which was unavoidable in such a large and complex ecosphere as the Ship's, showed in blue; and sectors where intervention was required were in red.

The Inner Deck was filled with green and blue fields, the usual readings. The nearly complete lack of plants guaranteed these results. The Middle Deck glowed in unbroken green. The Outer Deck was green except for one sector in the area of the bow.

"What's going on there?" the Naahk asked. He didn't have to state his question any more precisely. The Net knew what data to show on his display.

"I do not understand your question."

"In Sector XVI F of the Outer Deck, there has been a drop in pressure." What was the Net up to? Was it playing one of its games with him?

"I do not understand what you are referring to. All readings are normal."

"And what's this I have here on the display?"

"Green readings, of course. I said so already."

"Yes, of course, now I see it." Lemal's fingers trembled as he took a closer look at the sector. A system failure. The behavior of the Net could no longer be explained by the modifications he had made to its interface. The Net behaved like a human being as a result, often resisted and hesitated, but up to now Lemal had never noticed it had the ability to lie.

There was only one explanation for the Net's behavior: a system failure. That of the Net or the hardware that supported it. He hoped that was the explanation.

He manually connected to the sensors in that sector. With one exception, they responded to the diagnostic routine with green reports. They were operational. The failure had to lie within the Net.

Lemal ran the diagnostic routine a second and third time. Perhaps he had been mistaken, perhaps it was only a defective sensor, not the Net itself, on whose failure-free operation the survival of the community depended.

Greens, nothing but greens.

He didn't give up. He connected to the surveillance cameras in the sector. Not surprisingly, he got overwhelmingly red values. Most of the cameras had broken down over the centuries, and since they weren't critical for the operation of the Ship they had not been replaced.

The Naahk began his inspection with the functioning cameras that were installed on the surface of the Outer Deck. He looked at the fields in which plants grew that were optimized for yield and resistant to the cosmic radiation and higher gravity of the deck. Nothing stood out. Or did it? Something wasn't right. His unease grew, increasing with each new camera view. Finally he realized what was bothering him: the fields were deserted. At this time of day they should been full of working metach.

What was going on? Was it mere coincidence? Or had the metach themselves noticed the decreasing amount of oxygen in the air and moved to other sectors? Such behavior would be highly unlikely. A good metach stayed in the location assigned to him until someone directed him to a new one. It would take something much worse than a temporary depletion of the oxygen supply to make him deviate from his instilled behavioral pattern.

Lemal made a note to call the responsible Tenarch and demand an explanation for the incident. But first he had to get to the bottom of the phenomenon. The Naahk checked the cameras within the Outer Deck. To his relief, he determined that the two shuttles stowed in this sector were untouched. At least his fear that a second Venron had appeared turned out to be unfounded.

He continued his search. He checked corridors and rooms that no human eye had seen since the Ship set out. In the flickering gleam of lights that came on automatically, or that of emergency lights that turned themselves on when the regular ones failed, he went through one after the other.

The work was tiring. His neck began to ache. He automatically moved his head from left to right, up and down, and while he pored over the shifting images, his deteriorating joints were subjected to stress that they were no longer capable of withstanding. Though he wasn't going to give up his search entirely, the Naahk was at the point of taking a break when he connected to a camera that watched over a long-empty storage room against the Ship's outer hull. The spare parts that had been stored there when the Ship launched had been used during the first century.

He saw a leak.

There had been other leaks in the history of the Ship. Materials aged, after all. But this leak was different from any he had seen before. Lemal zoomed the camera in close. He saw a welded seam, circular and large enough for a man to pass through. The seam was irregular, as though it had been hastily improvised—which eliminated the possibility that it had been the work of the Ship's builders. Lemal switched the view to infrared. The seam glowed crimson. It must have just been made.

He acted immediately. He did not turn to the Net: the partial blindness of the computer network was unmistakable proof that he could no longer count on it.

Launt's face appeared in an inset window on the display. The Tenarch was even paler than he had been the day when Netwar had conferred on him the hunt for the traitors.

"Naahk!" Launt exclaimed. "Have you already heard about it?"

"About the disruption in the air supply?"

Launt shook his head. "I don't anything about that. About the strangers, I mean."

"Strangers?"

"I've just learned about them. Intruders are on board in Sector XVI E! The metach are running away from them."

It was the sector bordering the one in which Lemal had stumbled on the fresh welding seam.

Someone had discovered the Ship. The day he long had feared had come.

"Naahk!" Launt pressed as Lemal said nothing. "What are your orders? What should we do?"

"The metach must leave the Outer Deck. All of them."

"I'll see to it. What else?"

"Call the Tenoy together on the Middle Deck. In full battle gear. I'll join you as soon as I can."

Lemal broke the connection. He injected a dose of painkiller and stood. From a drawer he took a supply of the medicine that was enough to last him for many weeks, then put on his body armor.

As he glided toward the Middle Deck in the elevator and the gravity pulled him more strongly toward the floor, he checked his weapons. They were functioning and loaded. He holstered them, then his fingers found the chain around his neck and clutched the medallion. He felt how it stimulated him, reminded him why he had made all this effort, what he stood for.

It took away his fear.

At least the worst of it.

24

Solina Tormas had always been interested in the past. As a child she had pestered her father and mother, her grandparents, her great-grandparents, and her great-great-grandparents—every member of her extended family within reach—and asked them how things used to be. While the other children spent their days with each other on the beaches and dove for glowfish to sell to the tourists, Solina had spent her time at home, preferably with her great-great-grandmother.

Mesdaq was different from all the others. She didn't shoo Solina away, never admonished her to stop with all those infernal questions about the dead past and occupy herself with something useful, like cleaning the kitchen or making some money from the tourists. Mesdaq never lacked time.

Only years later, after Solina had grown up, did she understand the source of Mesdaq's patience. Her great-great-grandmother had been an old, worn-out woman waiting for death. The life-sustaining systems in her floatchair had denied her that relief while her mind gradually decayed. Finally, she was only a shadow of the woman she had once been, now living in the past.

"Mesdaq, what was it like when you were a child?" Solina asked.

"We were poor," the ancient woman said. "Bitterly poor. The ocean was full of glowfish, but nobody wanted to buy them. All you had to do was throw a net into the sea and pull it back out again, and it was filled with them. You needed a lot of strong arms for that. There were never enough of those. Many people died before we knew which fish we could eat and which not to. There weren't many we could."

"Why didn't you buy your fish in the stores? Or have them delivered to you?" Solina didn't know anyone who ate fish directly from the sea.

"There weren't any stores. And nobody who would have given us anything."

"Why weren't there any stores?"

"We were new on this world."

"You ... you weren't from Shaghomin?"

"No."

"And there weren't any stores, not a õne?"

"No."

How dumb, the little Solina thought, *moving to a planet where there weren't any stores!*

"Then why did you come here?"

"They forced us to."

"Who did?"

"The government. The Energy Command."

That's so silly! The government only does good things for us!

"Why did they do that?"

"Because they wanted us out of the way."

"Where did you come from?"

"From Drorah."

"Is everybody here from Drorah?"

"No, but many are."

"Then is Drorah where we really, *really* came from?"

Mesdaq always thought about that question for a long time. At first she answered with "yes," but once she thought about it for so long that Solina believed her great-great-grandmother had nodded off again until she whispered, "No, from Lemur."

That was the first time Solina heard the name of the world of their origin. It would never let her go.

The child grew into a teenager. She became cut off from others her age who sensed that she was different from them. Solina acted as though it didn't bother her and buried herself more deeply in her enthusiasm for the past. One day, she discovered that the computer terminal in her room was good for more than just silly games or mindless entertainment. The numerous generations that had come and gone before her lived on within it.

Before long, she had stopped spending time with Mesdaq. Despite the systems in her floatchair, her great-great-grandmother was now almost always asleep. If an antigrav field hadn't held her head up, it would have constantly fallen forward. The stories that Mesdaq told became more confused and incoherent, and Solina had already heard them anyway.

The computer, on the other hand, always had something new to tell her, and so Solina learned the history of the Lemurians, the ancestors of the Akontans and thousands of other races. They had all originated on one planet: Lemur, which was now called Terra or Earth.

Lemur was an inconspicuous world in a remote spiral arm of the galaxy. It was distinguished only by the fact that it bore life—a peculiarity that it shared with many hundreds of thousands of other planets in the Milky Way.

And yet, a long time ago, within a short (by historical standards) period of a millennium and a half, its inhabitants had risen to become the leading power in the galaxy. From the continent of Lemuria, the Lemurians sent ships of colonists to all parts of the galaxy. Soon the Great Tamanium, as they called their interstellar empire, included more planets than even the Arkonide Empire or the Terrans' Solar Imperium at their peaks. Ultimately, one hundred-eleven Tamans, or administrative districts, belonged to the realm of the Lemurians. Yet even that wasn't enough, and the Tamanium stretched its fingers out to the neighboring Andromeda galaxy.

It seemed destined to endure for all eternity.

Then the Beasts had come out of the void to attack the Lemurians, and within a few years the Great Tamanium crumbled. The continent of Lemuria, where the Lemurians' civilization had originated, sank beneath the ocean. The Tamans were wiped out. With the help of the multi-star teleporter, some of the Lemurians were able to flee to the Andromeda galaxy. Gradually they forgot their origins and became the Tefrodians. The Tamanium, from which Akon later grew, chose a different escape route, that of total isolation. The plan succeeded in that the Blue system was spared the devastation, but at a high price, as Solina learned later: the petrifaction of an entire culture.

In one last desperate effort, when the struggle had long been lost, the Lemurians dealt their enemy a decisive blow.

They did the worst thing possible to their enemy.

They made him content.

The Beasts had lived up to their name. They were giants four meters tall with four arms, three eyes, and two brains. One of the brains, called the Overbrain, was capable of performance comparable to a positronic computer. When the Beasts chose to walk on both their arms and legs, they could reach a speed of more than one hundred-twenty kilometers per hour—and keep up that speed for twenty-four hours. They could turn their bodies at will into a crystalline structure harder than any steel; their stomachs transformed even rock into usable nutrients.

The Beasts were born to kill.

The Lemurians changed them into peaceful beings of unmatched selflessness.

TheLemurians succeeded in developing a beam projector called the psychogenic-regenerator and, under its influence, the murderous Beasts mutated into sensitive philosophers. From the Beasts came the Halutians, who voluntarily limited their population to one hundred thousand members, retired to the planet Halute and from then on never again interfered in the affairs of other races. For the Great Tamanium, rescue had come too late, but it allowed many thousands of worlds settled by Lemurians to escape destruction. The Blue system of the Akonians was one of those worlds, and in all probability Lemur as well.

At first, Solina had tried to tell her great-great-grandmother the story of the origin of their people—no one else she knew would have cared to listen to even a little of it—but she had quickly given up. Mesdaq lived in one particular past, her own world, in which the Lemurians were nothing more than a catchword. Besides, the ancient woman was no longer capable of enlarging her world—with one exception that made Solina angry beyond measure.

One day, a woman tourist had emerged from the daily stream that flowed around the big round beach house of Solina's family and pressed a gift into the trembling hands of the pitiable old lady in her floatchair. It was a statue of Vhrato the Sun Herald, a messianic salvation figure who had been worshipped throughout the entire Milky Way fifteen hundred years ago in the hope that Vhrato would free the galaxy from the yoke of the Larean tyranny. The Vhrato cult derived from an old tradition of the Vincranians, Lemurian descendants who had survived the onslaught of the Beasts within the protection of a nebula. The Vhrato cult spread quickly, became a unifying symbol in the struggle against the Lares and subsumed other local cults.

After the retreat of the Lares, it had appeared at first that Vhrato would be forgotten, but the cult merely underwent a transformation. As a symbol of redemption there was always a need for him somewhere in the galaxy, and over the next millennium an entire family of redeemers grew out of the one Vhrato, whose outward physical form always resembled that of their worshippers.

The plastic Vhrato that Solina's great-great-grandmother had been given was accordingly in the image of an Akonian with velvet brown skin that was already beginning to flake off in places and long hair tied back in a ponytail, the arms widely outstretched in a gesture of bestowing grace. The family had let the old woman keep the statuette. What harm could a plastic Vhrato do? Mesdaq seemed happy to smile dreamily while running her fingers over its contours.

Some weeks later, the statuette had disappeared from the old woman's hands. Instead, Solina found it in the main corridor of the house. Someone had made an altar of driftwood, on which the plastic Vhrato now stood. And that was just the beginning: during the years leading up to Mesdaq's death, the altar grew in size, and soon there was an offering left in a bowl for Vhrato every day, usually glowfish that could have been sold to the tourists and which stank terribly.

No one would admit to knowing how the altar was growing or where the offerings came from. Everyone in the household complained about it, but no one worked up the courage to take the

Vhrato away from the old woman, who floated in front of it in her chair every day, smiling blissfully and making it difficult for the rest of the family to move past her.

Then Mesdaq died. They buried her in the catacomb beneath the house where all members of the family found their final rest, and when Solina came back up, she expected that her father, who had complained the loudest about the altar, would take it apart and throw it into the ocean. But the altar remained untouched where it stood, and a fresh glowfish lay in the offering bowl.

Solina hadn't been home in several years now, but she was convinced that the altar still existed, perhaps by this time taking up the entire hallway.

And now she stood before an altar once more. Solina looked past Perry Rhodan, who stood leaning on the guide bar of the vehicle he called a bicycle, at the small clearing between the bushes. The Akonian had the feeling it was a hiding place, as though the cult served by the altar was only reluctantly tolerated.

As in her family's house on Shaghomin, the altar was improvised. Instead of driftwood, the builders had used branches from the bushes and other nearby plants and assembled them into a larger structure woven together with plastic parts. The inconsistency of the materials that had been used as well as the differing methods for putting them together—Solina was mentally tempted to call them "styles"—suggested to her trained historian's eye that she was looking at a construction that may already have existed for generations, and many hands had been at work on it.

The result was an oval pedestal that Solina estimated to be about two meters long with a width of roughly one and a half meters. At the foot of the pedestal was a row of securely fastened offering bowls, most of them filled.

"I don't believe it!" Robol von Sarwar moaned when he saw the figured enthroned on the altar. "I simply don't believe it! That can't be, Solina—can it?"

The historian didn't reply. Nothing was impossible. "History" was always just a construct of what was known and what a society considered worth noticing. The average citizen's reflex was to dismiss as impossible everything that didn't fit the known picture.

Therefore it was the historian's duty to evaluate new facts with as little prejudice as possible and weave them into the picture so that it came a tiny bit closer to the facts. That is, to the extent anyone even believed in such a naive concept as "facts," as did only a few historians in the fourteenth century NGE ... .

From the corner of her eye, Solina saw that Pearl Laneaux and Hayden Norwell had taken up watch positions with their beamers drawn. That gave her the opportunity to take a closer look at this place of worship.

The Akonian stepped up close to the altar, knelt down in front of the statue and examined the offering bowls. Two of them contained food: a long pod that reminded Solina of the fruit of the nhemud tree of her homeland, while the second offering seemed to be a piece of bread. In the other bowls she found a primitive handmade chain, a wreath of flowers and a piece of grease-smeared metal. Solina picked up the last item and turned it between her fingers.

"Maybe it's a tool for their bicycles?" said Rhodan, who had knelt down beside her. "It would represent something very valuable—exactly what someone would offer to a god!"

"Sounds convincing." Solina picked up a folded piece of paper that had laid under the tool.

"For the Protector," she read, deciphering the Lemurian handwriting. She unfolded the sheet and on it was written a wish. "Mighty Protector, let me win the race tonight!"

Solina and Rhodan looked up at the statue of the being that the inhabitants of the ark apparently called the "Protector," then at each other in amazement. Solina was sorely tempted to follow Robol's lead and exclaim, "It can't be!"

But that was out of the question; she was a historian. Together with Rhodan she examined the other offerings. Under each one was a sheet of paper with a request for the Protector. "Let me be transferred to another Me—!" Solina couldn't make out the final word. "Let my toothache be healed at last!" "Let her yield to me!"

Solina and Rhodan stood up. The statue of the Protector was about a meter high, but because of the altar on which the being stood, they looked directly into its three eyes. They were bright red.

The statue had been made out of a kind of clay that was nearly black and mostly unpainted. The being was naked. It stood on two massive pillarlike legs and had four arms that it held half reaching out, posed as though holding its arms protectively over its worshippers. The head sat on the shoulders without any neck.

"No doubt about it," Rhodan said, expressing the thoughts of everyone else. "It's a Halutian!"

"Or a Beast," Hevror ta Gosz put in, having joined the other two.

"Improbable," Solina contradicted him without taking her eyes off the Protector's statue. She had never seen a Halutian with her own eyes, but the statue was startlingly similar to images she was familiar with from pictures and recordings. "This ship set out long before the Beasts attacked. The distance from its starting point proves that. Its inhabitants couldn't know anything about the existence of the Beasts."

"But what if there had been an encounter with Beasts along the way?" Hevror demanded.

"Then the ship wouldn't exist any more," Rhodan replied. "The Beasts never asked questions, not even after shooting. They would have destroyed the ark the second they found out there were Lemurians or the descendants of Lemurians on board."

"That leaves the Halutians," Solina said. "The ark must have met up with Halutians."

"That seems to me the only possible explanation," Rhodan agreed. "But to be honest, it doesn't satisfy me, either. For thousands of years, only one hundred thousand Halutians have existed in the galaxy, a vanishingly small number. And hardly any of that little group ever leaves Halute. The odds that Halutians happened to stumble on the ark by chance are right at zero."

"Perhaps it wasn't by chance?" Hevror suggested. "Perhaps the Halutians learned about the ark somehow?"

"Also extremely improbable," Solina said. "As far as I know, no one up to now has ever found any hint of the existence of a ship like this. If the Halutians had found one, they would have informed us. And besides, they actually would have helped the inhabitants during their visit instead of taking off again after a quick stop. Isn't that right, Rhodan? You know Halutians personally."

She was referring to Icho Tolot, who had been allied with the Terrans in a friendship that had lasted more than twenty-five hundred years. The Immortal nodded. "The Halutians are very concerned about atoning for the sins of their ancestors. They would have—" He didn't have a chance to finish his sentence.

"Perry!" Pearl exclaimed. "There's a na … a female Lemurian on one of those wheel-things!"

"Can you catch up with her?" Rhodan asked.

"Not necessary. *She's coming straight toward us!*"

A moment later, she had reached them. She sped on her bicycle into the midst of the team, brought it to a grinding halt and gasped in ancient Lemurian, "Please, strangers, you must help me!"

Rhodan was the first to recover from the surprise. "How can we help you?" he asked, also in Lemurian.

"Please help me, or they will kill me!"

25

For what seemed like an endlessly long time, the troll led Eniva ta Drorar through the corridors and decks of the *Palenque*. On the one hand, the Akonian was grateful for the opportunity to look around the foreign starship, and on the other she was amazed by the Terrans' technological backwardness. It was common practice on Akonian ships to use teleporters for even short distances. No one would have conceived of the idea of using an antigrav shaft to traverse more than two decks. Or did the Terrans have some sort of cult about physical activity and rejected teleporters for ideological reasons? She could believe almost anything of the Terrans, and she would have liked to think about it some more ... would have, if Alemaheyu Kossa had kept his mouth shut for even a second.

The *Palenque*'s comm officer talked as though his life depended on it. He talked about the weather on Terra ... asked if the weather control on Sphinx—the oaf used that ugly Terran name for Drorah!—messed things up as regularly as it did on Terra ... didn't give her a chance to answer ... complained about the shift assignment on the *Palenque*, which was rigged from the start to his disadvantage ... asked if it was the same way on the *Las-Toór* ... didn't give her a chance to answer ... informed her of his concern about the galacto-political situation ... and didn't she think the Ako ... Excuse me! the Arkonides were behind everything bad, maybe even the incompetent weather control … didn't give her a chance to answer … asked her if she had ever met Perry Rhodan … didn't give her a chance to answer … and then launched into a long and certainly far-fetched story of what good buddies he and Perry were … .

Alemaheyu's torrent of words was like a tidal wave. Eniva wished she were back in the shelter of her cabin, small and malodorous though it might be. Or better yet, back on the *Las-Toór*, which she should have never left in order to get to know the barbarians better from up close. Because that was what the Terrans were, no doubt about it: barbarians. No Akonian of position would behave so badly as to refuse to let a conversation partner get a word in edgewise, and certainly it never would have occurred to anyone to do what that supreme barbarian Sharita Coho had cooked up. She had rid herself of a comm officer who was probably insufferable when he had nothing to do, and at the same time neutralized her Akonian hostage in a way that was unassailable. Hadn't she taken care of her guest at great sacrifice and assigned Eniva one of her most important men as a personal adjutant?

Sharita Coho was a devil. If she ever had the chance, she would—

"Here we are, Eniva."

The Akonian had difficulty bringing herself back to the here and now. The Terran troll had stopped talking. What was going on?

"We're where?"

"This is my cabin."

"Cabin? You said you wanted to guide me through the ship!" She wasn't afraid of Alemaheyu Kossa. If the Terran dwarf tried physical force on her, she would demonstrate the close anatomical similarities between Akonians and Terrans with one kick between his legs.

"And that's just what I did! We went through the entire ship twice."

"What? Why didn't you say anything?"

Alemaheyu's eyes went wide with indignation. "But that's what I was doing the whole time! Weren't you listening?"

"Oh, of course." Eniva remembered that she was on board the *Palenque* as something of an official representative of her people. There was no excuse for being infected by the Terran's impoliteness.

"If you say so, I believe it. We Terrans are polite people, after all."
Alemaheyu pointed invitingly to the door of his cabin. "And that's
why it's customary for us to offer our guests something to drink."

Eniva looked at the door to Alemaheyu's cabin. It wasn't different in any way from the hundred others that the Terran had led
her past. With one exception: Someone, presumably Alemaheyu
himself, had stuck a hand-lettered cardboard sign on it at eye-level
with primitive adhesive strips.

"ALEMAHEYU KOSSA," Eniva read. "AIR GUITAR MAIL
ORDER SERVICE."

She was rather proud of her Intercosmo and understood each of
the words on the sign. Yes, she even had some idea what a guitar was,
but still, the words didn't make any sense when taken together.

Alemaheyu smiled at her with his perfect teeth, as though he
expected her to ask about the sign.

For that, she thought, *you can wait a few dozen centuries!*

"Very well," the Akonian said. "Let's get it over with. *One* drink."

"One drink."

Alemaheyu led her into his cabin. "I've been on the *Palenque* for
quite a while now," he said apologetically as he noticed that she was
mentally comparing his cabin with her own, "and my function on
the ship makes me irreplaceable. That's why Sharita assigned me a
more generous cabin. The extra maintenance costs are deducted
from my shares."

"Generous" was stretching the facts. On the *Las-Toór*, a cabin of
this size would have been allotted to a member of one of the lower
crew ranks. But the *Palenque* was certainly not the *Las-Toór*, and Eniva
thanked the spirits of her ancestors that at least she didn't have to
sit together with Alemaheyu on a couch.

The Terran leaped to a chair, cleared a pile of papers and empty
food packages from the seat, and motioned for her to sit down.
"Sorry. I wasn't expecting company, or I would have cleaned the
place up a little."

A poor excuse. What were housekeeping robots for? Eniva
reminded herself once more of the Akonian politeness that was
justifiably famous throughout the galaxy, thanked him, and took
a seat.

"You'll love it!" Alemaheyu announced as he opened a large refrigerator, which looked about as orderly inside as his cabin—in other words, it looked as though a transform bomb had gone off inside.

Finally Alemaheyu found what he was looking for. He held up two brown bottles, made himself comfortable on the chair opposite without any concern for the papers piled on the seat, and placed the bottles on the small table between him and Eniva. "Perfect temperature: 8.4 degrees." Alemaheyu pulled a tool from his pants pocket and used it to open the bottles. They hissed and some droplets of foam sprayed on the table. "Brace yourself, Eniva. You're about to experience an exquisite pleasure that the entire galaxy is crazy about—genuine Terran beer!" He clinked his bottle against Eniva's and raised it to his mouth. "Cheers!"

When Eniva didn't follow suit, he quickly murmured: "No, no glasses. You drink beer out of the bottle!" Then he took a fast swallow, as though to prove to her that it wasn't poisonous.

Eniva gathered all of her courage and drank as well. She was prepared for the worst. She had heard that the Terrans went so far as to fill bottles with animal milk and drink it.

The cold fluid washed across her gums and over her tongue. Then the flavor exploded on her tastebuds along with a thought in her mind: Kavla! They drank kavla! Much too cold—the temperature bordered on blasphemy—and too much carbonation, but Eniva's certainty grew as the liquid warmed in her mouth and the taste became more familiar.

Kavla! The Terrans knew about kavla! She was so relieved that she emptied half the bottle in one gulp.

"Do you like it?" Alemaheyu asked. For the first time, Eniva saw that he was uncertain.

"Yes, it's not bad. It's much too cold, of course, and being in a bottle doesn't show it off to best advantage. You should put it in a microwave and serve it in a bowl ... "

"A microwave? That would be ... "

"Just a suggestion," Eniva said to soothe him before he could pronounce the word *blasphemy*. She emptied the bottle with a second gulp. The kavla may have been served in an abominable fashion, but in her stomach it blossomed into its familiar warm blessing. All of a sudden, Eniva didn't feel so lost and out of place among the Terrans. "Do you have any more kav ... er, beer?"

"Sure." Visibly delighted by her request, Alemaheyu leaped to the refrigerator and came back with half a dozen bottles held together in a plastic sheath. "We call this a six-pack," he said earnestly. "For as long as the Terrans have known beer, they've been drinking it as a six-pack."

At first, Eniva thought Alemaheyu had brought out far too much beer in his eagerness, but she was wrong. After she had gotten used to it, Terran kavla ran down her throat just as smoothly as Akonian. And she had been wrong about something else: Alemaheyu wasn't really such a bad fellow as she had thought. The Terran wasn't a troll, just short and slender, and he was really rather charming. He told her how he had come to sign aboard a prospecting ship and that he hoped someday to visit Ethiopia, the region of Terra from which his ancestors had long ago emigrated. And he asked about Eniva's situation. How had she come on board the *Las-Toór* and how was it for her there? Eniva found herself pouring her heart out to him, and when she realized what she was doing, she didn't care.

The six-pack was emptied much too quickly. When Eniva asked for another one, Alemaheyu shook his head sadly.

"Sorry. Like I said, I wasn't expecting company, and if Sharita found out I was requisitioning beer from the central supply room in our current situation ... "

"She would have your head."

"Exactly." Alemaheyu stared gloomily through the neck of his empty bottle at its bottom. Then he jerked up. "I've got an idea!"

"And that would be ... "

The Terran was already opening a drawer and taking out a small bag. With practiced movements he pulled out several paper strips, added long brown shreds of what looked like dried plant fibers, then scrapings from a lump of something, and rolled up the paper.

"This is like ... well, not like beer. It's different. But the best thing is for you to try it yourself."

"If you think so. How do you eat it?"

"You don't. This is a joint." Alemaheyu's laugh was friendly. "I'll show you." He lit the paper assemblage at one end, put the other end in his mouth, inhaled the smoke, and with closed eyes held it in his lungs. When he opened his eyes again, there was a dreamy shine in them. Then he handed her the joint.

The idea of inhaling smoke disgusted Eniva, but she gathered all her courage together and did it. After all, she was here to experience a foreign culture. Immediately a second layer of warmth descended on Eniva and enveloped her. Just as Alemaheyu said. It wasn't like kavla, but ... oooh!

They smoked the joint to the end. Alemaheyu offered to make another one, but Eniva declined. Enough was enough.

For some time, the Terran and the Akonian stared happily into space, then Eniva gathered all of her courage—from childhood on, she had been instructed never to show her ignorance, and this went deeper than kavla, beer, or joints—and asked about the sign on Alemaheyu's cabin door.

"Oh, that," the Terran answered. "It's just a joke. I don't sell air guitars. You can't do that."

"Then they don't exist?"

"Oh, they exist, all right!"

"But I don't understand. Why can't you sell them? Is it illegal?"

"No, no, that isn't it." Alemaheyu rolled his glassy eyes. "Hm, how can I explain this to you?" He rolled his eyes for a few more moments, then leaped up again and cried out, "I know! I'll show you!" From one of the many cabinets that lined the walls of his cabin he pulled a bulbous object with a long neck.

"A guitar!" Eniva exclaimed, proud to have recognized the instrument.

"Correct." Alemaheyu held the guitar at waist-level, one hand around its neck and the other resting on the body so that it nearly covered the hole in the center. "You hold it like this." The hand over the hole ran along the strings and some sharp tones rang out. "And this is how you play it."

"All right. So that's a guitar—and what's the difference between it and an air guitar?"

"Watch closely!" Alemaheyu laid the guitar aside, gave the syntron a hand signal, and threw himself into a pose. He jerked his hips forward almost indecently while he positioned his hands as though they held a guitar. Then he closed his eyes and his fingers slid over the strings of the imaginary guitar.

A howling erupted from the cabin's acoustic fields. Eniva would have taken off running on the spot if hadn't been for the warmth within her making her feel safe. So she remained sitting where she was and let the sound of Alemaheyu's air guitar wash over her. *The cabin syntron must be programmed to follow the Terran's finger movements and convert them into tones.*

And then the miracle happened. To the same degree that the Terran threw himself into his playing, that he swayed to the rhythm and swung his hips in an unambiguous manner, Eniva opened up to his music, and from the howling came tones that left the Akonian with no other choice than to leap up and surrender to the beat.

Eniva was perspiring as Alemaheyu brought the song to an end. He sank to his knees as though thanking some unknown god for the blessing of his playing, his upper body bent so far backwards that the back of his head nearly touched the floor. As the last chord died away, he opened his eyes and saw the enraptured Eniva. A look of utter satisfaction spread across his face. "I'll bet the Akonians don't have anything like that!"

That's what you think! Eniva thought. She was about to turn to the cabin syntron and improvise a session of plejbek to show up Alemaheyu, who had turned back into a Terran with a superior attitude, but at that moment a holo appeared in the center of the cabin. It was Sharita Coho.

"Alemaheyu!" the Terran commander said abruptly. "The Terran Residence is asking for Perry Rhodan. You've got to cook up an answer. They can't be allowed to find out that we're in dilation flight or we'll have the LFT fleet on our backs! They'll have the Lemurian ship in tow faster than we can blink, and if we're really lucky they might pay us off with ten solars per person!"

Alemaheyu jumped up and tried to salute. "On my way! What about Eniva ta Drorar? She's here with me. Should I bring her along?"

"What kind of a hare-brained idea—?" The commander must have realized that Eniva was listening and swallowed the rest of the sentence. "Let her continue to enjoy your excellent hospitality in peace. I'll send a robot to give your corridor a thorough cleaning. It needs it, understand?"

The last hint was meant for Eniva. It was outrageous behavior by the Terran commander, but the Akonian was still too enraptured by the beer, joint and music to care. As Alemaheyu left the cabin murmuring innumerable excuses, she sank back into her chair, completely exhausted.

She quickly discovered that the chair could be extended into a comfortable couch. Eniva stretched out while the scratching of the cleaning robot at the door lulled her to sleep. The last thought that went through Eniva's mind before she nodded off was that she was happy she didn't go on board the Lemurian ship. Nothing that happened there could be nearly as exciting as her adventures among the Terrans.

26

The largest armed force ever assembled in one place in the history of the Ship was waiting for Lemal Netwar on the Middle Deck.

There were almost four hundred Tenoy standing in groups. No other metach could be seen anywhere. They must have decided either to take to their heels or to stay out of sight. To avoid the risk of setting off a panic on the Middle Deck, which had remained calm up to now, Lemal had not publicly announced that the Tenoy were being called together.

The gathering of the Tenoy was a confirmation of the rumors that were racing through the Ship: strangers were on board!

Against conventional projectiles, the Tenoy wore impenetrable body armor; they carried heavy weapons that had been stockpiled in the Ship's armories for just such an occasion. This was the first time they had been handed out. The weight of the weapons—many had to be carried by two or three individuals—didn't seem to bother the guardians. On the contrary: their mood was euphoric. From the elevator cabin, Lemal saw fists raised high in anticipation of victory, and he could read innumerable boasts on their lips.

Most of the men and women wore face masks painted with savage-looking caricatures that only left their noses and mouths uncovered. Those who didn't have masks had let their comrades paint grotesque designs directly on their faces. The warrior identities they assumed this way filled them with a self-confidence that bordered on intoxication.

The Tenoy had no idea what to expect, and it was just as well.

One of the Tenarchs greeted him. "The Tenoy have reported as you ordered." The man bowed. "They await your command."

It wasn't Launt. The Naahk would have given a great deal to have his most trusted Tenarch with him at this moment, but Launt was at the Ship's stern carrying out the execution of the traitors. Netwar had considered relieving him of the task, but ultimately chose to let him fulfill his duty: he had given this duty to Launt in order to make him an even more loyal Tenarch, who would serve him well for many more years.

"Are the strangers still on the Outer Deck?"

"Yes."

"Do you know their location?"

"Yes."

"Then take us to them."

"But ... " The man went silent as the Naahk's icy gaze rested on him. He turned away and loudly called out orders.

But that doesn't make any sense! the Tenarch had wanted to protest. Netwar could read it in his face. Marching toward the enemy in formation was madness. They knew the Ship; it was their home. It would be simple for them to fan out and surround the strangers undetected.

But the Naahk held to his decision. If he had guessed the strangers' identity correctly, only unity could save them, if anything could.

The descent to the Outer Deck took long minutes. In order to arrive as a group, the Tenoy had to use a single elevator. Netwar had gathered them at one of the big freight elevators, but because only fifty Tenoy could be transported per trip, it took more than half an hour for the entire force to reach the surface of the Outer Deck.

Lemal went with the first squad, and as the rest of the Tenoy arrived in stages behind him, he looked out over the Outer Deck. It had been a long time since he had come here. The relatively high gravity usually kept him off this deck, and only the pain medication made it possible for him to be here now. He hated to imagine the damage he was causing to his joints by being here, and he had no idea how much longer his body would hold up. Even though he understood what was inevitable, he couldn't face the idea that someday he would be unable to move, leaving the Ship without guidance.

The Outer Deck appeared peaceful. The well-ordered rows of fields stretched into the haze, and no metach or strangers could be seen anywhere. But appearances were deceptive. They were hiding down there somewhere.

Lemal wondered how the strangers had found them. Even between the vastness of space and the hyperdetection shield with which the builders had equipped the Ship, their discovery couldn't have been by chance. He was suddenly overwhelmed by the feeling that the high gravity was trying to drag him to the ground and crush him. He recognized it as primarily an emotional reaction to stress.

"Transport is complete." The Tenarch's report pulled him back to the present.

"Then we don't want to waste any time." He pulled at the chain around his neck, bringing his medallion of office into view from under the body armor. He positioned it on his chest so the Tenoy could see it clearly. Then he drew his weapon, released the safety and took his place at the head of the guardians.

***

It took long minutes for the Lemurian to calm herself enough so that she could explain matters with relative coherence.

Solina Tormas used the opportunity to take a closer look at the woman, who called herself Denetree. She was young, practically still a girl, and shorter than an average Akonian, though with her fair skin she could have easily passed for a member of one of the Terran races. She was unusually strong; her sleeves and trouser legs stretched over well-developed muscles. From that, Solina concluded she spent much of her time in the increased gravity of this outer deck. She probably worked in the fields. Denetree had tied her long, black hair into a ponytail so it didn't fall into her face. Her eyes were pale blue and in constant motion at that moment, she was looking back and forth between Solina and Rhodan, who had both shown they were fluent in the Lemurian language.

"You must take me with you!" Denetree begged. "They want to kill me!"

"Who wants to kill you, and why?"

"The Naahk … the entire Ship!" The Lemurian trembled.

"But why? Have you done something that … ?"

"No, we didn't do anything! All we did was dream of the stars!"

"And that is a crime?" Solina took an involuntary step toward the Lemurian, perhaps thinking to take her consolingly in her arms. Denetree drew back, one hand on a bulge in her belt.

"Yes. The Naahk is afraid for the Ship. But we didn't do anything—we only dreamed! I never wanted to leave the Ship!"

Rhodan spoke up. "You say 'we.' Who is that?"

"My friends and I. And my brother. We met secretly and dreamed of the stars. Now they've caught my friends and are going to kill them. And soon they'll catch me. You must help me! You must help us!"

"And what about your brother?"

Denetree lowered her eyes. "He is dead. He tried to flee in a small ship. The Tenoy shot it down. You can do nothing more for him."

Rhodan stiffened. Solina wondered if there was something the Terrans were hiding. They had reported the wreck of a shuttle that had put them on the trail of the ark. They had not said anything about a passenger. Had the Terrans taken a prisoner, perhaps?

"No, Denetree, we can't do anything more for him." Rhodan shook his head sadly.

The Lemurian wept softly. Again she rested her hand on her belt. When Denetree raised her hand to wipe the tears from her face, Solina saw she had taken a rectangular plastic case out from under her belt.

"So your brother did more than dream?" Solina asked.

" Venron was never content with what he had. He always wanted to know more. He believed there was a better life among the stars than there was here." She looked at Rhodan and Solina. "Is that true?"

"I don't know," Rhodan said. "I don't know anything about life on board this ship. But I can assure you that there is life among the stars—and that we will take you with us if you wish."

Denetree's "thank you" was drowned out by Pearl's exclamation. "Rhodan, I think you'd better come and see this!"

"What is it? More Lemurians?"

"Yes, a *lot* more!"

Rhodan went to stand next to Pearl, who as before was keeping watch at the edge of the altar clearing. Solina gave Denetree an encouraging glance and joined him. She was happy to finally have spoken with an inhabitant of the ark, but if they wanted to find out more about the ship, they needed to make contact with the command level. Perhaps now there would be an opportunity to do that.

Pearl had stationed herself between two bushes, an observation post from which she could look out over an adjacent field that recently had been harvested. At the moment, several hundred armed individuals had taken up position. Solina couldn't tell much from their faces—they wore masks or had exaggerated their facial features with paint to look frightening—but that wasn't necessary. The determination with which they aimed their weapons at the joint scouting party spoke volumes.

There was an exclamation behind her back. "The Tenoy!" Denetree cried. "They've found us!"

"Now what?" Pearl asked. "Do we wait until they open fire, or do we beat them to the punch?"

Solina was surprised that Pearl had suddenly turned to Perry Rhodan as the leader after she had so determinedly acted as if she was in command of the group. But it was the only reasonable thing to do: Rhodan had much more experience in such situations than all of them put together, probably more even than the hundreds of opponents facing them. But in Solina's eyes, Pearl Laneaux had been behaving like someone who was much more status-conscious than rational. Had she misjudged her?

Rhodan didn't answer immediately.

"They can't crack our shields," Pearl went on. "We can knock them flat with our paralyzers for a few hours—and then maybe they'll see reason."

"I doubt that." Rhodan seemed to have come to a decision. He turned to the Lemurian. "Denetree, don't let them see you, no matter what happens! Understand?" Then he said to Pearl, "It's hard to have a conversation with a headache, and that's where we'll be if we paralyze them. Not a very good beginning for a friendly relationship. I don't know what kind of weapons they have, but if they open fire on us, there's a danger they could damage the ark beyond repair." He straightened up. "We have to talk."

Rhodan lifted both arms, held out his empty palms toward the armed group facing him, and started walking.

For a moment, Solina looked at him in amazement, then leaped up indignantly. What was he thinking? Did he believe that just because he was immortal, he had a monopoly on dramatic gestures? She stretched out her own arms in the same gesture and caught up with Rhodan. He greeted her with a smile. "Thank you for the company."

They continued on together.

As the armed inhabitants noticed the two strangers approaching them, they stiffened. The clinking of metal on metal that accompanied the positioning of their weapons faded away. No one said a word. Solina thought she heard a faint humming she hadn't been aware of before. Perhaps it was the background noise of the ship's operating systems.

Rhodan hadn't activated his personal defense shield. Solina didn't, either. She thought she knew the reason for the Terran's decision: their armed opponents would have noticed the shields due to their flickering glow, and perhaps opened fire on the spot. The Lemurians facing them must be extremely nervous and frightened if even only a fraction of what Denetree had told them about the ark's society were true.

It was a calculated risk. If they were fired at, their suits' syntrons would activate the shields in time to protect them. In all likelihood, at least; they didn't know what kinds of weapons their opponents were carrying.

About twenty paces in front of the armed front line, Rhodan and Solina stopped. Rhodan lowered his arms, taking care to continue showing his empty palms, and called, "We come in peace!"

Rhodan spoke in Lemurian.

The barrels of the weapons did not move.

"We come in peace!" Rhodan repeated. "We wish to speak with you!"

A single man emerged from the mass, armored the same as the rest, but wearing neither mask nor facepaint. He stopped halfway out to them and laid down his weapon. His steps were strangely stiff, as though he wasn't used to moving his legs, or the high gravity was affecting him adversely. His nearly bald head sat frozen on his neck and didn't move even when he bent to lay his weapon on the ground. His rigidity gave him the appearance of a robot. Only his eyes betrayed the turmoil raging within him.

But Solina hardly noticed the man as such. Her attention and Rhodan's was entirely focused on the chain the man wore around his neck. From it dangled a dull metal egg.

A cell activator!

The man coming toward them was an immortal!

The man stopped two steps in front of them. "I am Lemal Netwar, Naahk of the *Nethack Achton*."

In her mind, Solina translated the name of the ark: *Far Horizons*. A hopeful name, at odds with the atmosphere of fear Denetree described.

Perry Rhodan and Solina gave their names. Solina pronounced hers in a state of numbness. A cell activator! It was impossible! By some unlikely chance a Halutian might have stumbled on the ark and gone down in their legends as a protector, but this ... it was impossible. It was only long after the ark had set out that the Tefrodians, descendents of the Lemurians, had cell activators ... .

"You say you come in peace. Why should I believe you?"

"Because we are human beings like you. We come from Lemuria."

"From Lemuria? Then Lemuria still exists?"

"Yes."

Rhodan didn't tell the Lemurian that the civilization from which he originated was gone. That knowledge could have thrown him into complete confusion, and events already were overwhelming Lemal Netwar. His hands trembled. He slowly lifted his right hand to the cell activator at his chest, as though he was seeking strength there. Which could be the case: Solina knew that at times of heightened stress, cell activators increased their life-sustaining impulses and so made their wearers better able to cope.

The Lemurian closed his eyes. What would he decide? Solina wondered what more they could say to convince them of their peaceful intentions.

Rhodan spoke again. "Your cell activator gives you strength."

Lemal Netwar opened his eyes wide. "You know about ... "

"Yes," Rhodan said. "I used to wear one like yours, but it was replaced by a new one implanted in my shoulder."

"You are ... "

The Lemurian sized up Rhodan. Solina understood that an instant bond now existed between them. Only an immortal could appreciate what immortality felt like.

They had won.

Lemal Netwar trusted Rhodan. It would not end in a battle.

In that moment, Solina heard Pearl cry out from behind her, "Denetree, no!"

Solina Tormas turned and saw the young Lemurian running toward her.

27

Hartich van Kuespert was assigned a console in the lower ring of the *Las-Toór*'s control center, one of those reserved for the Akonian scientists, the Yidari. The console offered the Terran a welcome refuge. The conversation with the Ma-Techten, the ship's first officer, had been a mixed pleasure. The Akonian's manner had perfectly matched Hartich's image of these people: self-controlled and reserved. But behind Echkal cer Lethir's mask of cool politeness, the Terran thought he sensed something seething. Disapproval. Distaste. Or had it only been uncertainty? It was hard for Hartich to trust his own perceptions. Hadn't the same man generously given up his own cabin?

Hartich suspected that much more time would pass before he began to understand the Akonians.

Fortunately, their technology was much easier to understand. The syntron responded to Intercosmo, and some kind soul had set his menus and outputs to the galaxy's lingua franca before his arrival.

Hartich quickly made himself familiar with his new workstation. It was astonishing how much Akonian technology resembled Terran: evidence that the two races were more alike than they wanted to admit? Or that Akonian economic espionage wasn't a fabrication of the Terran secret service after all, as the hyperphysicist had assumed up to now? And each system and piece of equipment on the *Las-Toór* seemed to be that little but decisive bit better than its counterpart on the *Palenque*. Evidently, the Akonian government was not quite as stingy as the private owners of the *Palenque*.

Hartich felt comfortable at the console. During the short transfer flight to the *Las-Toór*, Hartich had come up with a new idea concerning the Lemurian ship's hyperdetection shield, and now he spent a few minutes with the syntron developing an appropriate computer model. When it was complete he tested it, which took longer than expected since some of the Akonian scientists were just then tying up a large percentage of the computing capacity.

Hartich leaned back and soaked up the atmosphere of the control center. Silent concentration reigned in the hemispherical room. The most prominent sound was the low murmuring of the various ventilators, interrupted now and then by muttered instructions to the various syntrons. Jere von Baloy seldom took an active part in the control center crew's work. The men and women were apparently an experienced team used to working together, and they made most of their decisions autonomously.

The maphan seemed engrossed in a syntron report, but he suddenly turned to the comm officer positioned on the middle level of the ring. "Netkim, have you been able to reestablish contact with the exploration team?"

A translator integrated into the console translated the question for Hartich with almost no delay into Intercosmo.

"No."

"Keep trying."

"Yes, Maphan."

The brief exchange of words tore Hartich out of the complacent mood into which his unexpectedly open reception on the *Las-Toór* had lured him. Communications with the Terrans and Akonians who had gone on board the Lemurian ship had been broken off? That was bad! They had to get help to the team—fast!

He wanted to ask Jere von Baloy what could be done, but while he was still formulating the words, the first officer spoke up ahead of him. "Maphan, we must do something!" Echkal cer Lethir urged. "Contact has been broken off for almost an hour!"

Jere von Baloy turned in his seat toward the officer. "And what do you suggest?"

"That we send in a second team, more heavily armed."

"And what do you wish to accomplish by that?"

"What else? They could get our people out of there!"

The maphan looked at his deputy almost pityingly. "That's based on the assumption that the team is in danger. There is no indication that is the case."

"But we've lost contact with them!"

"That doesn't mean that anything has happened to them. It is very likely that we are merely dealing with a side effect of the Lemurian ship's hyperdetection shield. Hartich, is that probable? You've been working on a model of the ship's detection shield, am I correct?"

In his surprise, Hartich was only able to manage a stuttered, "Yes, I have ... " The commander of the Akonian ship was asking for advice from him who, despite all the polite talk of hospitality, was really just a hostage?

Jere von Baloy was satisfied. "See, Echkal? We'll wait. We agreed with the Terrans on a period of twelve hours for the scouting mission. We will of course honor the agreement. We are Akonians, don't forget. We are the good guys." The maphan grinned at those around him, as though he had made an excellent joke. But no one laughed. The Akonians accepted his words as though what he had said was self-evident.

Once more silence returned to the control center, but Hartich was now aware of a tension in the air that he had not sensed before. He had the feeling he had witnessed a scene in a play that had already been going on for some time. Otherwise, the openly spoken objection by the first officer and its brusque dismissal by the commander could not be explained.

Hartich wondered when the curtain would go up for the next act.

"Maphan!" the comm officer exclaimed. "The Seventh Fleet is calling again! Takhan Gartor von Taklir wants to speak with you immediately!"

The commander thought for a moment. "Give the highly respected admiral my best regards. I am unavailable at the moment."

They were polite words such as were expected between highly placed Akonians, but Hartich had a critical advantage over the admiral: he could read Jere's expression. And there was expressed a very different message: *Get lost, Admiral!*

"Of course, Maphan," the comm officer said and transmitted the message. He listened to the reply with an expression of concentration, then turned back to the commander. "Maphan, Takhan von Taklir wishes to state that nothing could be so important as to make the commander of an Explorer unavailable for hours on end, unless there is an emergency condition that exceeds his and his ship's limited capabilities."

Jere stiffened in his chair. The jab had not escaped him. Hartich was slowly coming to the conclusion that the Akonian language consisted entirely of jabs. Everything else that was said was merely incidental, the framework that carried the actual message.

"I see, I see," the commander said lowly. Then, louder, he said, "Switch him over to my avatar, Netkim. Let the honorable Takhan work off his ill-manners on it."

The comm officer didn't react.

"What is it? Didn't you hear my order?"

"I did ... " Netkim rubbed the back of his neck, at a loss. "It's just that the admiral added something else to his message: 'And don't try to foist me off on an avatar! Otherwise I'll see to it that you spend the rest of your days scrubbing deck floors on the fleet's ships.'"

"Very well." Jere von Baloy stood and assumed a stiff posture. "Well, who can refuse such a friendly request? Put him through, Netkim!"

The holo, which up to now had been showing the Lemurian ship and the *Palenque*, changed. Hartich looked an Akonian admiral in the face and involuntarily hunched his shoulders. Gartor ta Taklir was a brawny man, perhaps past his best years, but his uniform still bulged over his muscular chest and arms. His gray hair was cut short in military fashion.

Jere von Baloy started to greet him but the admiral cut him off. "Damned civilians!" he blustered. "Can't even make a simple hypercom connection! Get off the channel, neelak! I want to speak to the commander!"

Neelak. The Akonian term for a common spaceman. Hartich was curious to see how Jere von Baloy would react to the insult.

"You already are," the commander said calmly. "What can I do for you, Takhan? I must request that you make it short. My duties really do make me unavailable, as I have already had my comm officer inform you."

At a glance, the admiral sized up the commander in his simple overalls and muttered, mostly to himself, something like: "No wonder these civilians can't make a comm connection, with this lack of discipline!" Then he said aloud, "The *Las-Toór* has orders to give the Seventh Fleet status reports at regular intervals!"

"Which, of course, we have done."

"With inexplicable delays!"

"As you may be aware, the Ochent Nebula represents a region of space comprised of extreme physical conditions. It is quite common here for comm signals to suffer interference, distortion and or delays. I am certain the Yidari can provide you with exhaustive statistics … "

"Spare me your gabbling professors! I don't need a scientist to smell something rotten here. Physical conditions are a factor—but there's also the human one!"

"By that, do you mean to say—"

"I am merely doing my duty, and I expect the same from you. You are a civilian, but you have also sworn to serve the Akonian people!"

Jere von Baloy's face turned red. The admiral must have hit a sensitive spot.

"That I have done. And that is what I am doing, I assure you. Now if you will excuse me … "

"One moment more. As you may be aware, officers of the fleet receive supplementary scientific training. We have analyzed your reports. And guess what we've found out? The *Las-Toór* has been in dilation flight for nearly thirteen standard days. What is the meaning of this? Is the journey too long for the ladies and gentlemen of the Yidari?"

"I can assure you that the ladies and gentlemen of the Yidari are working hard. The dilation flight is part of a series of scientific experiments that are too complex to explain in a simple hypercom conversation."

For several moments, the two men stared at each other. Takhan ta Taklir possessed the merciless glare of a man who did not allow errors and had been in a position of power for so long that he had forgotten how to excuse one.

Jere von Baloy held his gaze.

"I am glad that your Yidari are so diligent," the admiral said at length. "I am certain that your experiments are of the greatest interest and in the long run will contribute to the welfare of our people."

Hartich couldn't believe his ears. *The admiral was giving in?* He quickly found his suspicion was justified.

"And nothing lies closer to our hearts than the welfare of our people, am I correct, Jere von Baloy?" the Akonian admiral went on. "Since your work is so important, I will be glad to provide reinforcements."

"Takhan, that is too kind. You—"

"No, please ... no polite protestations. We are coming." The admiral leaned forward, filling the entire camera range. His gigantic, enlarged face hung over the men and women of the *Las-Toór's* control center. "And in the interest of our people's welfare, I *order* you to remain on your present course until our arrival. Until then, Jere von Baloy."

The face vanished.

Perspiration appeared on Hartich's forehead. The Akonian fleet was on its way to their position, and he was stuck as a hostage on an Akonian ship! Perry Rhodan, Pearl Laneaux and Hayden Norwell were lost on the Lemurian ship, and the commander of his own ship was a known Akonian-hater.

The next few hours would be ... well ... interesting.

But there was a very different thought that made the Terran sweat: what was driving Takhan von Taklir to take such drastic action? Injured pride? A need to show civilians spoiled by the government who really ran things? Or did the admiral know more than he was saying?

28

"Naahk! You must save them!"

Denetree ran at the Naahk without incident. Solina assumed that even the ... Tenoy, Denetree had called them, sensed a fundamental change had taken place. The catastrophe warned of for generations had occurred: strangers had found the Ship and boarded it. The End of Time had come.

And now the Naahk stood together with the strangers and spoke with them as though they were friends. The world must not be making much sense to the Tenoy at the moment.

Solina Tormas had to admit that she felt pretty stunned herself. Before her stood a human wearing a cell activator, the commander of a ship whose technological level limped along thousands of years behind the level required to manufacture the life-prolonging devices. What was more, there was no civilization currently existing in the galaxy capable of developing an activator. No one was even close.

How had this man ended up on a rust bucket like the ark? Was he fleeing something? Was he hiding? Was this ship, mighty despite its backwardness, built solely to provide him with a comfortable hiding place, where he could live as the ruler of a people kept in fear and ignorance? Or did the ark have an unknown destination? But if that were the case, then why had the Immortal chosen a means of transport that would require tens of thousands of years or more to reach a destination?

Questions and more questions burned on the historian's tongue, but remained unasked since Denetree's interruption. Solina consoled herself with the thought that she would have an opportunity later to ask the Naahk her questions. After all, now that they had established contact, they had all the time in the world.

At first, the Naahk ignored the young Lemurian woman. Lemal Netwar seemed transfixed by Rhodan's revelation. It was obvious from the Naahk's expression that he was trying to absorb and understand the implications: *An activator carrier ... a brother who shared his fate, who knows the loneliness that is the inevitable price of immortality. Could he trust the man in front of him? Was he a brother, or a cunning deceiver?*

Denetree refused to be put off.

"Naahk!" she cried again. When he still didn't react, she reached for his hand. "Naahk!"

Solina heard a seemingly infinite clicking of metal as the Tenoy released the safeties on their weapons. Denetree had touched the Naahk! She had crossed a line.

Netwar made no effort to shake off Denetree's grasp. His eyes were unfocused, he was caught up in his whirling thoughts. His face had frozen to a mask. When he became aware of her touch, life slowly returned to his eyes and expression. The powerfully built man trembled as though he were shaking off the implications of the meeting for the moment, and angled his body to face the young Lemurian woman.

"You ... are ... Denetree," he said slowly.

"Yes, I am," she answered defiantly.

"The ... traitor."

"The former traitor!" Denetree spoke with the determination of someone who had chosen her path, even if the price of walking that path was her life. "Where is the treason in dreaming of the stars, when even the Naahk speaks with strangers from the stars? Where is the treason when metach seek a different life than their ancestors?"

"I ... " Netwar shook himself. "I ... " His closing lips silently brought the sentence to an end. Solina watched Lemal Netwar collapse. His shoulders slumped. His head, which he had held unmoving, fell forward until his chin hit his chest. It was as though a burden was pressing down on Netwar, a burden heavier even than the increased gravity of the outer deck, a burden that he had carried for thousands of years. That he had shouldered with a strength beyond that of any normal mortal. A burden that, faced with the young Lemurian woman standing fearlessly before him, threatened to overwhelm him.

"You … you understand?" Denetree seemed too surprised to release Netwar's hand from her grasp. Which was probably a good thing: the Naahk was depending on her for support. Solina doubted that he could have stayed on his feet without the contact of Denetree's hand.

The Naahk nodded slowly. Stiffly, as though his neck vertebrae were incapable of accommodating any other movement.

What was wrong with the Immortal? Had the shock literally struck him immobile? Or was he ill? Impossible, Solina decided. Activators prevented the aging of a living being, including natural wear and tear, and protected it from chronic diseases.

"No," Lemal Netwar managed to say. "You are no longer a traitor. You need no longer fear for your life."

"Thank you, but … "

Denetree was saved, but she had not relaxed. What else was going on?

"What about the others?" the Lemurian woman asked the Naahk.

"The others?"

"The other traitors. The *former* traitors. The Star Seekers."

Lemal Netwar's eyes went wide. "No … their execution … " He raised his free arm and looked at a metal armband. "It isn't too late!"

He put his wrist to his mouth. "Net!" he called. "Cancel the execution!"

No answer.

"Net!" he called again. "Listen to me!"

No answer.

"It … it isn't working," the Naahk said. "The Net seems to be out of order. Before you came, it was already showing signs of system failure. It must have switched itself off."

System failures in the net.

"Perhaps the problem is in your armband," Rhodan suggested. "You could try it with another one." Rhodan pointed in the direction of the armed guardians.

" None of them carry a communicator."

System failure ... When Solina had hacked into the net, she had slipped in a few harmless Trojan horses to protect her ability to access it. Could her actions be the cause of the breakdown?

"Here's a stationary terminal!" called Pearl, who had been listening to the encounter from a short distance away. The translator in her suit converted what she said into Lemurian with virtually no delay. "Try it here!"

The group moved in Pearl's direction. Solina went along, feeling numb. She suspected the effort would be in vain. She had programmed simple sleepers that should have become active only at her command. She felt sick. She had only wanted to ensure the team's safety. Now, she might be responsible for the loss of other lives.

With stiff movements, the Naahk manipulated the display's touch screen. "Nothing," he whispered after a few seconds. "The Net isn't reacting. I can't send any messages."

"How long until the execution?" Rhodan asked.

The Naahk stated a time period that translated to about seven Terran minutes.

"Where is it taking place?"

"At the stern. It is too far away to get there in time on foot. It could not be managed even on a bicycle."

"That isn't what I was thinking of." Rhodan activated his suit's antigrav. The Terran shot upwards.

And then just hung there.

Solina saw the soles of Rhodan's boots, heard him swearing—or at least thought she did; she would have thought that after thousands of years a person could break himself of such bad habits—then he dropped back to the deck and landed hard.

"The antigrav isn't working right!" Rhodan exclaimed.

One after another, the Akonians and Terrans tried their systems. None of them went further than two meters. Pearl did the best, but even then had the bad luck of coming down in one of the bushes.

Denetree first watched their attempts at flying with an open mouth: the strangers could fly! Then, as they failed, with growing desperation.

"That means they're doomed!" she cried out. Tears welled up at the corners of her eyes. "No one can save them now!"

The only answer was silence.

Hevror ta Gosz stepped forward. "Now, that seems a little premature," he said and pulled the long bag off his back.

***

Hevror knew that he didn't dare waste any time. The Terrans, Rhodan included, and the two Lemurians looked at him as though he had lost his mind. Solina and Robol, who knew the theory of his hobby, looked less astonished.

Hevror turned to the two Lemurians. "There must be a ventilation system on board this ship. With huge air shafts, right?" His suit's built-in translator converted his question to Lemurian.

Denetree and the Naahk nodded.

"Is there a big air shaft somewhere close by that transports warm, used air to the fields?"

To his surprise, the young woman answered, not the immortal Naahk, who should have known the entire ark like the back of his hand.

"Yes," Denetree said. "Two fields further up."

"Excellent. Take me there at once."

The Lemurian woman, eager to save her comrades, immediately started off. Hevror followed her, along with rest of the group.

"What are you planning?" asked Rhodan, who caught up with him seemingly without effort. His cell activator seemed to keep Rhodan totally fit; in contrast, the Naahk hobbled stiffly at the rear of the group.

"One of us has to get to the ship's stern."

"You?"

"Yes."

"And how will you manage that?"

"With wings."

Denetree stopped near a round hole in the ground. It had a diameter of about two meters. Through the grating that secured it against accidents came a warm if not particularly fragrant stream of air.

Hevror held his arm over the shaft, testing for the updraft. Yes, it could work. With a little luck, a push from his antigrav ... .

The Akonian dropped to his knees, opened the clasp on his bag, and took out the Akon-steel struts. Each individual strut was narrower than his little finger and weighed only a few grams, because it was hollow, like a bird's bones.

"Naahk!" he called to the Lemurian leader, who was the last to take his place in the ring of spectators closely watching Hevror's movements. "Naahk, how do I find the execution site?"

"It is at the stern in a former cargo hold—"

"I need a description from outside!"

Hevror had fully unfolded the struts and fit them together. He pulled a thin sheet of fabric from the bag.

"The hatch is marked in red. It—"

"Can it be seen from above? From the air?"

"I think ... yes."

While the Naahk described a series of landmarks for him, Hevror stretched the fabric over the struts, lifted the finished construction to examine it, then threw it on the ground to test its durability. It held. The wings were ready for use.

Now came the difficult part. Hevror's wings were intended to be worn over tightly fitting clothing or the naked body, which was Hevror's preferred method of flight. Despite its compact design, his protective suit got in the way. But he couldn't take it off: he needed the antigrav to give him his initial altitude.

Hevror slipped his arms through the arm loops, but he couldn't reach the rear fastenings with his suit on. The Akonian struggled for a moment, then felt a strong hand pulling on the fastenings for him. The Immortal had seen the problem, and together they managed to fasten the harness. The Akonian prayed that they would hold over the bulk of the suit. For the sake of Denetree's friends—and for his own. The "sky" of the outer deck might be relatively low, but it was high enough for him to fall to his death.

He nodded to the others. "Be right back!" he assured them with a grin and a confidence he didn't feel. He took a deep breath and leaped, his arms—the *wings*—stretched out to catch the rising stream of air from the shaft.

For a fraction of a second nothing happened, and he fell toward the grating. It wouldn't kill him, but he would look ridiculous. Then the antigrav kicked in, yanked him up, and failed again.

It was enough.

The experience of decades told Hevror that he had enough air under the wings. He began to circle in the warm air current as it fanned out. He climbed higher and higher. His companions, along with the Naahk's flabbergasted guardians, shrank to the size of toys. Hevror looked out over the strangest landscape he had seen since he had buckled the wings on his back for the first time. That had been a half century ago. On that same day, he had resigned his position with a minor government agency—a rank that generations of his family had been working toward—and turned his back on Drorah. Whenever someone expressed a sincere interest in his passion, he described his decision as having "flown out of the cage."

Since then, Hevror's wings had felt the winds of a hundred worlds. Hevror had looked down on buildings and ocean waves, on deserts of sand and ice, on endless plains and bottomless ravines. But nothing so far compared to the vista in the ark. It was gigantic and tiny at the same time.

Tiny in its physical dimensions. It was just a few kilometers long, not even half a kilometer in diameter, and housed a number of inhabitants that wouldn't have merited being termed a village on Drorah. If he applied himself, as he was doing now, he could fly through the ark's entire length in a few minutes.

And yet it was gigantic, too. Its dimensions dwarfed everything the Akonian shipyards produced using far superior technology. What an enormous effort! It was the physical expression of the indomitable will, the determination of the hundreds of thousands of people who must have worked on its construction. But where had that determination come from? Hevror could only speculate, and the answers eluded him like the haze-shrouded horizon of the outer deck.

The Akonian continued to fly in circles. The toy-size figures beneath him were now gesticulating, pointing in the direction of the stern with frantic movements. They were afraid that he had lost himself in the rapture of flight and was now flying in circles without a thought for his actual mission.

"Hevror!" he heard Solina's voice call from his suit's acoustic field. "By all the stinking glowfish of Shaghomin, what are you doing up there?"

Hevror was surprised that their comm units were functioning within the ark. He turned his comm unit off without replying. They weren't flyers and wouldn't understand. Hevror needed all the altitude he could get, because altitude meant distance and speed.

He spiraled further upward until his wings almost scratched the underside of the sky. As he was about to go into a dive, he thought he saw a face in a space helmet.

The Akonian circled once more, but the face was gone. Perhaps he had only imagined it. The light, whose source he could still not locate, grew slowly weaker. Night was falling on the ark.

Hevror pulled in his arms, abruptly ending his circling movement. Then, spreading his wings again to control his angle of descent, he dove toward his goal. He was running a big risk. He didn't know if he could hold up to the stress of the speed and direction. His concern wasn't for his wings: the Akon steel and the sheeting would have tolerated many times the stress. No, Hevror was worried about his own body. His arms could break. If that happened, he would lose control over his wings and fall to his death like Malit Balak, the inventor of the wings. His death made Malit a legend, and with one catastrophe catapulted flying from lunacy to a way of life. Hevror wondered what would happen to him if he failed now. The Akonian doubted any monument would be erected to his memory.

The desperate Lemurian woman, the Naahk, the Tenoy, Perry Rhodan and the others fell quickly behind him. Like an arrow, Hevror shot over the outer deck toward the haze, to the place where people would die if he came too late.

The description that the Naahk had given him proved accurate. Hevror corrected his course by slightly bending his arms, a bit of precision work that had taken him long years of training.

When he had almost used up his altitude, the red hatch, his destination, emerged from the haze. The stern that must have towered before him remained hidden.

The Akonian came down hard, stumbling before he shook off the numbness from landing so abruptly. Then he pulled the quick-release latch and slipped out of the wings, leaving them behind—a painfully difficult thing for him to do. A flyer never left his wings behind: they had borne him into the heavens! He ran to the hatch. It was locked. A touch screen shone dully at eye level next to it. Hevror hit it with his fist. Nothing better occurred to him. He had no ability to finesse computers. He only knew that they *never* did what he wanted them to.

This one did.

The hatch slid to the side. Hevror ran through. A large, empty cargo hold opened up before him. At the back wall stood half a dozen armed guards, and at a distance of a few paces, a slender man wearing some sort of one-colored suit. He seemed to be looking at the floor.

"Stop! You must stop!" Hevror ta Gosz cried and ran toward the group. The guardians raised their weapons and aimed at him, but Hevror continued to run, as though still propelled by the force of the dive that had brought him here.

"Stop ... please!"

The guardians didn't fire. When Hevror stopped in front of them, the man in the suit raised his head.

Hevror read the answer in his eyes even before he saw the display screen built into the wall. It showed the area of space just beyond the stern of the star ark—and the corpses frozen into grotesque positions.

The man's eyes seemed to be sunk deep in their sockets. Tears ran down his cheeks.

Hevror had come too late.

The Akonian activated his comm unit. "Solina?"

"Yes?" came the immediate answer.

"They ... they're dead."

29

"They ... they're dead."

Denetree froze when she heard Hevror's translated words. Then, as though in slow motion, she buried her face in her hands and wept. Her knees gave way. She sank to the ground.

"Denetree!"

Solina started toward the Lemurian woman to comfort her—but an exclamation shifted her attention.

"Up there!"

The Akonian looked up and saw soldiers raining down from the sky.

They weren't like Hevror. They weren't flying. Hevror swam through the air, played with it, made himself its toy ball, put himself in the power of the elementary forces. The soldiers cut through the air as though it didn't exist, propelled by the overwhelming force of their pulse drives.

There were hundreds of them. Solina turned her head and saw small dots everywhere racing toward the ground in standard loose formations that denied an opponent an easy target.

But no one fired. The Naahk's guardians cried out in fear when they saw the soldiers, then the first of them lost his nerve, threw down his weapon and ran off. The rest quickly followed his example. The soldiers let them flee.

The band of guardians was not their objective.

The soldiers landed. A dozen of them surrounded the group of Akonians, Terrans and Lemurians; a second dozen braked their fall over the ground and floated above the group.

Their antigrav units operated flawlessly, and as was shown by the shining, transparent field that surrounded each soldier, so did their defense-shield projectors.

How can that be? Solina asked herself. *Why does their equipment work and not ours? What—*

"Takhan, we have them!" one of the soldiers reported into his acoustic field. Solina didn't hear a reply, but the soldier must have received an answer because he signalled his comrades to keep their weapons held ready. The soldiers belonged to her people, but they seemed ready to deal with anyone taking what they could interpret as a hostile action. A few moments later, Solina heard a humming. She turned her head cautiously and saw two more dots racing toward her.

The dots expanded and landed near the group. They were officers. One of them was short and burly and wore more rank symbols on the chest of his battle suit than Solina had ever seen in one place before. The second was of average build and had thick, black hair combed smoothly away from his forehead. His symbols of rank Solina could interpret; she knew them from the departure of the *Las-Toór*, when Jere von Baloy had worn his uniform for the first and only time. He was a maphan, the commander of a ship.

The two men were unarmed, a demonstration of their power. If they had a notion to use force, their soldiers would take care of it.

The brawny man bowed slightly. "Takhan Gartor von Taklir, Commander of the Seventh Fleet. I see that my instinct has not betrayed me!" He stepped in front of Rhodan and saluted. "It is an honor to meet you in person, Perry Rhodan."

"Thank you." The Immortal accepted the admiral's expression of respect with the reserved composure of a man who had experienced similar situations a thousand times before. "And to what do we owe the honor of your visit?"

"Duty, what else? I wish I had the opportunity to chat with you, but that is impossible. Your very presence aboard this ship demonstrates the urgency of my mission." Takhan von Taklir drew himself up. "I declare this ship to be the property of Akon."

"How so?"

"Evaluation of the hyperdetection data from the *Las-Toór* and the *Palenque* will document that our ship detected this vessel first. Hence it falls under Akonian jurisdiction. Its inhabitants—"he bowed in the direction of the Naahk"—will naturally enjoy the care and protection of the Akonian Empire. We will ensure that they suffer no harm."

Solina listened to the admiral's statements with her mouth hanging open. *No!* she wanted to scream. *You can't do that!* She knew that if the military confiscated the ark, she would never set foot on it again. She would die of old age before they allowed access to an insignificant historian of doubtful loyalty to the Empire.

But Solina said nothing. She'd dealt with people in uniforms often enough in her life to know that it would only hurt her. People in uniforms loved to shout at others, and couldn't stand it when the tables were turned. If she protested now, she herself would destroy any slight chance that still remained for her to explore this treasure.

Rhodan seemed to have been thinking along the same lines. With remarkable calm, he said, "With all due respect, Takhan, I doubt that your version of events would stand up in court."

"We'll see about that. We are of course ready to appear before an independent court of law. I am certain that, assuming willingness to cooperate on both sides, we can have a judgment within a few years. Until then, this ship will remain in Akonian custody. Its inhabitants urgently require our assistance. As we stand here talking, a repair team has already begun installing a supplementary air supply system. The existing system is so worn out that it could break down at any moment. And I don't have to explain what that would mean, do I?"

No one said anything.

"I see we understand each other." He turned to the Akonian ship commander, who had followed his statements with an absent look as though his thoughts were somewhere else. "Achab, escort our Terran guests to the teleporter. Their ship is already waiting to take them out of Akonian territory. I assume that your violation of the frontier occurred unknowingly, so I will waive the penalties that are normally deemed appropriate in such cases."

The maphan stepped forward and pointed in the direction of the ark's bow. "If you please!"

Pearl Laneaux swore under her breath in a strangely melodious language that seemed unsuitable for obscenities. Her hand rested on the grip of her beamer. It was clear from her manner what she thought of Taklir's "politeness," but Solina had come to know her well enough to know she was too intelligent to do anything stupid. She only rattled her chains a bit to let her tormentors know that she could see right through them.

Hayden Norwell's shoulders sagged. His was not an aggressive personality. And Rhodan? The Terran looked at her pleadingly. *Do something!* he begged. *You're one of them, aren't you? Do something!*

Solina turned her head in shame. What could she accomplish? She was just a tiny, insignificant cog in the vast workings of the Akonian Empire. This mission, these pathetically few hours, had been the only time in her life in which she had attained a position of influence, in which she been involved in something great, not as an analyzing spectator separated from events by the abyss of millennia, but as an active participant.

It had felt so damned *good*.

She didn't want it to stop.

She had to do something. She couldn't watch idly while the chance of her life slipped through her fingers. She had to make at least an attempt to do *something*; just so she could live with herself.

Use your brain! she urged herself. *You've always been so proud of it, haven't you?*

Two of the Akonian soldiers stepped to the side to allow the maphan and the three Terrans to pass through.

Solina watched them blankly. The Takhan had the whip hand—two hundred warships and several tens of thousands of soldiers to carry out his orders without question. The Seventh Fleet had secured the ark within minutes. One gesture from Gartor of Taklir, and only a cloud of stardust would remain of the *Palenque*—and that applied to the *Las-Toór* as well, if the scientists made too much trouble.

No. Resistance was not only futile, it was suicidal.

Rhodan, Pearl Laneaux and Hayden Norwell joined the maphan. They were passing through the ring of soldiers when Solina had her inspiration.

Resistance was futile, but even the weak had weapons.

"Takhan!" she called, turning to the admiral. "May I congratulate you in the name of all the Yidari on board the *Las-Toór* for taking initiative so resolutely?"

Gartor von Taklir chose to acknowledge Solina for the first time. There was an impatient gleam in his eyes. The admiral didn't seem to care for flatterers, especially when their flattery had no definite aim. Solina had to keep talking, and quickly.

"But you shouldn't act so half-heartedly."

"What?"

"If you expel the Terrans—which is the only appropriate thing to do—you should expel all of them."

"What do you mean by that?"

Solina pointed to Denetree, who had been watching events as though stunned. "You forgot that one here."

"That's a Terran? She isn't wearing a spacesuit like the others."

"No, she's a specialist. The Terrans slipped her in hoping to put one over on us."

Noticing that she was suddenly the center of attention, Denetree woke from her paralysis and murmured some words in Lemurian.

"She isn't speaking Terran," the admiral declared suspiciously.

"Of course not. Not now. She's trying to maintain her cover. But look at her closely! She has a Terran's fair skin! Is this secret agent to be allowed to remain on board and spy on this artifact?"

"The Terrans can't be that stupid."

Solina held the Takhan's gaze. "Oh, yes, they certainly can be. And they're arrogant, too. The Terrans have considered themselves lords of the galaxy for much too long, and they've gotten lazy and sluggish. If you ask me, it wasn't an accident that an *Akonian* fleet appeared first."

"There's something to that. Achab, take her along!"

The commander hesitated, then said, "But Takhan! What if she isn't a Terran? We—"

"What does it matter? Look at the terrified little thing—what could she tell them? Let them take her with them!"

Denetree said something in Lemurian again, louder this time. Solina stepped to her side and hissed into her ear, "By all the star gods! Get moving, girl! Go, or I'll … "

She gave her a shove in the direction of Rhodan and the other Terrans. Denetree went.

***

When Rhodan, Pearl Laneaux, Hayden Norwell and Denetree emerged from the teleporter on the bridge of the *Palenque*, they were met with outrage.

"So here you are at last!" The uniformed Sharita Coho stamped up and down, her cheeks flaming red. "Didn't I tell you? You can't trust those Akonians! They tricked us! It's a miracle that they let you go without a scratch and … " The commander broke off as she noticed Denetree. "Who the hell is that girl? Another Akonian? I've had my fill of them with the one we've got, with all her special requests! I … "

"She's a Lemurian," Rhodan said.

"A Lem … how did you pull that off?"

Before Rhodan could answer, Alemaheyu Kossa broke in. "Sharita, comm message from Takhan von Taklir. We're supposed to get out of here at once, or else…"

"Oh, let the old man blather!"

"But … "

"Did you finish my avatar? We can put it on for the admiral, the same way Jere von Baloy used his on me."

"Just about. We've got a very decent beta version."

"Run it. Let's see how the Akonians like the taste of their own medicine." The commander turned back to the newcomers. "All right, out with it. How did you smuggle this Lemurian out? Is she a spy?" She looked at Denetree suspiciously. The young Lemurian woman trembled. Perspiration stood out on her forehead.

"It wasn't us," Rhodan replied. "An Akonian woman from the *Las-Toór* managed it."

"Oh, come on! Why would she do that?"

"I'm wondering the same thing." Rhodan went to Denetree and took her hands. "Can you hear me?" he asked in Lemurian. "Can you help us?"

The Lemurian whispered an answer, but it was lost in the roar that suddenly shook the *Palenque*'s hull.

"Intimidation fire!" Harriett Hewes called. "The Akonians fired a salvo. They must not have found your avatar very convincing."

"Shield load?"

"99.3 percent of capacity. They know exactly what they're dealing with."

Sharita shrugged. "Very well," she then said. "We shouldn't refuse such a polite request. We'll leave."

Denetree reached under her belt and pulled out a black plastic rectangle. It was so small that the Lemurian could close her fist around it. She held it out to Rhodan.

"What is that?" Sharita asked.

"The reason why Solina Tormas saw to it that Denetree went with us," Rhodan replied. "A memory chip."

The hull of the Palenque shook a second time as the Akonian fleet gave it a blazing farewell salute, then the ship transitioned into hyperspace.

Rhodan barely noticed it. Let Takhan von Taklir imagine himself as the victor and tow the ark to the Akon system as a trophy. The Terran believed he held something much more valuable in his hands—the key to the mystery of the ark.

epilogue

The sun sank below the horizon.

Alemaheyu and his companions watched the setting of the giant sun Pollaco Hermi on the helmet displays provided by their ship's syntron. Watching with their naked eyes, the prospectors would have seen only the light fading from the haze that had stubbornly persisted in the streets of the capital city of Kreytsos ever since their arrival on Maahkora. The haze consisted of a mixture of ammonia, hydrogen, methane and various trace gases, heated to a temperature of 98.7 degrees centigrade—moderate for local conditions.

Despite his protective suit, the comm officer thought he could feel every one of those degrees. Sweat covered his body in a sticky film.

Now and then, massive shadows emerged from the mist, paused for a moment to look at the group of humanoids, and then went on their way, always in a hurry. Because Maahkora was the Maahks' embassy planet in the Milky Way galaxy, strangers were the exception, rather than the rule. There was always something urgent to be done here.

Still, Alemaheyu and his companions caused something of a sensation.

Had the news spread that Perry Rhodan, the immortal Terran, was in Kreytsos?

Unlikely. No one knew of Rhodan's presence, not even the Terran Residence.

Or was it the size of the group that attracted attention? There were more than forty Terrans, two Blues and a Gurrad striding through the streets of Kreytsos. Only a skeleton crew, commanded by Harriett Hewes, remained on the *Palenque*. She was also looking after Denetree, who was still very depressed by the death of her friends.

Or was it the group's attitude, which seemed at odds with their destination? The prospectors determinedly set one foot in front of the other. A look through their helmet faceplates would have revealed strained expressions and firmly set jaws, as though they marched toward an unpleasant, unavoidable task. This expression was overlaid by a hint of curiosity.

The prospectors were headed toward Meklaren in Kreytsos' pleasure quarter, but they didn't give the impression that they were anticipating pleasure.

As the light from Pollaco Hermi faded away, the street lighting brightened correspondingly. And as the prospectors increased their distance from their ship, a new sun rose before them: the lights of Meklaran.

Alemaheyu's throat felt tight. Perry Rhodan appeared beside the *Palenque*'s comm officer and asked, "Nervous?"

Alemaheyu looked at the Immortal in surprise. "You know about it?"

Rhodan nodded. "Of course. You know how it is—there are no secrets on board a ship."

"Very true, very true." Alemaheyu swallowed. "Yeah, I'm a little nervous ... "

"You'll be okay!" Rhodan raised his left arm, as though to slap the comm officer encouragingly on the shoulder, but dropped it again without making the gesture.

"Thanks," was all Alemaheyu said. His thoughts, which were not, as Rhodan suspected, entirely devoted to the evening that lay before them, caught him up again in their vicious cycle.

Before they left the *Palenque*, Alemaheyu had checked his console one last time. Out of habit, without any particular reason. And while he was archiving the log files from the past few days, he had stumbled on an anomaly. He hadn't had the time to investigate it more thoroughly—Sharita Coho didn't stand for lack of punctuality—but everything indicated that the antennae of the *Palenque* had received a hypercom impulse during that time. The ship's syntron had categorized it as a natural phenomenon of the Ochent Nebula and so hadn't notified Alemaheyu.

Alemaheyu had quickly reached a different conclusion: the signal was artificial—and it had originated on the ark.

Which was impossible.

Completely impossible.

Hypercom was five-dimensional technology. The ark's technical level was centuries, if not millennia away from that.

The signal couldn't have come from the ark.

Alemaheyu only peripherally realized that they had reached the edge of Meklaren. A shaped energy dome vaulted over the district, creating a tolerable atmosphere inside for oxygen breathers.

The prospectors took off their protective suits and left them behind in the monitored storage locker area, revealing widely idiosyncratic and colorful casual clothes. Air saturated with sweet fragrances, the lures of widely diverse establishments, filled the comm officer's nose. Alemaheyu loved this aroma, but this evening he was too entangled in the whirl of his thoughts to enjoy it.

Assuming that the comm signal really had come from the ark, then what did it mean? Was it a distress call? Or an invitation?

Perhaps that was it. An invitation that the Akonian fleet had answered.

You couldn't put anything past the Akonians.

Perhaps that also applied to artistic taste? Alemaheyu would find out this evening.

Sharita took the lead of the prospectors and navigated confidently to The Drunken Sailor. Was she familiar with the location of their destination? Or following directions from her picosyn? After just two thousand years in business, The Drunken Sailor wasn't Meklaren's oldest night spot, nor was it the most famous or the most notorious—nor, as Alemaheyu discovered when they entered its dim interior, was it the most clean. It was simply a very typical run-down bar in a very typical run-down pleasure quarter.

In other words, The Drunken Sailor was the ideal place for what they had in mind.

Tables for about a hundred people had been set up in the main room, the chairs arranged to face the raised stage. Just the sight of them made Alemaheyu forget all thoughts of mysterious hyper-com signals.

Just half an hour more and … .

The doors at the other end of the room slid open and the crew of the *Las-Toór* streamed into The Drunken Sailor. For several long seconds, the Terrans and the Akonians eyed each other, silent and uncertain, then the bar owner took pity on them and laid down a carpet of Maahkish music over the uncomfortable scene—a clever choice, since no non-Maahk could stand such so-called music. Sharing their disgust at the abrasive noise, the Terrans and Akonians found places at the tables.

The Terrans sat to the left of the center aisle and the Akonians to the right. The Akonian commander made an effort to approach his Terran colleague, but Sharita sent him back to his chair with an icy look.

The bar robots swarmed out. Both sides ordered as if there were no tomorrow, glad to have something to do, and soon the tables were piled high with bowls and glasses. Both sides shot more fre-quent covert looks across the aisle, but still no one dared to invade enemy territory.

The show program began with the inevitable duo of an Ertrusian (humanoid, copper-colored, two and a half meters tall, with Mohawk-style hair) and a Siganesian (humanoid, lime green, eleven centimeters tall). Terrans and Akonians alike applauded courteously. Maahkora was out in the boondocks, and as long as something was happening on stage, no one was inclined to be too critical.

Alemaheyu hardly paid any attention to the unmatched pair on the stage. He looked around and found Eniva ta Drorar. The Akonian woman gave him a friendly wave, pointed to the stage, and grinned encouragingly.

The Terran wished he could be as uninhibited as Eniva. He would have liked nothing better than to stand up and run away. Or pour so much beer into himself that couldn't even stagger to the stage. But there was no turning back.

And besides, someone had to break the ice.

Then it was time. While a shape-shifting Morphing Willie attempted to break through the audience's inhibitions by making himself into living caricatures of prominent politicians—among them Rhodan who, unrecognized in the audience, laughed louder than anyone else—the bar owner came to Alemaheyu's table and said quietly, "Okay, you're next."

Alemaheyu stood up and made his way through the tables to the side entrance to the stage. He felt as though thousands of eyes were boring into his back, and his sweat-drenched shirt stuck to his body. One of The Drunken Sailor's employees approached him. "Nervous, eh? Don't worry. I'll get you a new one!"

"A new what?" Alemaheyu asked, confused.

"Shirt. Yours is—"

The comm officer shook his head. "That's all right. It fits with what I have in mind."

The assistant shrugged. "It's up to you."

Alemaheyu tested The Drunken Sailor's syntron while the Morphing Willie finished its performance with an impersonation of the Arkonide Imperator Bostich stumbling over his ceremonial rapier during one of his beloved military parades.

The syntron checked out. The software he needed had been correctly initialized. Now there was only one risk factor remaining: Alemaheyu Kossa himself.

The polite applause for the Morphing Willie died out. Alemaheyu took a deep breath and stepped out onto the stage. The spotlight blinded him, making it impossible to see his audience. Eniva waved to him from the other side of the stage.

The comm officer unbuttoned his sweat-damp shirt, took it off, and rolled it up. Then he tied it around his forehead to keep his mane of hair out of his eyes.

Alemaheyu bowed. "Dear … " He faltered. Dear *what*? Friends? Allies? Ex-archenemies? Rivals? He left the salutation unfinished. "This is a piece that some of you may already be familiar with. An old Terran folk song called 'All Along the Watchtower'."

He closed his eyes and concentrated on his fingertips. He had to *feel* the guitar in his hands.

Shouts came from the Terran side. "Show us, Alemaheyu! Give us your air guitar!"

Alemaheyu gave it to them.

His fingers, which up to now had only felt the air, now felt the strings of the air guitar as though they existed as physical objects. He drove the first tones screeching into The Drunken Sailor's main room.

Alemaheyu opened his eyes. The bar owner had dimmed the spotlight, so Alemaheyu could see the audience. The Terran half was already out of its seats. And the Akonians? Alemaheyu thought he could see some of them covertly tapping their feet in time with the music.

Good, they're getting warmed up. And now ... he gave Eniva the signal.

The Akonian walked slowly out on stage. Tiny antigrav projectors kept her styled hair in constant, snakelike motion. She bowed, opened her mouth, and soundlessly moved her lips.

The syntron caught her movements and converted them into song. Alemaheyu heard "Watchtower" as he had never heard it before. As a wonderfully rich, husky song. Overpoweringly feminine, overpoweringly passionate.

The Akonian audience couldn't stay in its seats a moment longer. Men and women leaped up, spurring Eniva on, calling louder and louder, "Plejbek! Plejbek! Plejbek!"

Frenetic applause washed over Alemaheyu and Eniva. The Terrans clapped and howled while the Akonians stamped and howled.

"Encore! Encore! Encore!" came from all sides as they finished their first number.

It was an unnecessary request. Alemaheyu had no intention whatsoever of stopping. Not now. They alternated between Akonian and Terran songs, and eventually they began letting them flow together.

Terrans and Akonians danced everywhere: on the floor, on the tables, on the bar and a few who had brought their antigravs on the ceiling.

Only one area remained clear: the central aisle, the boundary between the two crews. No one dared to dance there, let alone cross it.

Alemaheyu, who after more than a dozen songs could barely stay upright, was beginning to think it would stay that way when something happened that astonished him more than the appearance of an entire fleet of Lemurian generation ships: Sharita stood up, unbuttoned her uniform jacket and hung it carefully over her chair. She took a few steps back, then ran forward and leapt onto the stage shouting a word that Alemaheyu couldn't quite understand: "Karaoke!"

Alemaheyu would learn what it meant that evening, which became a very long night. He and the crews of the *Palenque* and the *Las-Toôr* staggered back to their ships in the gray dawn in small groups and pairs, bellowing the words to songs or engaged in quieter pursuits.

The comm officer was the last to return on board the *Palenque*, more exhausted but more mellow than he had ever felt before in his life, not least because of the kiss that Eniva had brushed against his lips before disappearing into her cabin on the *Palenque*. Alemaheyu took it as the promise of a most pleasant future.

As he staggered through the *Palenque*'s hangar, he pinched his arm to reassure himself that he hadn't dreamed the past few hours—and banged his head against a metal wall.

The comm officer stumbled back.

"Watch out, Alemaheyu—that thing is harder than your head!" came an amused voice from one side. The comm officer turned his head and thought he could make out Hayden Norwell, who had voluntarily stayed behind on the ship.

"Uh ... what thing?"

When his vision focused again, he saw it: in the *Palenque*'s hangar stood a brand-new space-jet, the auxiliary craft for which they had been waiting in vain for years.

"That ... that's ... "

" ... a space-jet!" Norwell finished happily.

"How did it get here?"

"Oh, I thought we could use one. So I got in touch with the ship's owners, talked to them very reasonably, and ... well, you can see the result."

Alemaheyu nodded. "Yes, I do see."

A ship full of Lemurians; the prospect of further discoveries that would make them all rich; people who cheered him; Akonians who weren't really so bad, and in one case not bad at all; Sharita relaxing in front of the crew; Perry Rhodan, who treated him like an old buddy—and now a space-jet for the *Palenque*, provided by the cheapskate owners.

Nothing was impossible.

PERRY RHODAN'S ADVENTURES CONTINUE IN:

LEMURIA 2
COMING SPRING 2007